The Fox
"The Sheep in Wolf's Clothing"

A novel by

Janet Lee Carpenter

Published by

Brighton Publishing LLC

501 W. Ray Road
Suite 4
Chandler, AZ 85225
www.BrightonPublishing.com

Printed in the United States of America

Copyright © 2011

First Edition

ISBN 13: 978-1-936587-00-1
ISBN 10: 1-936-58700-9

Cover Design by: Tyler Rausch

All rights reserved. No part of this publication may be reproduced or transmitted in any form or by any means, electronic or mechanical, including photocopy, recording, or any information storage retrieval system, without permission in writing from the copyright owner.

The Form Benders
"The Sheep in Wolf's Clothing"

A novel by

Janet Lee Carpenter

Published by

Brighton Publishing LLC
501 W. Ray Road
Suite 4
Chandler, AZ 85225
www.BrightonPublishing.com

The Form Benders – Janet Lee Carpenter

♽ Dedication ♽

*T*his book is dedicated to my dear family who supported, loved, and believed in me.

For my youngest son, whose imagination exceeds my own, and my eldest, who helped me with all those pesky questions I had about computers.

For my daughters who repeatedly told me, "Go for it, Mom. You can do it!"

To my husband, whose levelheaded trust pushed me into following my dream.

To my mother-in-law who supported my creative endeavors with her wholehearted love and kindness—bless you and thank you!

To my mother who, although she is gone, will never be forgotten. Thank you for believing in me, always!

To my sister who helped me perfect my story and kindly read it almost as many times as I did. I am so glad you are in my life!

To my college English professor, Mr. Borofka, who told me I was "quite talented." Thank you for your support—I would have never done this without you!

To my delightful and cherished publishers, Kathie and Don McGuire of Brighton Publishing, who through their tireless and gifted efforts, their attention to detail, and their overflowing fountain of knowledge, helped bring this special child of mine into publication. Bless you both for believing in me—you two are the best!

And finally, thank you to all my friends and readers who turn the pages of this adventure of Ripley's and find enchantment in your life. It's always fun to find the magic in each day—you are my magic! Thank you!

The Form Benders – Janet Lee Carpenter

The Form Benders – Janet Lee Carpenter

Chapter One

A pregnant silence shrouded the sun-dappled pine and oak forest as if in anticipation. The dogwoods' scarlet seed pods hung from a background of flame-colored leaves. Each pod was filled with spring's promise as it awaited the winter's blanket of snow. Hints of autumn whispered through the silent forest as Ripley walked quietly through the giant trees, an uneasiness snaking through him. He could feel the hairs on the back of his neck stand on end. He stepped up his pace a bit and headed toward the end of the path that would lead him out of the suddenly sinister woods. A cool breeze tossed the leaves in front of him into a dust devil, spooking him even more and adding to the anxiety already pulsing through him. He was too unnerved to look over his shoulder to make certain nothing was there…that *nothing* was following him. He kept his eyes trained on the path before him and continued to move forward, each successive breath creating a shallow rhythm.

A twig snapped, making a resounding *C-R-A-C-K* behind Ripley in the silent forest. He jumped and flashed a glance over his shoulder in spite of his trepidation and quickened his pace. He tried to walk briskly without seeming to be frightened. His heart revved up into hyper-drive as he made his way down the well-worn path…*was that a movement in the bushes behind him?* He wasn't supposed to be in the forest, but it was so much easier than having to walk all the way around it to get home from school. Besides, his mother would never know which way he came home; she didn't pay much attention to those things. *The truth was he didn't think she noticed anything about him,* he mentally shrugged. Bringing his thoughts back to this moment, he thought about where he was. Strange things had happened here in the forest…*maybe this hadn't been such a good idea after all,* he reflected. He could *feel* something watching him, moving with him. *But…what was it? If only he had the courage to look!* He forced his thoughts back to the present moment. He couldn't get sidetracked and he couldn't shake the foreboding that something was here with him…and it meant to have him no matter what. *What was it waiting for?*

The Form Benders – Janet Lee Carpenter

He adjusted the backpack he carried over his left shoulder with a shrug, trying to act calmer than he felt, moving steadily toward the light at the end of the trail. It was all he could do to keep his feet from flying down the pine needle and leaf-strewn path he knew so well. However, his father had taught him *never* run from a wild animal…it just makes them chase you. That's what it *had* to be, he tried to convince himself. It was a wild animal stalking him. He cautiously stepped over the gnarled tree root almost covered with leaves and gained momentum as he neared the edge of the thick grove of pine. His hands were shaking from the adrenalin as it pumped through him, but he kept his eyes on the light ahead. He was almost there!

Then another twig crackled in the silent forest and he heard the heaving breath of something—or someone. It was moving faster now, its footfalls pounding out a rhythmic beat, matching his. Whatever it was, it was not stalking him any longer, but ready to make its move…he sensed it! His heart pounded and picked up the beat of the footfalls behind him. With the sound of pursuit in his wake, Ripley felt the adrenalin pump from his heart into his arms and legs, forcing him to break into a wild run. He gripped the strap of his backpack so he wouldn't drop it and let his feet eat up the distance between freedom and heaven knew what! He couldn't control the beating of his heart or his flight any longer. His long strides carried him forward as he neared the clearing. His hearing became sharper as the footfalls behind him seemed to move in unison with his gait. Too frightened now to turn around, he pounded down the trail. He was no longer sure if it was *his* breathing or someone else's he heard. His fear impelled him forward, ever closer to the clearing ahead. He mentally counted the footsteps…it sounded like two…no, maybe four footfalls behind him. It or *they* were getting closer, what*ever* that sound was!

Maybe it was Joshua and Michael playing a trick on him, he thought to himself, trying to keep himself calm. Then he remembered that Joshua's mom had picked the boys up from school. *It couldn't be them!* It would be just like Joshua to pick on him when Ripley's friend Pete wasn't around.

Ripley never did find out what happened that day between Pete and Joshua over a year ago. All he knew was when Pete came out of the boy's locker room after school, Joshua wasn't with him. When he'd asked Pete about it, he'd told him Josh had forgotten something. Ripley thought it was odd, but didn't press him on the issue. They'd continued

The Form Benders – Janet Lee Carpenter

on their walk home together. He hadn't given it much more thought. That is, until the next day when he'd gone to school and seen Joshua in the locker room in his first period P.E. class. Josh was unusually quiet and wouldn't look at him. It wasn't until they were playing football on the field that he noticed the black eye Josh was sporting. Josh never bothered him again, and Ripley never asked Pete about it. Ripley allowed himself a grin before the seriousness of his situation brought him back with a jolt. *If it isn't Josh, then who is it?* He almost panicked more.

His mind raced over the recent newspaper headlines as he plowed through his final few feet to freedom. *Two Children Lost in the Woods, Hennessey Found Mauled by an Unknown Creature, Sally Brunswick, Vanished in the Woods.* He put the brakes on those thoughts and shivered as he burst into the late afternoon sun and onto the dirt baseball field. The hairs on the back of his neck stood at attention and an electric charge made its way down his spine and back up again. He could still feel those eyes on him as he ran.

The baseball diamond, once well cared for, was a mere memory of its former glory. Tiny tufts of grass clung stubbornly to the dry landscape in a pathetic attempt to add some color to the unrelieved, earthen-colored dust bowl the ballpark had become. Ripley used to play here; he threw the meanest screwball Shaver Lake had ever seen. However, that was a long time ago, when he had dreamed of becoming a pro ball player. He rarely came here anymore. Not since everything happened seven years ago. *That* was when his life changed. *That* was when he quit playing Little League baseball.

His breath came in gasps, but he forced himself to keep running. He had to slow his pace due to a sharp pain in his side. Head back, gasping for breath, Ripley continued to run as he grabbed his side with his right hand. When that didn't work, he pressed his fist hard into the muscle in spasm. The huge, uneven ball diamond was eaten up by his flight as he made a direct beeline for the apartment beyond. He flicked another look over his shoulder. Seeing nothing there, he stopped in his tracks gasping, the fear gradually seeping out of him as he realized he was safe...for the moment. He dropped his backpack carelessly to the dusty ground and leaned forward. His damp, silvery hair hung down from his forehead. He placed one hand on his knee, and his chest heaved while he sucked in the fresh mountain air in large gulps. He tried to still his racing pulse and knead the stitch in his side with his fist at the same

The Form Benders – Janet Lee Carpenter

time. He filled his starving lungs several times before they finally drank their fill and his heartbeat slowed to a steady rhythm. Ripley looked around him. No sign of anything following him, but he could still feel someone or something watching him from the woods even now. He shook himself and wondered...*was it his imagination?* It couldn't have been...he had heard the thing's breathing, the twigs snapping and the sound of footfalls had been unmistakable. Oh yes, something was there all right...and it was stalking him, trying to reach him...*but why?*

As he stood there, bent over, trying to catch his breath, he covertly studied the forest's edge, trying to detect any movement. Satisfied that nothing was there now, he reached down, picked up his backpack, and raised his fist in the air at the unseen enemy.

With the autumn sun pouring its waning warmth across his back, Ripley turned and slung the pack over his left shoulder as he headed for the apartment. Dust puffed from under his tennis shoes with each step as he shuffled the rest of the way across the field, each stride taking him closer to home and all the changes he'd been through. Sweat ran down his back and forehead unheeded. He almost turned and fled to his friend's house, but his mother would be expecting him; she would need him. He wouldn't tell her what just happened...*I've learned my lesson*, he thought. And with resolve, he continued toward their apartment.

He wiped the sweat from his brow once more as he reached the hallway and stairs leading to his apartment. He frowned when he realized a strange car sat on the street in front of his home; one he was almost certain he'd never seen before. Very little went unnoticed in this small community. He took the steps two at a time to the second floor, shrugged his backpack off his shoulder and let it slide down his arm to reach its destination. It landed neatly in his coiled fingers. At the same time, he shoved his right hand into his jeans pocket and pulled out the key. It slipped into the lock easily, as it had so many times before. But he paused when he heard voices coming from inside the apartment. One was his mother and the other he didn't recognize. He let go of the key and started to back away from the door, just as it swung open to reveal a stranger. He held out his backpack as he stepped away from the door...and then, leaned back to check and make sure he hadn't made a mistake in the apartment. But the key worked, so it had to be right. His mother was inside. Confusion filled him. The woman smiled and reached out a hand, taking hold of the pack as if he'd offered it to her.

The Form Benders – Janet Lee Carpenter

"Come on in, Ripley. We have a lot to talk about." *Who was this woman inviting him into his own home?* Her body took up the entire doorway...she was humongous! She was easily the largest woman Ripley had ever seen. This stranger's clothing was pulled so tightly across her chest that Ripley was certain if she took a deep breath every button would pop off her silky, purple shirt. Her jacket was as tight, if not worse, than the shirt she had on underneath it. The sleeves were a full two inches above her wrists. Her skirt was a deep purple to match the jacket, but it was much too short, he decided, because he could see that her thighs kind of pooled around her stocking-clad knees. She reminded him of a large, ripe plum with too much juice inside, ready to explode! She waddled forward with a kind of rolling motion, huffing and puffing, her severe hairstyle adding to his already odd impression of her. Her tiny probing eyes in that gargantuan round face seemed to assess him.

Ripley still held onto the pack in a brief struggle over its possession, and then gave up and released it. He almost laughed as he let the full weight of the pack go and she suddenly struggled to hold herself upright. He recovered himself and coughed into his hand instead, eyes sparkling, the flight of only moments before fading into the background. He had all his books in his backpack, in addition to probably three hours of homework. In addition, since he hadn't done the special project Mr. Hanks had asked him to complete today, his backpack must have weighed a solid seventy pounds!

Okay, so it *felt* like seventy pounds after the run he'd just made through the woods from school, but it was probably half that! Now he'd have to work all weekend to get it done! Ripley frowned at the thought. He grabbed the key from the doorknob and inched past the woman into the room, sliding around her as she ineffectively blocked his path. Finally, he saw her...*Mom*. She was half-lying, half-sitting on the couch in her pajamas, covered with the filthy robe she'd been wearing ever since he could remember. A cigarette clung precariously to her lower lip, and her silvery blonde hair was still bound up in the ever-present curlers. He sneezed at the pungent odor of cigarettes.

"Bless you," the heavy-set woman said immediately.

"Yesh—bless you, Rippy. Honey, come on in." She attempted to sit up and waved from her throne on the couch as she let her eyes roll a bit from side to side, and then closed them. All the while, she was giving

The Form Benders – Janet Lee Carpenter

him a limp-wristed beckon to get him to join her on the couch. "Come give your momma a kissh..." She left the words hanging in the air.

He could tell she was having trouble staying awake, as well as staying upright. Ripley slid a quick glance at the stranger, and then went dutifully over to kiss his mother on the cheek. At the same time, he deftly removed the burning object from her mouth. As he leaned over, the smell of alcohol and cigarettes emanated from her. He sneezed again and almost gagged, but kept his face passive as he gave her a quick peck on the cheek, aware that the stranger was still scrutinizing him. He crushed her cigarette out in the ashtray on the marred trunk, which acted as their coffee table, and stood up. He ducked just in time to avoid the arms that snaked out too slowly to embrace him, all in one fluid motion.

"Hey!" was all she managed.

Ripley ignored her outburst and said, "I have a lot of homework to do." He stated it to no one in particular as he moved smoothly away from her. "I've got to get started on it."

His mother frowned as it took her a few moments to realize how he'd outmaneuvered her, but recovered nicely. "Aw, come on, Honey...come and sit by your momma and tell me how your day went." She patted the couch beside her invitingly.

Why was she acting like this? Who was this stranger who seemed to have such an odd effect upon his mother? She usually said hello to him, and he went right on through to his room without stopping. She never said more than that to him when he got home from school. He didn't know what to think now. *What kind of power could this woman possibly have to cause this sudden interest in him from his mother?* Ripley could feel the stranger's eyes on him, watching every move he made with her.

"Oh, I've forgotten my manners," she managed. Ripley was confused at his mother's words. *What manners were in order here? Who was this woman?* "This is Msh. Washington; she's here from CPS," the last came as she whispered behind her hand. Though it was meant for only Ripley to hear, she spoke louder than she'd intended. The entire room echoed with her words. "You know...Child Protective Shervicesh," she continued.

The Form Benders - Janet Lee Carpenter

He felt the anxiety as it washed over him, but he didn't let on that the presence of the CPS employee worried him. He winced at his mother's statement. "Yeah, I know what CPS stands for, Mom." He couldn't keep the annoyance he felt out of his voice. He snuck a peek at her as he cautiously reached out toward Ms. Roly Poly and shook her hand while trying to decide what she wanted here. It looked as if his mother was beginning to tilt on the couch again. His hand was immediately engulfed in the woman's pillow-like grip. He extricated his hand from hers and slid it down his pants, a gesture not lost on Ms. Washington if her frown was any indication. Then he ran his hand back up his pants and stashed it in his pants pocket, as if he wasn't genuinely trying to wipe the clamminess from it.

Ms. Washington slowly walked to the mantle and picked up last year's school picture of him, scrutinized it, and then placed it back on the mantle. Sometimes he wondered if he hadn't been randomly dropped into this life...this family...because it was so hard to relate to who he was compared to his mother. If he didn't have her nose and eyes, he might have truly questioned where he came from. Where his mother was short, he was tall; he thought that maybe her drinking might have caused the frailty he now saw in her. He, on the other hand, was extremely fit and strong. The only other thing they had in common was a thick, full head of silvery blonde hair.

"Nice picture," Ms. Washington said, trying to make conversation.

However, Ripley wasn't buying it. Ignoring her attempt at small talk, he shook off his earlier thoughts and said, "I'm gonna put my stuff away." When no one seemed to object, he headed to his room to put away his backpack and take off his shoes. He reminisced as he did these chores automatically.

The doctor once told him it was hereditary for a young man like himself to become prematurely gray. It didn't happen often, but sometimes that gene would be predominant and spawn a child who would have gray hair early in life. It usually happened near their coming of age; his started much sooner. He had coal-black hair when he was born, but by the age of nine, his hair began to turn silver. By the time he was twelve, his hair had turned entirely to the silvery, blondish hair he now sported. The doctor thought it might have been because of the

The Form Benders – Janet Lee Carpenter

Scarlet Fever he'd contracted shortly after his father left. But he wouldn't think about that.

He was the brunt of a great deal of ribbing at school; that is, until the other kids realized he was smart. They called him "Old Man" and "Silver Streak." Nevertheless, when they finally figured out how smart he was, they started laughing *behind* his back, not to his face anymore. Ripley didn't know which was worse.

There were two reasons for the change in their behavior. One was that he helped a lot of the other kids with their homework. The other was Pete Cranston. In their freshman year in high school, he and Pete met and became fast friends. Pete was tall and lanky, and in the last year or so, he'd begun to gain muscle. Since he was over six feet tall, no one bothered him. They didn't want to be on the wrong side of a conversation which included Ripley as the butt of the joke when Pete was around either—and certainly not after the episode with Josh and Pete in the boy's locker room.

Ripley smiled, and then changed his train of thought. He thought about his father often, more often than he cared to admit, trying to remember what color his hair had been. The black and white photo was so worn it didn't confirm whether his father's hair had been black or brown. It was unquestionably dark. He wished he hadn't touched the picture so much when he'd been younger. Now he could only vaguely see the features which had once held him so captive. He wondered if the scarlet fever had robbed him of all memory of his father. Ripley's brow furrowed as he thought about the night his mother destroyed all the pictures of *him* in a drunken fit when he was ten years old...all but the one he kept hidden in the envelope under his bed. Then she'd fallen asleep on the couch, tears streaking down her face. She hadn't been sober since...at least, not for long. That's when he'd learned to hate *him*.

The one thing that differed so much with him and his mother was that she liked to lie on the couch all day and he was into sports: running and track, backpacking, hiking, baseball, basketball, fishing. He loved to play games...ones that required him to push his physical limits! Studying heredity in school made him question so much about his father and his mother that he'd rather not think about. He shook himself to jog the memories loose as his thoughts wandered back to his mother.

The Form Benders – Janet Lee Carpenter

She hadn't always been this way...a drinker. It was after his father...he caught himself before he remembered all of the awful things that had happened after he'd left them. *Why was it that thinking about his mother always seemed to lead to thoughts about his father?* He wouldn't think about it anymore; it didn't change anything. He hadn't thought about *him* for an unusually long time. It was just the *stupid* chapter in class today that led him down this path of reflection!

Ripley made his way back to the living room; he could hear his mother's slurred speech as they talked softly. However, when Ms. Washington spoke again it was a bit of a shock after being lost in his thoughts. She cleared her throat and began, "Well, Ripley, let me explain why I've come here. I'm here because there has been a complaint lodged against your mother about how she cares for you. I am here to decide whether or not the allegations brought to our attention have any merit or not." He watched in studied fascination as her several chins rippled while she spoke. *Why is it adults always talk to me as if I'm such a child?* he wondered. *I am almost sixteen...a man!*

Then the light came on, and he finally understood. So *this* is why she's here...*who had said something?* He tried a different approach on her...and tried desperately to change the direction of this conversation.

"Do you mind if I make something to eat? I'm starving." Ripley felt strange as he asked for permission in his own home to make himself a snack. He waited for her to say something while he instinctively decided this woman could not be trusted. She merely stared at him with a blank look. Not sure he wouldn't say more than he should, he gave up waiting for her permission. He turned away so she couldn't read his expression as he headed for the kitchen.

She was so serious, and perhaps she looked strange to him because everything on her jiggled like a bowl of Jell-O as she spoke and moved. Ripley tried not to look at her. She made him uncomfortable, and he wasn't sure why yet. She toddled along behind him as he made his way to the dark kitchen.

She seemed to have finally come to her wits and said, "No, not at all; we can chat for a bit while you make yourself something to eat."

"Yesh, tell her son. We do fine here..." his mother chimed in from her perch. *What on earth did that have to do with anything?* He wished she'd just shut up. She was just adding to the tension he was

The Form Benders – Janet Lee Carpenter

feeling. He was hoping his replica of a saunter conveyed a relaxed state, though he felt anything *but* comfortable as he went into the kitchen. This woman made him tense.

He went to the cupboard, opened it, and shoved aside the macaroni and cheese boxes and the half-filled oatmeal container to find the jar of peanut butter. He moved the close-to-empty brown sugar bag out of the way and removed the jar of Skippy. In his other hand, he grabbed the loaf of bread from the bread drawer and noted that his mom, once again, hadn't eaten anything today. There wasn't a dirty dish anywhere in the kitchen. The counters held no debris indicating she'd pulled out something to eat. Heaven knows she rarely put anything away...she just left it up to him to clean up her messes. Attempting to hide his discomfort, he turned to the refrigerator, pulled out a jar of jelly and began to make a PB&J. They were his favorite. He waited for her to speak again, because he wasn't about to volunteer any information.

Since PB&J's were about the cheapest thing he could find to buy with the money his mom gave him when she was feeling in an expansive mood, they covered most of his meals. He got free lunches at school, so that helped to round out his nutritional needs. He noted she'd left twenty dollars on the counter for him with a shopping list. He quickly scanned its contents and slid it into his pocket when he saw the first thing scribbled in her handwriting on the list...wine. That was *all* he needed Ms. Washington to read. The last thing he wanted was for Ms. Washington to see the list and put two and two together. *It wasn't as though she hadn't already figured out his mom had a drinking problem,* he thought derisively. He suspected his mom gave him the money as a kind of payoff for going to the store to get her the wine instead of her thinking of him or his needs. If they lived anywhere else, he wouldn't have been able to buy the wine, with or without the note she'd penned for him to give Mr. Richardson at the grocery store. Here, in this tiny community, lots of things went unnoticed...like the fact that he wasn't old enough to purchase wine. But because his mother had befriended the store owner, he overlooked that tiny detail.

Lucky for him he liked PB&J sandwiches. The lady in 2A, Mrs. Schaeffer, sometimes gave him some eggs, but that was rare. She only got them when her nephew visited her from Fresno, and usually she would share her bounty with him. He liked her. She'd brought him a

The Form Benders - Janet Lee Carpenter

dozen this past Tuesday and he had saved some for his birthday tomorrow.

Since his mother had left the money for him, he decided that when he picked up her wine he might splurge and buy himself a cake mix. After all, it couldn't be too hard to bake a cake and at least he'd have one for his birthday. Probably wouldn't be enough for frosting, but he didn't care, the cake was the most important. Maybe he could use one of the votive candles his mother had placed on the fake mantle for his celebration and make it a real birthday cake! He could feel his mouth water at the thought of a delicious lemon cake. He hadn't had one for ages! Not since his dad had been here...regret and sadness washed over him before he could stop it. Shaking himself, he put the lid back on the jam and returned it to the refrigerator. *Why could he remember details about their life together, but was unable to recall a single detail of his father's features?*

Most of the time he was dependent on his mother for the food he had each day, since every penny he made from his paper route went to help pay the rent. *There was nothing left over each month; there was never anything left*, he thought sadly.

Ripley put the peanut butter back into the cupboard and turned to the woman. "So, what is it you wanted to talk about, Ms. Washington?" he asked as he took a giant bite of his sandwich and lifted the handle to the tap, filling his glass with cold mountain water. *At least the water is free*, he thought with satisfaction.

"Your mother and I have been chatting, Ripley," she stated with an all too uncomfortable familiarity. *How long had she been here?* Ripley wasn't sure he liked her presumption, but at the same time he wasn't going to say anything until he found out what was going on. Having been silent while he'd made his sandwich, it was kind of a surprise to hear her speak again in the tiny residence, her words echoing off the walls in the sparsely furnished apartment. "There has been a complaint lodged stating your mother is not capable of taking care of you...*and,*" she paused for emphasis, "that you have been taking care of her and yourself for some time. The report also states that she is unfit and we have to check it out...you understand," she continued as her kind but small, beady eyes stared straight at Ripley, gauging his reactions as she spoke. Something in her eyes, however, told him all was not as it appeared to be. Though there was a kindness in them, her eyes also held a steely intent Ripley didn't trust.

His mother piped up. *She must have "come to" for a moment,* he thought in embarrassment. "Yesh, Baby…tell her how good I take care of you."

Ripley glanced over at his mother, and then back at Ms. Washington, careful not to reveal anything as he took another gulp of his water and another mouthful of his sandwich. He knew he was eating fast, but he was *starving*. Slow down, he reminded himself, *she'll think you're lying*. He couldn't lie…*wouldn't* lie for his mom. Instead, he said, "We do okay…got enough food and stuff," while he forced himself to meet her probing stare without a flinch.

"I would like to see your room, if I may." Ripley looked at her askance, shrugged his shoulders and led her to his small bedroom, sensing he would have to show her whether he minded or not. He munched on his sandwich as he led her to his room. It used to be his parents room, but since his father left, it had become his exclusively. His mother claimed the couch for herself instead. His bedroom was next to a tiny bath with just the necessities: toilet, sink, and shower. He opened the door to his small room and she leaned in next to him to peer into the room. Damn, he'd forgotten to make the bed! He leaned into the wall to keep her from pushing him into it, but to no avail…her billowy body pressed against him, forcing him against the wall. It would have been clear to Ms. Washington that he wanted to get out of the hallway…*fast*, if she had been paying any attention to him at the moment. Instead, she appeared to inspect his tiny room with the utmost interest. He held his breath while he lifted his sandwich and glass of water high above the two of them to avoid smashing it between their bodies. The scent of her cloying perfume was making him lose interest in his sandwich.

Ripley craned his neck to look back into the living room to see if he could see the bottle of wine he was sure his mother had been steadily consuming since she'd awakened this morning. There was no evidence she'd had anything, which mildly alarmed him. What had she done with the bottle?

Ms. Washington stopped leaning into his room, turned about and returned to the kitchen. Relieved, Ripley took a deep breath once she'd left the hallway. He followed her at what he thought was a safe distance.

The Form Benders – Janet Lee Carpenter

She moved closer to the breakfast bar while he maneuvered himself across the kitchen from her. As she toddled around the counter, she effectively put the slab of Formica between them as he leaned his long frame back against the opposite counter, thankful for the barrier she'd put between them. She sat down gingerly on one of the bar stools. Ripley heard the groan of the wood as she lowered her girth precariously onto the cheap stool. He was waiting for the legs to snap beneath her mighty weight; but to his surprise, they simply creaked in protest and remained strong. She leaned across the bar, crossing her arms in front of her. Her blouse was now seriously in danger of exploding and spilling its contents all over the counter. Ripley flinched.

She began speaking again and he had to force himself to look at her and not watch her chins as they rippled and moved. "I can see there isn't much food here and when you opened the refrigerator a few moments ago, there was only a small carton of milk and a few odds and ends. I am concerned for your welfare, Ripley." *She seemed overly preoccupied with food,* Ripley noted...*his food! Her tiny eyes missed nothing!*

He shrugged and moved away from the kitchen counter, heading for the light switch on the wall. He reached over and flipped it on. It was getting darker in the kitchen as the afternoon passed into the evening. He wasn't about to explain that he saved the milk for his cereal in the morning when he had it. Instead he said, "I'm fine; can I go do my homework now? I've gotten all A's and B's since I started this semester. I'd like to continue. And...if I don't get this project done, I'll get a "D" in the class...it counts for half my grade."

"Yes, I think I've seen and heard all I need to here," she said as she shoved the objecting stool backwards with a scrape. "I'm going. I will need to make a report to my office, and then we will contact your mother as to our decision." He looked at her, trying to gauge what she meant by that last comment, but she was already turning away from him. Ripley shoved the remains of his sandwich into his mouth and set his empty glass down on the counter beside him.

That sounded ominous to him! He watched as Ms. Washington walked ponderously toward the makeshift coffee table, picked up her purse and briefcase, and made her way to the door. Maybe she didn't toddle as much as she teetered; but whatever it was, she looked rather

The Form Benders – Janet Lee Carpenter

like a sailor who'd had too much to drink. He started for the door to let her out of the apartment, but she waved him away.

"I'll just see myself out," she announced as she opened the door. She seemed to have some trouble getting through the door, but when she finally managed she said, "Thank you for your time, Ms. Adams, Ripley."

As she pulled the door shut behind herself, he heard a loud crash in the hallway beyond. He stifled the urge to laugh, or to run and see what had happened, and instead stood quietly listening. Ripley finally heard footsteps on the metal stairs leading down to the street beyond. Instead of going to the door, he turned to his mother, who had slid sideways sometime during Ms. Washington's perusal of their apartment. She was already asleep on the old green couch someone had given them. He let out a large sigh, picked up the afghan lying across the back of the divan, and spread it over her. He shook his head and went to the kitchen to wipe the crumbs from his sandwich off the worn Formica counter top, and wash his glass. He dried it and placed it back in the cupboard next to her wine glass, the door making a hollow sound as it closed. Strange he hadn't noticed it there earlier; she mustn't have bothered with the glass and just drank straight from the bottle. A much worse day than he'd thought at first. He put the bread back in the drawer and turned off the light.

"I'm going to my room Ma, to do my homework. I'll see you around suppertime," he said to the quiet room. The soft snores from his mother the only other sound. *He never could stay mad at her*, he thought to himself.

Ripley went to his tiny room and flopped down on the mattress on his floor. With a lanky arm tossed recklessly over his eyes to shield him from the westerly sun shining through his bedroom window, Ripley thanked the heavens he kept the apartment clean. He hated clutter and dirt. Hopefully, Ms. Washington hadn't noticed that he hadn't made his bed this morning. He had two blankets, one for the mattress and one to cover him...it was enough. He stared up at the ceiling and wondered about all the events which had just occurred. *What did it mean to him? What did she mean when she said she'd contact them when they'd made their decision...decision about what? Who had reported them? And why did she want to see his room?*

The Form Benders – Janet Lee Carpenter

The questions floated around in his head unanswered as he closed his eyes, listening to the sounds of the forest. A chickadee chirped his objection to some intrusion into his territory, while a neighbor's dog barked somewhere in the distance. The otherwise harmonious, quiet afternoon sounds soothed him as song birds joined in. He imagined they were singing their gratitude to the day…his birthday was tomorrow!

"No big deal, as usual," he whispered to no one in particular, and tried to prevent himself from becoming excited at the prospect…but he was. A soft breeze flowed through the open, screened window and tickled his hair. Maybe he would take the twenty dollars she'd left on the counter, buy a bus ticket and leave this place. What would she do then, he wondered; find someone else to take care of her? His breathing came in deep, slow, rhythmic beats as his consciousness slipped away and faded into dreams. Tomorrow…

Chapter Two

Eyes still closed, in that place of twilight where you are half dreaming/half awake, Ripley floated in the waning sunlight. The sun's rays dappled his face as he watched the tiny dots of light on the screen of the back of his eyelids dance with the gentle breeze. Each movement of the soft zephyr brought the peace of the forest to soothe him. He could feel the light brush of the gentle wind against his cheek. He loathed the thought of moving and spoiling the blissfulness of the moment; instead, Ripley clung to sleep and the dream. The brush of something tickling his face finally moved him to brush his hand against it. When he encountered something cold, fuzzy and wet, his eyes flew open. He sat up.

There before him was a beautiful white wolf, with the bluest eyes he'd ever seen. For some reason, after his initial surprise he realized he wasn't frightened. He was, however, curious. *Where did this creature come from? Was he dreaming?* He somehow realized he was. *Don't fight the dream...it's rather pleasant,* he thought to himself. He didn't know how he knew, but he sensed this wolf was a female; she seemed to be waiting for something. He stood up and looked about him; he noticed an ethereal quality to the woods around him, and his eyes came back to the wolf. *How could he know she was waiting for him? Or did he know? Maybe he just wanted it to be so.*

What do you want? he thought to himself, and was surprised when the answer came.

She didn't speak; instead, he heard her soft, melodious tones in his head. Thoughts of a female wolf were verified when he heard her say, *"You must follow me, please."*

"Lead on," he thought in an uncharacteristically reckless moment. Gesturing with his hand, he did a little bow and indicated for her to lead the way. All the while, he was thinking this was indeed an odd dream.

"Who are you?" he queried.

The Form Benders – Janet Lee Carpenter

The wolf's gaze pierced his own as she stared deeply into Ripley's eyes, probing his thoughts. Without further thought, she turned and began walking away from him without dignifying his question with an answer. There was something about those eyes that was vaguely familiar. He was compelled to follow, wondering who she was and if she would say anything more to him. He wanted to hear her voice again, even if he could only hear it in his mind.

They walked companionably for a while in the forest, not speaking. There was nothing to intrude on the quiet but the sounds of the birds and the rustle of the forest floor as they trod softly upon the blanket of pine needles. Ripley recognized it as the forest behind his home, but somehow it looked different—more colorful and alive. In fact, it was as if all of his senses were heightened. They had been walking for quite a while, following the twisted path when she finally turned to him and spoke. He heard her gentle voice in his mind again. *"It's not much farther now."*

Who was this wolf who spoke to him in such a melodious voice? If she could read his mind as he thought she could, why would she answer none of the questions she must know were burning inside of him?

"Where are we going?" The thought formed in his mind.

"You'll see," came her cryptic reply as she picked up her pace and led him forward at a quick trot, deeper into the woods. This was by far the oddest conversation he'd ever had, or...he'd *never* had...he wasn't sure which.

"What is your name?" he questioned her. "Please tell me..." She turned her head toward him as she continued forward, and he could swear she smiled kindly at him.

"All in good time, Ripley...all in good time."

Ripley felt a jolt go through him as he realized she knew his name. Suddenly he hesitated, no longer so sure he should be following her deeper into the forest away from his home, yet he couldn't seem to stop himself. His curiosity was driving him onward; toward what destination, he didn't know.

"You don't have to worry. I mean you no harm," she read his thoughts again as she spoke softly in hers. "*I am not at liberty to explain*

The Form Benders – Janet Lee Carpenter

at the moment. All will be revealed in time, my dear Ripley. Just be patient a little longer."

It was eerie that she could read his thoughts, that she was in his mind listening to whatever dialogue he had going on. *What power did she have that she could see through him so clearly?* She flashed a look back at him as she continued onward. Still, Ripley followed her, his curiosity piqued; he could not turn back even if he wanted to. There were too many unanswered questions. They walked a short distance farther, and then crossed a small stream where a beautiful waterfall trickled down and dribbled between the nooks within the moss-covered stones. They were piled high to create the picturesque falls. It was then he realized they almost looked as if they'd been deliberately placed there. He slipped once on the slimy, slick stones as he stepped from stone to stone in the small stream, but righted himself quickly. He continued behind her as he jumped from the last stone, landing nimbly on the other side of the stream.

They must have gone nearly five miles when she finally began to slow down to a lope, her tongue lolling out of her mouth as a giant grove of aspen, young willow trees and Elderberry bushes blocked the path ahead of them.

"*This way,*" she said and appeared to step into the bushes and vanish.

Ripley stood there for a few moments, trying to discern how she had gone through the seemingly impervious wall of plants. Just then, she poked her head through.

"*Come on, Ripley,*" she urged.

"*How did you do that?*"

"*It's an illusion, Ripley...just WALK through it!*" Her voice, for the first time, seemed to convey impatience with him, as if he should have understood all along how she did it.

She disappeared again through the bushes and Ripley tentatively stuck out a hand to touch where she had disappeared. He rapidly removed his hand and shrunk back when it disappeared into the thicket. What kind of magic was *this*, he wondered? His fingers still tingled from their contact with the shrubbery. He started to put his hand in again to test the illusion when he felt a firm grip close over his hand to pull him

The Form Benders – Janet Lee Carpenter

through to the other side. As he went through, his heart slammed into his chest and the blood pulsed through his veins, giving him the fight or flight response he'd heard so much about in school. It felt like static electricity was running all over his skin, causing the hairs on his face and arms to rise.

Pure adrenalin coursed through him until he saw what was on the other side of the wall...it was *unbelievable!* The hand belonged to her! Then, just as he started to take in her appearance, she turned back into the familiar wolf companion. *What was this*, he wondered? He caught a flash of snow-white hair, and for a moment thought she was old; but she was young...close to his age! *What was going on here? How had she changed? What kind of crazy dream was this, anyhow?* Before he could assimilate what had just happened, a young girl in a bright red dress caught his eye, and he turned his head to look at her. He finally began to register what was going on in his surroundings. So much was happening at the same time; it was hard for him to process it all.

He knew his mouth was hanging open, but for the life of him, he was unable to close it. His astonishment was complete. There before him was an entire town, or village, or whatever you wanted to call it. Many people filled the area, all dressed in various attire, bustling to and fro. Animals were everywhere...wild and tame alike. The young girl, the same one who had caught his eye earlier, was running down the cobbled street with a puppy following her. She looked as though she was going to fall forward, when suddenly she changed into an owl and flew off after another boy who turned into a wolf. The puppy was still trying to catch up with them. What an odd place! There were older people and younger, giant bears and wolves, and a great deal of commotion; but he felt a quiet peace inside him in this place that defied words. Everyone seemed to walk purposefully by him, tipping hats and smiling as if seeing him there was a common occurrence. How could this place even exist without his knowledge? He knew every nook and cranny within miles of Shaver Lake...he had explored all of it!

"*What is this place, or should I say,* where *is this place?*" He scanned the street and the small buildings in front of him, trying to comprehend what he was seeing.

Ignoring his question, the wolf who had led him here stood passively, waiting for Ripley to adjust his thoughts. *"Come on, Ripley, the Elders will want to meet you."*

The Form Benders – Janet Lee Carpenter

Ripley blinked, and let himself be led by the wolf, in a daze. He was still wondering what kind of place this was. More importantly, *why was he here?* It was like coming home in a way, which unnerved him even more. He looked everywhere, trying to assimilate everything he was seeing, his bright mind grasping at all the images around him.

Finally, he realized what she had said. *"What Elders?"* He questioned her in the same internal dialogue, beginning to come back to himself. He felt disoriented, as if he was floating, and nothing was real; yet it felt like it was at the same time.

"The Elders are a group who will help you, Ripley. You can trust them with your life." She seemed amused then. She eyed him up and down, and then finished. *"Guess you already have."*

He followed his newly found wolf friend down the street, trying to take in everything and make sense of what she'd said to him. Finding it impossible, he gave up. He had the faint impression of lots of windows and an imposing log building. It sat neatly within a nest of giant Sequoias, which towered over them. Where there were pine needles and leaves strewn about on the ground at home, here it was pristine, with no natural evidence on the ground that the trees ever lost their leaves in this place. Again, he noted that everything was more colorful and deeper in hue and contrast than at home. The sky was so intense it was almost violet; tiny clouds scudded across the unfamiliar sky.

The building had large doors with stained glass in them. The panes depicted four different animals: a wolf, an owl, a bear, and a cougar. Each had their own pane within the two doors, which opened automatically. There didn't seem to be an electric eye reading their presence. *Fascinating,* Ripley thought as he studied the doors to see how they opened. A young boy he thought to be no more than twelve years old ushered him in front of the Elders, while the white wolf with the strange aqua eyes followed close behind him. As they headed into the Town Hall, they found several older people sitting around a large, community meeting table. He wasn't sure how he knew, but he felt as if he'd been here before. *How could that be?* Ripley was puzzled.

"Ripley, my boy, it's so good to have you here. Welcome to our little sanctuary." The big man with cinnamon colored hair, sitting at the center of the table, stood up. He turned instantly into a giant bear as he walked around it in an upright position, and then clasped him gently on the shoulder. Ripley blinked several times in an effort to wake himself from what he had just seen. However, the image persisted as the bear's massive paw easily covered Ripley's entire shoulder. The giant claws sprouting from his paw caused Ripley some trepidation as they neared him, so he stood perfectly still. When he stood on his hind legs, the man was easily eight feet tall. He towered above Ripley's six feet two inches with ease. Again, nothing was said outwardly; the entire conversation was taking place in his head. His booming voice echoed in the confines of Ripley's skull. As he slowly looked up at the mammoth bear's chest, he was struck by just how vulnerable he was and stepped backwards just a fraction to look into this bear's face. Seeing no threat there, Ripley relaxed, only slightly. No matter how friendly he seemed, caution seemed to be the prudent course of action here.

What is going on here? he wondered. *How is it possible for children to turn into birds and wolves? Full-grown people to change into bears? Speaking without words? Where* was *he?* Ripley was beginning to feel like Alice must have felt when she fell down the rabbit hole. Only this was a whole lot stranger, because it all seemed so real, and it was happening to *him!*

"Yes, come on in." A sandy haired man also stood...the one who was sitting next to the bear/man. In his human form, he was handsome in a regal way. His eyes were wide set and his straight nose and thin lips gave one the impression that he might be stern. He would certainly be a worthy adversary for anyone who cared to test his mettle against him; of that, Ripley was certain.

Upon ending that thought, he immediately turned into a cougar to greet him warmly. "I am known as Prince Valiantheart. This is Oren Trueblood," he said as he indicated the bear with a toss of his massive head. "Also, this is Remenion the Wise." He nodded to the largest owl Ripley had ever seen. He must have stood at least six feet tall! The owl seemed somewhat preoccupied with cleaning his feathers with his beak. He was the only one there who hadn't changed his form yet. *Maybe he can't change?...hmm, that's an intriguing thought...*

Bringing him back to the moment, the Prince said, "We are pleased to meet you in person, *finally,* Master Ripley."

"Yes, yes...," Oren said, and Remenion chorused his agreement around a mouthful of molting feathers, along with the other Elders.

The Form Benders – Janet Lee Carpenter

"Just Ripley will do. Thank you, sir," he said with a little bow…playing along with whatever game it was that appeared to be amusing them. For the first time in a very long time, Ripley didn't feel in control of his environment, and it made him terribly uneasy. Therefore, he tried his best to seem unaffected by all of this.

"Very well, Ripley…," the Prince acknowledged his request with a slight incline of his head.

He wasn't sure he liked the owl much. He had the unnerving feeling he could see right through him. In fact, he was afraid his thoughts were so transparent they could *all* hear them, yet no one had mentioned anything. He wasn't sure why they were choosing not to say anything about his thoughts. Were they too polite? On the other hand, could they only hear parts of what he was thinking? The bear, Oren, seemed quite warm and welcoming; the cougar, or rather the Prince, was a bit reserved, though he also seemed genuinely kind. Ripley started to let his guard slip.

"I'm sure you are wondering what you are doing here, Ripley. So, let us explain what is to happen here."

That's the understatement of the century, he thought to himself! "Okay," he said aloud, thinking this had to be a dream; it was just too weird to be actually happening. It had an *other-worldly* feeling to it.

"Tomorrow is your sixteenth birthday. You will be returning to us in the wakened world."

How did they know he would be sixteen? He chose to ignore the thought for the moment. "So this *is* just a dream, right?" Ripley asked the owl, not certain he understood his meaning. "That's what you're saying…right? Am I getting your drift?"

Remenion stared at the boy and Ripley felt as if he'd asked an extraordinarily dumb question.

"May I go on? There isn't much time…" He let his thoughts trail in Ripley's mind. He felt he'd just been reprimanded, but he just wasn't sure how…or why.

"Please, continue." Ripley was scared inside, which made him angry, but he kept it to himself. *Why are they talking to me like this…? It's just a stupid dream! Better yet, why was* he *taking it so seriously?*

The Form Benders – Janet Lee Carpenter

Remenion continued as if he hadn't heard his thoughts. "As I said, tomorrow is your birthday. You will return to us in the wakened world, only not in this form you wear now. You must go home, and then when the time comes, and you will know when that is my young friend, it will be time to fulfill your father's promise."

At the mention of his father, Ripley stiffened. It would be an intensely cold day, indeed, before he would keep any promises his father had uttered to these imaginary people...animals...*whatever they are!* What was he thinking? *NONE* of this was real!

Remenion acted as if he hadn't heard Ripley's emotional outburst, or had chosen to ignore it. *Maybe they couldn't hear everything.* "You are not to answer the door in the morning, young man, but you must return here on your own on the morrow. You will find a welcome here *and* a home." He batted that weird, one-eyed blink only owls have, and then continued. "Remember, nothing is as it appears, and you know little of what is to come. Your new form will begin at midnight this eve...be prepared for a new life."

Ripley thought this was the weirdest and *oddest* dream of his life. What silly nonsense this all was. He started to laugh, but the Council of Elders and the young female wolf stared at him. Her voice came to him. *"Be cautious, young Ripley. The Elders will teach you much, but do not laugh at them, for their patience can wear thin with disrespect."*

"Okay," he answered her. "At some point will I get to know your name? I mean, you know my name, I think I should know yours."

Her crystalline blue gaze turned to him then and she spoke, "Soon Ripley, you will know. For now, you must heed my warning."

Ripley calmed himself and looked quietly at her, wondering if it was possible for him to control his emotions so as not to reveal how silly he thought all of this was. A teeny, tiny spec inside of him was trying to be cautious, in case this *was* real. He shook his head in denial at the fantasy and decided to test whether he was dreaming or awake. He pinched himself. Okay, that *hurt*...but he wasn't sure if it hurt because he *thought* it would, or if it hurt because this was real. He was so confused!

The test was an absolute failure in regards to finding out if this was real or just a dream after all, but he was hoping she would disclose her name to him. She was the first *person* he'd ever met, or *wolf* rather,

The Form Benders – Janet Lee Carpenter

who had the same genetic hair thing the doctor had told him about. *What was she? Was she a wolf or human?* He wanted to know a lot more about her. She must have taken pity on him, because in the next moment she answered his earlier question.

"*I am known as Whitemane, but I had another name once. Maybe someday I will share it with you, Ripley, but for now let's leave it at that.*" She seemed perturbed at him, and he tried to smooth her ruffled scruff.

"*Very well; Whitemane it is.*" Ahh…a secret…he loved figuring out puzzles and delving into secrets! He reached out a hand to her, and she delicately placed her paw in his outstretched hand. Perhaps she forgave him his outburst with the Elders. "*Pleased to meet you,*" he offered. Somehow he would find out her other name…he swore it to himself!

"*Likewise,*" she said, and he could swear he saw that elusive smile cross her features.

He turned to the Elders earnestly then and bowed in his most courtly fashion. "I apologize if I have offended you, Prince Valiantheart, Oren and Remenion. It was not my intention. You have obvious regard for someone for whom I have little or no respect. Do not expect me to change my mind so easily," he said formally. *How did they know his father? Who were these characters?*

"And do not expect, young Ripley, to hold on to old grievances in the face of new information," Remenion said. "Your vision has yet to expand to include all things, so I suppose you can be forgiven this time. We will see you here tomorrow," Remenion stated, and then turned his back to him. He spoke softly to Oren and the Prince, and though he strained to hear, Ripley couldn't make out what they were talking about. He had been dismissed. *If only he could hear their thoughts…*but they obviously hid them from him. *How could they do that,* he wondered?

"Return him to the wakened ones," Remenion said as he turned his head 180 degrees and spoke to Whitemane, who stood behind him, "and we shall find him here tomorrow…whether it is for good or ill remains to be seen."

The Form Benders – Janet Lee Carpenter

Whitemane's thoughts spoke softly to him, *"Come Ripley, it's time to take our leave. Tomorrow will be soon enough to answer your questions."*

"But I still have questions." His thoughts came simultaneously with Whitemane's directive. A quick glance at her revealed that nothing more should be said and he would have to satisfy himself with what he knew so far. For the moment he would let it go, but they *would* tell him what he wanted to know at some time in the near future; he was counting on it.

Ripley could feel his steps lighten as he felt the weight of what Remenion said slowly lift from him. He knew each step toward the apartment and home would take him further and further from his thoughts of the village with its odd inhabitants and the dream. What kind of promise could his father have made to these...what should he call them...beings?

As he pondered what he'd been told, Ripley found himself in that weird haze again as he turned and followed Whitemane from the Town Hall, down the village street and back into the thicket. Once again the feeling of static electricity tingled all over his body as he stepped into and through the illusion of the wall. They crossed the tiny stream and backtracked through the woods. Ripley found himself not only pondering over everything he was told, but more importantly, pondering over the things he wasn't told. *What is an awakened one? How do they know my father? What form are they talking about and how do they have knowledge of what will happen to me tonight at midnight?*

This was the strangest dream he'd ever had. He could hardly wait to get to school tomorrow and share it with Pete Cranston. He and Pete had been best friends since they'd met at Sierra High School. They would have fun talking about all this fanciful stuff. Oh, wait! *Tomorrow is Saturday*...his disappointment was palpable. Since Ripley's phone had been disconnected some time ago, he would have to wait to share his dream with Pete until Monday. Maybe he could go to his house after he finished cleaning the apartment and doing the laundry tomorrow morning. The walk into the little town would do him good, and he could pick up the lemon cake mix from the grocery. The exercise would be a welcome respite from all the homework he had to do.

The Form Benders – Janet Lee Carpenter

Whitemane looked back only once as she made her way back to the clearing on the forest floor, making certain he was following her. *"Now what do I do?"* he thought to himself. They had returned to the place where he'd first seen her.

When they reached the spot, her voice came in loud and clear. *"Lie down here in the forest and close your eyes. When you open them again, this will all be gone. Remember, you are to return to the Elders tomorrow. Do not forget, nor make them wait."* Her voice echoed in his head.

Ripley shook his head and smiled. *"No, I won't keep them waiting."* He could swear he saw her frown, but she said nothing. He would awaken in the morning, and this would just be a silly dream to recount to his friend.

"Lie down and close your eyes. It will all be over in a moment."

Ripley lay down on his back; he didn't know why he trusted Whitemane, but he did. With his eyes facing the canopy of leaves above him, he started to feel a little dizzy. He fought the feeling. He wanted to ask her if he would see her again or if they would meet only in his dreams. Was she the one in the forest following him after school, or was it someone or something else? *Did she know? Would she tell him?* Before he could say anything to Whitemane, his eyes became extremely heavy. He closed them to stop the world from spinning, and when he opened them again, it was dark. He was in his room, and the forest was only a memory.

The Form Benders – Janet Lee Carpenter

✺ Chapter Three ✺

"*Damn...homework!*" Ripley bolted upright from the bed...reality urging him to his feet. Yet the dream stubbornly clung to him, trying to delay his entry into reality. He flipped on the light switch beside his bed and determinedly rifled through his backpack, shoving away the tendrils of the dream which clung to him as he took his history book out. *How long had he napped?* he wondered. He glanced at the clock on his nightstand; no more than forty-five minutes had passed. It seemed as if he'd been asleep for hours. He thumbed through the book until he found the picture of the battle of Gettysburg, and laid it on the dresser. He grabbed the diorama he'd made last week and put it on his desk. He began to place the tiny Civil War figurines Mr. Hanks gave him to complete the project on the hill in his diorama. He had been at it for over an hour when he heard his mother rummaging through the cupboards. His dream had been temporarily suspended in the back of his mind, forgotten until his homework was finished, at least. Then it slipped even further away from his memory as his mother called to him.

"Ripley?" he heard his mother call from the kitchen. "I need you...*Ripley!*" Whatever vestiges of the dream might have persisted in his thoughts were shattered when his mother called his name, and they fled just like he had in the forest earlier that day. He put the last few touches on the battlefield, set it carefully on his bookshelf and went to see what she wanted. It sounded like she was sober again.

"Yeah, ma, what do you need?"

He quickly headed for the kitchen before she tore it apart looking for whatever it was she wanted. She stood next to the kitchen sink, silver hair tousled and mussed, since her curlers threatened to come undone from her nap. She swayed with her robe open as she moved methodically through each cupboard, searching.

"What do you need, Ma?" he questioned again as he stepped up behind her and shut the two cupboard doors she'd left open.

The Form Benders – Janet Lee Carpenter

"What did you do with my wine, dear? I've looked everywhere, and I can't seem to find it." She was kind at first; sweet and cajoling...she always was. She finally turned and looked directly at her son. As soon as her eyes made contact, however, they slid away from his knowing gaze. He was unsure if she actually saw him, or if it was his father she was seeing, whose eyes were as sea-colored as his own.

"I haven't seen your wine, Ma. I was gonna ask you the same question. I wondered where it was when Ms. Washington was here. I looked for it, but I couldn't find it." He closed the lower cupboard door as he moved about behind her, still shutting the doors in her wake.

"You're the only one who takes it. *Where* did you put it?" Her voice was beginning to change pitch as her ire rose. "*Stop doing that!*" She snapped at him as he closed yet another cupboard door.

SSDD, same stuff different day, Ripley thought to himself. The more she needed a drink, the meaner she became, especially when she thought he was standing between her and her booze.

"Stop doing, *what*? Ma, I don't know where it is..." he said, deliberately misunderstanding as his voice trailed off. He *did* stop following her around the tiny kitchen though and watched her as she walked to the living room, robe flying out behind her, moving quickly to the couch. She bumped her toe on the edge of the old trunk and snapped, "Damn" as she grabbed her throbbing foot.

"Well, don't just *STAND* there! *Help me find it!*" she ordered and whirled toward the couch. She looked behind it, and then her hands clawed at the cushions, throwing them off of the couch.

Ripley made no move to help her as he watched the scene he had witnessed so many times before. His arms were linked across his chest. With his legs casually crossed at the ankles, he leaned back against the kitchen counter. He watched calmly from what he thought would be a safe distance, when he genuinely felt anything *but* calm. He wanted to yell at her. Instead, he let her vent her ire at fate. He was waiting patiently for her tirade to be over; then he would go to his room and wait for her to drink herself into a stupor. Then he'd return to straighten out the mess she made before he went to bed.

"*Aha...here it is!*" She raised the bottle triumphantly from inside the couch, between the arm and the seat, where she most likely had stuffed it when Ms. Washington showed up. At least she'd had the sense to do that. The look of utter success on her face was beautiful in a sad way. She used to look like that when *he* was around, Ripley remembered. Now, however, this was the only time he saw her face light up. Ripley turned away, unable to bear the sight of her joy in something that could so nearly destroy them both. She trotted to the kitchen and pulled her wine glass down from the cupboard. She unscrewed the cap, poured the blood red liquid into her glass, and took a long drink. Her eyes closed as if she were drinking ambrosia, not rotting grape juice.

Ripley turned from her then, realizing she didn't even know he was there. He walked into his bedroom and gently closed the door. He picked up his English book and tried to read. He stared at the book for a long time before he realized there were tears dotting the page in front of him, and he hadn't read a word on it. He rubbed the offending tears from his eyes with the palms of both hands, and then slid them on his blue jeans to dry them.

I am NOT *crying,* he swore to himself, denying the evidence even as he brushed his hand over the page. He sat there quietly listening, but there hadn't been any sounds of movement from the living room for some time now. He heard nothing but the nondescript strains of music barely discernible through the closed bedroom door. Ripley got up to check on his mother. He opened the door and he could hear the small, portable radio softly playing *Sixteen Candles*. It sat with books on either side of the shelf above the TV. Of course, the TV didn't work for two reasons: one, because they had no reception here; and two, they couldn't afford to pay for cable. So the TV sat alone and forgotten in the living room. He used to watch movies on it before the VCR quit working.

The books on either side, however, were well read through the summer months when Pete and his family went on vacation; that's when Ripley would amuse himself with reading and walking to the nearby lake, usually with fishing pole and tackle box in hand. His favorite book was "*Gone with the Wind,*" by Margaret Mitchell. Oh, he loved them all, but the well-worn pages slipped through his fingers as Scarlett O'Hara and Rhett Butler took him on a Civil War adventure. He loved stories about the Civil War and how the United States was divided in its stand against slavery. He respected President Lincoln and all he stood for. Lincoln's quest for equality and freedom for all the people of the United

The Form Benders – Janet Lee Carpenter

States eventually united an entire country, and for that, Ripley truly admired Lincoln.

He smiled as he pulled the afghan over his mother again. He tugged the empty bottle from her lax hand and placed it gently on the table. At some point, she must have returned the cushions to the couch because they were back on it. She must have fallen asleep on the couch as she listened to the music. He could still see the trails of the tears on her cheeks as he gently brushed her hair from her face, leaned over her, and kissed her forehead affectionately. They had probably played "their song" on the radio, he thought as he shook his head. That's most likely why she insisted on listening to this channel. It was the only one around that played sixties and seventies music, bringing back the early days when she and his father were together—when they were so much in love.

She stirred briefly, slipping deeper into the pillow and the afghan, and then mumbled so softly he almost didn't hear it, "Rafe…"

Ripley wasn't prepared for the sharp stab to his heart when he heard his mother cry out softly for his father. He hadn't expected her to confess her thoughts in her unconscious state, but she had, and for some reason it made him even sadder.

He checked the lit clock in the kitchen from where he stood…10:30. It was time to get ready for bed. He tiptoed to the radio and gave the knob a gentle twist until he heard the click. The silence was deafening. He went to open the sliding glass door to let in the fresh mountain air, and checked the screen to make certain it was locked. The breeze played with the curtains as they bellowed into the room and then fell back into place against the glass partition. Crime was almost nonexistent here, but one couldn't be *too* careful, he decided.

He picked up her empty wine bottle on his way back to the kitchen and tossed it in the trash can at the end of the counter. He would have to take the trash out tomorrow morning, he reminded himself. Then he walked into the tiny bathroom to brush his teeth and get ready for bed. He took a quick shower and wondered if anything would be different tomorrow. Or, would his birthday come and go without much fanfare? Well, he'd have to see. He'd go to the market in the morning and fill his mother's list, buy the cake mix he'd promised himself, and bake it. It couldn't be *that tough*. He turned off the light, stepped into his room and plugged in the tiny night light for the evening. His feet made their way to his bed by memory as he finally lay down on it, and pulled the covers up as he curled into a ball on his side to dream.

Ripley was breathing hard and fast...sharp pains wracked his body, as sweat drenched him. This was like waves of nausea, only worse. It was waves of pain instead! He couldn't catch his breath and everything seemed to ache on him. Pain coursed through him. He watched as his arms elongated and alarm filled him. *What is going on? I can't move! This has to be a dream...but, why does it hurt so much? I don't ever remember feeling pain in my dreams. Well...except for that pinch earlier.*

He felt his body changing all around him. His face hurt and it was stretching. He wanted to cry out, but no sound was issuing from him. The darkness around him seemed to press down, smothering him. He glanced at the clock...12:15 a.m.; this had been going on for *only fifteen minutes*, but it seemed like *hours!* The first pains awakened him at midnight. Another wave struck him as he gasped for breath. He didn't know how much more he could stand! He wanted to move...he wanted to scream, but he was pinned to the mattress. His vocal chords wouldn't respond to his thoughts! *If only I could get to the front room, maybe I could wake Mom. Maybe she could help me*, he thought, as another spasm hit him.

Tears streaked his face, and once again the wracking pains gripped his body, sending intermittent shivers—and then hot flashes—through him. His spine hurt, his face ached, and his whole being was a mass of nerve endings waiting to snap. He wanted to vomit, but couldn't. Waves of nausea assaulted him. He closed his eyes tightly, willing himself to make a sound, to cry out. He focused on making a noise. Anything to take his mind of off the excruciating pain he was experiencing. He tried to calm his breathing, hoping some control would alleviate a bit of the pain. Concentrating on making a sound, Ripley finally felt a cry coming from deep inside of him. It started as a rumble deep in his chest, almost a growl. Then it turned into a howl as his vocal chords finally responded to his will.

"Aowwoooo..." came his first utterance in over twenty minutes.

Suddenly the horrific pain stopped and he felt like he was on the ocean...floating without destination, to somewhere unfamiliar. He was

The Form Benders – Janet Lee Carpenter

amazed at what he saw when he opened his eyes. His room was no longer dark. He shot a quick glance at the clock...*2:30 a.m.! Wait...it had to be dark...strange*, he thought. He could see vaporous trails across his bedroom. Everything seemed so much more intense. *Gah!...were those his tennis shoes he smelled?* A quick glance at the vapor trail leading from the shoes back to him confirmed his suspicions; it was *definitely* those shoes!

He tried to get up from his bed but suddenly realized something wasn't right. Instead of his two feet landing solidly on the floorboards, four feet—or rather, *paws*, landed on the hardwood flooring next to his bed and spread out from his body. Alarm coursed through Ripley as he tried to get his four legs under him instead of spread out beneath him. When they finally took hold and were underneath him, he shook his head to clear it. Then he tentatively walked a few steps to try out his new legs. When he felt he was able to maneuver himself, he walked to the bathroom to look in the mirror hanging on the back of the door.

Thank heavens he hadn't closed the door to the tiny room, he thought to himself. He wasn't sure he would have been able to get it open otherwise. He nudged the door open with his face. Then he turned around to see his reflection. He was certain he couldn't maneuver anything with his paws. *PAWS? Omigosh! What just happened?* It was too dark in the small room to see, even with his new sight, so he rose up on his hind legs and attempted to flip the light switch on the wall. It took a couple of tries to get his paw positioned perfectly, but when he finally did and could see himself in the mirror, another low howl escaped him.

Oh my God! he thought to himself. Ripley couldn't believe what he saw. There, staring back at him was a full-fledged silvery wolf with deep sea-green eyes and a long snout. *That's not me! It can't be me!*

He denied the image, even as he backed away from the mirror...horror wreaked havoc in his mind. He bumped into the toilet, and the seat came down with a loud, hollow clang. It captured his tail as he swung around. "Aowwoooo," he howled in pain, and then stifled the urge to cry out again. *I can't wake up, Mom!* Thoughts came frantically as he stood perfectly still, his ears pricked forward as he listened intently. Hearing nothing from the other room, he calmed himself and looked into the mirror again. *What is going on here? How did this happen? Why me? Why now?* Then a thought hit him...*maybe I can just go back to bed and when I wake in the morning, everything will be back to normal!* He clung to the soothing thought, trying desperately to convince himself this was true. Deep inside, however, he didn't really believe it.

Then the dream came flooding back to him, in full color and detail.

Hadn't...what was his name again? Oh, yes...Rem... Remenion...that was it! He was certain that was the owl's name. *Hadn't he said something about a different form? Was this what he'd meant?* It was just a dream; it couldn't really be happening! Nothing in his life had prepared him for *this!* There was *no way* to prepare for what was going on at this very moment.

Ripley worked at the switch a couple of minutes, got it to go off and stood in the bathroom doorway, not certain what to do. *I'm going to go back to bed, and when I get up in the morning, this—like Remenion and Whitemane and all the others—will just be a bad dream...just more fairy tale for me to share with Pete!* He was finding it harder and harder to believe as the minutes ticked by.

He went to the bed, walked around on the mattress several times plumping the area and tried to decide which way to face, exactly...which way danger might come from, and then finally flopped down on the bed facing the doorway and curled his body up into a ball. His tail brushed against his wet nose, tickling it. His tongue darted from his mouth and licked it to stop the itch that formed there. *Eww...gross!* A profound sigh issued from deep in his chest as he licked his nose one more time in resignation before closing his eyes to fall asleep on the bed. *This was just so weird*, he thought to himself. Tomorrow would be better. Everything would be fine in the morning...

However, Ripley was not that fortunate. Instead, he found himself watching the clock as the hours swept by. He was aware of every sound out in the forest, the rustling of leaves, and a logging truck winding its way down the highway...its air brakes letting out a long, low hiss as the truck slowed for the turns in the road. Why couldn't he *relax?* Maybe because he could still smell those tennis shoes near his bed, as well as the odor of the wine his mother had consumed earlier, coming from the other room. The scent of something out there in the forest beckoned to him...something familiar. *What was it?* He was too distracted by the scent of his well-worn tennis shoes to remember, but it pulled at him, nevertheless.

The Form Benders – Janet Lee Carpenter

Ripley finally gave up and got up to pick up the tennis shoes. He picked one of them up in his mouth and carried it cautiously into the front room, letting it drop quietly from his mouth onto the floor near the TV. He went back and got the second, keeping an eye on his slumbering mother. She'd never awakened after he'd covered her earlier in the evening; at least, he didn't think she had. *What would she think if she woke up now?* He couldn't let her see him like this. *Never mind that he would never be able to explain it to her in his condition!*

He almost made it back with the other shoe when she moved. He froze dead in his tracks as he waited in tense silence for his mother to resituate herself on the couch, and then settle back into the cushions and lie still. Ripley hadn't dared to breathe during this whole thing as he waited in perfect stillness for her to begin softly snoring again. It seemed like hours as he stood paused there like a stone statue with the stinky shoe in his jaws, waiting. His newly acquired muscles were straining to their limit from the lack of movement as he remained there, hoping he wouldn't be discovered. Even his heart slowed its beat to accommodate his desire to be still.

It was amazing how his body responded to his will so perfectly. It would be nice if he could get it to do that when he was human. Sadness gripped him. *Will I ever be human again? How will my mother react in the morning? Will she scream? Will she know it's me? Will she think I'm some stray dog that found its way into the apartment after she fell asleep last night? Worst of all, will she hate me for what I've become?* he wondered in anguished silence.

She started to snore, signaling that she was deep in her alcohol induced sleep again. Cautiously he moved forward on silent paws. Slowly, he lowered the shoe and padded softly across the floor, making sure to hit the area rugs so the clicking of his toenails wouldn't be heard on the hardwood floors.

He made it back to his room in relative safety, and then climbed back on the mattress and turned several times only to find himself back in the same position as he curled into a ball on the mattress. His snout faced the door where he knew the danger would come from in the morning. He closed his eyes and swore he could still smell the tennis shoes out in the front room. He was beyond caring as his tired eyes sought their rest.

The Form Benders – Janet Lee Carpenter

His mind wandered to the dream and to Remenion and the Prince. *What did today have in store for him? Where was Whitemane at this moment?* Was that *her* familiar scent he'd latched onto earlier, coming from the forest? *Was she out there? Was she waiting for him?* The thought of her waiting for him made him smile inwardly.

Happy Birthday, Ripley, he thought sarcastically as the last vestiges of awareness slipped from him.

The Form Benders – Janet Lee Carpenter

∽ *Chapter Four* ∾

A loud pounding at the door woke Ripley from his dream.

"Open this door!" The authoritarian voice from the hallway boomed louder, "Open it *now!*"

Ripley immediately jumped to attention, his feet hitting the floor before he realized too late that he still had four feet, not two. His disappointment was momentary as he grappled with the adrenalin pumping through him at a speed faster than light. He could hear his mother stirring in the living room…the hair on the back of his neck rose in warning.

"Whaaa?" she croaked to the voice in the hall outside their apartment.

Ripley knew she was trying to awaken—probably with a hangover. He was certain the pounding on the door was *nothing* compared to the pounding in her head. He padded across the floor of his room to the bedroom door and nosed it open a tiny bit to survey the scene. For some reason, he felt an urgency to get out of here, out of this apartment…and it had to be soon. The immediate problem was…*how was he going to get out without his mother seeing him?*

The banging on the door persisted as a disembodied voice once again demanded, "Open this door! This is CPS! Police officers are with us! *Open it, or we'll knock it down.*"

That finally got a response from his mother as she moved from her sitting position, still managing to hold her head with one hand. She staggered to her feet and massaged her temples with both hands as she tried to navigate her way to the door. She managed a strangled, "Wait…" then seemed to find a stronger voice and said, "I'm coming."

Ripley watched with anticipation as she stumbled a little past the coffee table, her back to his bedroom door as she approached the entry. *Now was his chance!* Before she could see what he'd become, and without hesitation, Ripley burst into a full run, flashing across the living room floor. He hit the screen door he'd locked last night at a speed to which he was unaccustomed. He didn't have time to reflect on the feel of the velocity of his movement, however. The shattering of the screen against the porch railing as he hit it made his mother stop her uneven path to the door. She whirled around just in time to watch in horror and amazement, as he scrambled up the screen. She couldn't have seen more than his tail disappearing over the railing. At the same moment, the door crashed into the apartment and men were swarming all over the tiny space. Ripley could hear the barrage of questions they shot at his mother in rapid-fire staccato.

"What happened in here? *Who was that?*"

Another voice asked, "Are you hiding him?"

"Hiding who?" she questioned indignantly. "What are you doing here? Look what you've done to my *door!*"

Another voice shouted, "There he goes, men...*get him!*"

That was the last thing Ripley heard as he hit the trash dumpster below their apartment, and then the ground—hard. He lost his footing and slid sideways before he righted himself. He gave his body a quick shake and took off once again. He continued to run at breakneck speed across the field. The feeling of the air in his furry coat was invigorating. He could hear the voices behind him now—they were after him, trying to capture him as he ran swiftly toward the forest and anonymity. The pounding of his feet kept him moving toward the safety of the woods. *Once inside, I can slow my pace*, he thought. However, that thought was short lived as he burst into the glen and heard another sound in the distance. The men had given up their foolish foot chase and a low rumble began, causing him even greater alarm.

*Vroom...vroom...*he knew that sound! His pursuers had a motorcycle! Not one, it sounded like several! They were coming after him...*where to run, where to hide?* As he dashed through the pines, the adrenalin pumped through him, forcing his feet to fly down the uneven path. There was no time to enjoy the scent of musky bear clover. They were coming closer. He had to find a safe place to hide. Ripley couldn't remember the way to the place he'd been shown in his dream, but his feet seemed to have a will of their own as they moved quickly in unison. With all four feet off the ground, they landed again and again to repeat the process, eating up the distance as he pounded onward. He was running aimlessly, pine needles flying from behind his hammering paws, his tongue lolling out of his mouth as he pressed forward—he kept going. The motorcycles were further away. He had gained some distance!

Then abruptly, he saw it! There ahead of him was the tiny stream, mossy rocks and all. Ripley didn't think he'd ever seen anything as welcoming as that little tributary of water was right at that moment. It had seemed larger in his dream. It couldn't be more than a few feet across. He *had* to drink...he was parched! He lapped at the water quickly, and then he stopped briefly and looked over his shoulder. His ears pricked forward as he listened for the cycles and the signs that they were on to him. When he heard them still in the distance, he decided he had a few more moments to quench his thirst before he picked up the pace. He drank greedily, wondering how dogs ever got their thirst quenched when they could only drink what they could catch on their tongues!

The sounds of the cycles were getting closer. He had to go! He lifted his head, picked his way across the small stream and headed more deeply into the forest at a canter. This time, however, he knew the way. He picked his way across boulders and grassland and across the forested floor without any hesitation in his step. His feet found what his heart already knew—*sanctuary!* He came to the grove of aspens, and without a thought for the illusion he stepped through it into the town he'd come to think of as his personal haven. Remenion told him he would find a home here...he hoped that was right, because right now he was homeless and about as confused as anyone could be. The only home he'd *ever* known might as well be a million miles from here. He flopped onto the ground, panting—praying he'd lost them.

The sounds of the motorcycles came very near and then stopped unexpectedly. Ripley tensed; he sensed they were looking for him. He didn't know how he could sense such things; he just knew he could. Another of his new abilities, he assumed. It must have something to do with the fact that he was a wolf. He was quickly becoming aware of many new attributes as he briefly studied his new form. He heard footsteps outside the grove and closed his jowls to quiet himself as he waited. They seemed to stop right outside of where he lay.

"He just...disappeared," one voice said.

"His tracks just end here," another spoke.

"He has to be here, somewhere," the first one said emphatically.

"Oh yeah, well where is he then, *Mister I know everything?*" The second voice snarled at the other man.

There was a pause and Ripley could almost see the man trying to control his temper. *"I...don't...know,"* he clipped out. "There! You happy? I don't know where the hell he is!" Seeming to gain some control, he snapped, "Fan out and let's find him!"

Ripley could feel him on the other side of the barrier...he laid there so still that even his breath stopped for a moment. He knew the man was waiting—and listening; so was he. Ripley watched the entry point, wondering if he would find his way in, but nothing happened. Finally, he heard the footsteps of the man on the other side of the wall of aspens. He was walking away from the wall...*he was safe!* He let out the breath he'd been holding, and then stood and turned back toward the scene of the small town.

"Head down near the lake! See if he's down there!" The man's voice faded away. Ripley didn't think he would ever forget the raspy voice of the man who chased him; the one who got so angry. He was the one in charge, and Ripley getting away didn't sit well with him. His scent was strong. He smelled of cigars and sweat—and of something else, too. Maybe it was apples? He wasn't sure, but he would never forget the scent. It was etched in his mind forever.

Now what? he wondered as he stood up, and then loped down the hill and into the quaint settlement of odd people. Wooden and brick buildings stood side by side on the main thoroughfare. Ripley didn't notice any cars; mostly there were horse drawn carriages and wagons. It was like a scene from the old West, sprinkled with a dash of an English village, and a touch of the South spattered in for color. White shutters lined most of the buildings, and there was no disrepair here to be seen. The old-fashioned boardwalk must be swept daily, as the boards gleamed with cleanliness. He suddenly noticed her. Whitemane was walking down the boardwalk and looked up, just as he entered the boulevard.

"Haloooo," she howled in greeting.

"Haloooo," he howled back, laughing to himself at the funny way in which he spoke.

The Form Benders – Janet Lee Carpenter

Whitemane trotted up to him, a bounce in her step as she approached him, obviously overjoyed to see him. She jumped, ever so slightly, off her front feet and gave him a friendly nip on the back of his neck.

"I thought I became lost, but then I found this place," Ripley thought to her in amazement.

"You will always be able to find this place, Ripley. It's in your heart, your blood."

"I was so scared. Those men...they were after me. Who are they? What do they want with me? What is happening to me? I don't understand..." his thoughts trailed off as he waited for answers from her.

"What men, Ripley?" she continued speaking to him in her mind as a frown marred her lovely features. *"Perhaps we should go see the Elders. They can answer your questions better than I. Maybe the Elders know who the men are and why they were chasing you...,"* she answered evasively, worry etching her brow.

Disappointment covered Ripley's features. He wanted answers, and he wanted them *now!* She must have sensed his disappointment and frustration because she sent her thoughts to him, *"I'll take you to them. I believe Remenion and the Prince are at the Town Hall right now. We can probably catch them before the meeting. You're early; we weren't expecting you until a little later."*

Ripley blinked at her, confused as to how they could know he was coming at any specific time, or at all, for that matter. *He* hadn't known he would even come here, or be able to find it this morning *in any case*, so how did *they* know? He probably shouldn't be amazed, though; he knew that. These beings seemed to know much more than *he* was aware of. He was beginning to realize they worked on a different plane of awareness than he did. He was also starting to get an inkling of what this was all about. After all, last night after he'd changed forms hadn't he known on some level that he would have to run from the apartment, not just because Remenion had told him so? Or that he would run and hide from his mother and everything he'd ever known when he heard the knock on the door only an hour or so before?

The Form Benders – Janet Lee Carpenter

He didn't know what had happened to him, or what was in store for him—but one thing he did know: Remenion had answers, and he wanted them!

He followed Whitemane as they picked their way through the people on the boardwalk and crossed the cobblestone street at a quick trot, heading for the one building Ripley was beginning to know so well. They trotted in silence as his mind went over the questions plaguing him. *Who were those people this morning? What did they want with him?* He unconsciously picked up the pace as he got closer to the Town Hall where the Elders were awaiting his arrival…he hoped.

He briefly admired the log building as they approached it. With its huge glass windows ringing the building, and the stained glass in the heavy oaken doors, it was impressive in itself. As they approached the doors, once again they opened of their own accord. No doormen were there to greet them as they stepped into the cool interior of the foyer. The small entryway opened into a massive common room with a large marble fireplace, which almost covered the back wall. There were vaulted ceilings, and rows of tables and chairs were set up before the stage. In the center of the room was a large, spotlessly clean chandelier. Delicate teardrop crystals hung from the wired frame, sending rainbows about the room in a profusion of light and color.

At the very back of the hall, in front of the imposing fireplace, stood a podium on a stage wherein the Elders presumably sat when conducting meetings. Today, only Remenion was there, sitting perched on the massive podium, watching as the two of them approached. There was no Prince in sight.

Their toenails clicked in unison on the slate floor as they made their way to the stage area. Remenion eyed Ripley curiously as he approached. He felt Remenion's scrutiny as he made his way to the dais with Whitemane, wondering what the elder was thinking as he watched them come to him. They stopped abruptly at the stage, which was raised two feet above the floor, forcing the pair to look up into the stern visage of the owl.

Remenion continued to stare at him intently, and Ripley could feel himself grow more uncomfortable under his inspection. When Ripley could stand it no longer, he cleared his throat, but before he could speak, he heard Remenion's words ring through the hall.

The Form Benders – Janet Lee Carpenter

"You are here early. What has happened, please? Do not leave anything out, as everything that happened in the last twenty-four hours is important in the extreme."

He forgot what he was about to say, so he spoke instead about what just happened this morning. "Well...," he began reluctantly, and decided to give him the short version of what had occurred, "last night, when I arrived home after my 'dream', I fell asleep. When I awoke, I was in horrible pain—and my body...well, it did this...," he said incredulously, and indicated his shifted form. "I thought it was a dream, but as you can see, I am still a wolf." He returned his gaze to the owl and watched Remenion carefully. He wondered if there was something they weren't telling him. Then he blurted, "Why didn't you tell me this would happen?"

"If you recall, Master Ripley, I *did* tell you. I said you would return to us in a different form. I'm afraid I didn't know which form the magic would choose, only that you would NOT be in your human form. The magic is never wrong."

"Ripley...," he said as he began to correct him. Remenion nodded to acknowledge his request. Unprepared for this simple reasoning, however, Ripley didn't know what to say.

Remenion continued with his interrogation, watching him closely. "Perhaps that is too far back, young Master. What I really need to know is what happened this morning." Remenion continued while his gaze pinned him in place.

"Well, I had trouble getting to sleep after I changed into this form. I wasn't sure what was happening to me." Ripley felt as if he was going to cry as he stood there. He swallowed audibly and looked down at the gray slate floor as he took a couple of deep breaths to get the tears under control. When he felt stronger, he looked up again at Remenion.

Once, several years ago, his father had questioned him about an incident at school when he was caught fighting the school bully. He was sent home with a note and suspended for three days, even though it wasn't his fault. His father questioned him the same way Remenion was doing now...with that same intent stare, delving deep into his private life. It made him extremely uncomfortable. As it turned out, his father backed the principal and not him. His father told him that fighting, no matter what, was *not* acceptable behavior from an Adams. Why could he remember things like this, but was unable to recall his father's features? The mystery disturbed him.

He shook the memory off. As the story suddenly began to pour out of him, he felt the strength flow back into him.

"I woke up this morning to someone banging on the door. Actually, I think I was awake before that, because I sensed something. I can't tell you what it was, but it made the hair on the back of my neck stand up."

"Yes, go on," Remenion encouraged him.

"I remember being worried about how I was going to get out of the apartment without my mother seeing me in this condition. When she got up to go answer the door, she turned her back to me and I saw my chance. I flew across the room and barged through the screen door. It landed on the porch railing, and I scrambled up the screen like it was some kind of ramp. I flew over the railing and down onto the trash bin, and then into the parking lot. I remember thinking how amazing it was that I didn't hurt myself, since I'd just jumped almost one full story!" Ripley shook his head, still amazed at the feat he'd performed.

"Did you see who was at the door?"

"Well, that was the strange part. They identified themselves as CPS, but I've never heard of them breaking down a door before." Ripley frowned and stared off into space for a moment when he was abruptly brought back to the present as Remenion asked him another question.

"Did you see them?" he asked urgently.

"Well…yeah—I saw them, but not when they broke into the apartment. I saw them later, when they chased me on motorcycles. I made it through the forest and into the entrance to this place. That's when they lost me."

Remenion frowned and cast a quick look at Whitemane, who also looked concerned. "Did they see how you got here?"

"Um…I don't think so."

"You don't *think* so?" He moved now from the podium and flew into Ripley's face as he stared deeply into his eyes. "I need to know,

The Form Benders – Janet Lee Carpenter

Master Ripley. You must be certain! Think carefully—did anyone see you enter, or where you entered? Answer me, boy!"

Ripley stepped back in the face of his intensity, drawing his head back as he tried to think.

"No…no one saw me enter," he stammered. "They came looking for me, and said that my tracks stopped at the wall of aspens. They seemed furious that they couldn't find me. They went on down the road, looking for me. One of them stayed behind for a little bit before he left too. I got the impression he was their leader."

"Did he have the scent of rotting apples about him?"

"Why, yes…yes he did!" Before he could ask how Remenion would know such a thing Remenion twisted his head and, continuing to stare at Ripley, he flew back to the podium, seemingly satisfied. Yet it was obvious to Ripley that he was still unsettled. He looked at Whitemane and nodded once.

Ripley watched the exchange, trying to figure out what just happened, when Whitemane bowed and whispered she would return shortly.

"Where are you going?" He watched as Whitemane turned and her nails clicked their way across the floor once again.

"I'll be back later. Your meeting isn't over," she replied. The doors opened for her and she stepped out into the mid-morning sun.

"Where is she going?" he asked Remenion.

"She is going to cover your tracks…just in case. She'll be back within the hour." Remenion seemed completely unconcerned as he walked about on the podium, as if he was trying to figure out how to say something.

When he spoke, Ripley frowned at the information. "I was not in favor of telling you some of the things the Prince and Oren suggested I tell you. Since they are not present for this meeting, however, and are attending other affairs, I must make a decision I am loath to make right now. However, this cannot be helped, and I believe with my whole heart that you need to be prepared for some things which will come to pass shortly. So, I must follow their advice and tell you a story in the utmost confidence," he continued, "trusting that you will not mention this to anyone outside of this room, or anyone but the Elders." He waited for Ripley's assent before beginning. Ripley nodded to him.

"About a month ago, on the night of the new moon," he began, "two of our most beloved members of this place disappeared. By 'disappeared', I mean they simply did not return from their forest forage. This wasn't the first time we had an uneasy feeling there might be an evil in the forest; it was unlike anything we've ever had to deal with. It was the first time it actually came after one of us and touched our lives." He shifted on the podium restlessly before he continued. "If the townspeople were to know of this, it might cause unnecessary panic."

Ripley's thoughts flashed across the screen of his mind as he remembered the presence he'd felt in the woods only yesterday. He wondered if that presence was the same one Remenion was speaking of now.

"One of these people was Whitemane's natural father—the other was Oren's younger sibling—his brother. We searched the forest and found evidence of a struggle. One of our best trackers, Malador, followed their scent. He went all the way into the city, hiding in the alleys in Fresno. While creeping around at night, he found where the trail ended. He couldn't get in, but he could taste the scent of our loved ones inside the building. He was almost seen by one of the men who came outside to smoke a cigar, but he escaped just in time. This man reeked of cigar smoke and, as you may have guessed already…rotting apples."

"Rotting apples," they said in unison. "But why are you telling me all this, Remenion?" Ripley questioned the owl.

"Because we believe the people who chased you into the forest this morning were part of that organization. That this man is one of the leaders of the group."

"No, it couldn't be," Ripley denied. "They were with the woman who came from the Child Protective Services yesterday."

"Would that have been a very large woman with dark hair and ill-fitting clothing?" His piercing gaze once again locked onto Ripley's as he waited for an answer.

"Well, *yes*…as a matter of fact, it was." He couldn't hide his confusion. Remenion's comment brought back her appearance in

The Form Benders – Janet Lee Carpenter

amazing and startling detail. Ripley shivered at the image of her standing in his mother's living room.

Remenion picked up the story again, "She is the head of the organization we are watching in the Fresno district. They are attempting to destroy those of us who are able to bend our forms into others. Why this is, we are not certain. So far we have been able to outrun, outmaneuver, and outsmart them. You have come to us to help, though I am concerned about how much help you can be when you know so little." Remenion turned away from Ripley and shook his head.

"I don't know what help I can be, but if I can help in *any* way, I would be willing..." Ripley's comments trailed off as he remembered the beady eyes of Ms. Washington yesterday. *Was it only yesterday when she had stood in his apartment?* He was surprised he'd made the offer, but even more surprised when he realized he meant it. In such a short time, he had come to trust these funny people, or animals, or *form benders,* as Remenion called them.

"As you wish, Master Ripley...if you indeed mean what you say...," he paused as Ripley nodded and finally gave up on correcting Remenion about the title he'd bestowed upon him, "then there is much we must do. When Whitemane returns, we shall go over the plans. You must meet Malador and preparations must be put into motion."

"Who is Malador?"

"He is our best tracker—a wolf bender like you. He has a lot of street smarts, but he is one of the only ones who came to us from the city; most came from the forest area surrounding this place."

"May I ask one more question, Remenion?"

"Speak, child," he said, not unkindly.

"Who are these people?"

"They call themselves the FBEF."

"What is the FBEF?" Ripley questioned.

"That is *two* questions, Master Ripley, but I shall answer." His eyes twinkled with repressed humor and Ripley warmed to him at that moment. "They are initials representing, 'Form Benders Eradication Force'. You must be careful, Master Ripley; much rides on your shoulders. Your future and ours is irrevocably intertwined in such a way that we cannot be separated."

"I will do what I can, Remenion."

"Good, then there is no time to waste. We must get you started. I shall contact your mentor to begin your lessons. You must learn each of the forms before too much time has passed."

"I noticed Oren and the Prince were able to change forms. Am I able to do it as well?"

Ripley's face fell when he heard the answer. "Eventually, you shall be able to change forms at will, but that time has not yet come. With each quarter cycle or full cycle of the moon, there will be another period where you are able to take on another form, but for now, you shall remain in your present form. This is the most important form for you at this moment. You must trust the form and the teachings of that form. You will be able to shift from wolf to human in a short while; it is all up to the Great One. There is another…" he started, and then seemed to think better of saying anything at that second. Ripley let his comment slide for the moment, though curiosity burned inside of him. He focused on what he'd been told only moments before.

"Eventually." Remenion's words hung in his mind as disappointment filled Ripley. He never got to say goodbye to his mom. No matter how estranged they had become these last few years, he loved her deeply, and it was going to be hard not seeing her. And now, from what he understood about what Remenion said, he wouldn't be able to change back into his human form for some indeterminate amount of time, so he wouldn't be able to return home anytime soon. He wondered who would take care of her and if she would worry about him. She would probably think he'd just gone to Pete's house for the weekend. He wished he'd done more to let her know he cared about her…that he'd communicated with her better. Now it was too late. The thought saddened him immeasurably. Who was this *Great One* Remenion spoke of with such reverence?

Then a thought occurred to him. "You said cycle or quarter cycle of the moon. What does that mean?" he questioned Remenion.

The Form Benders – Janet Lee Carpenter

"The quarter cycle of the moon is the four cycles of the moon in a month, waxing, waning, and the full and quarter moon. The full cycle would include all of these."

"How will I know which cycle will find me in another form?" Ripley asked the Owl.

"Again, it is up to the Great One. There is only one before you who has mastered the quarter cycle; it is a very rare phenomenon."

"I see," Ripley muttered, though he didn't see at all.

"Ringer!" Remenion called to someone just out of sight. It was the same young boy who escorted him into the hall only yesterday. *Wow, had only one day passed since he'd been here?* It was hard to believe. "Take Master Ripley to the Johns' house. They will give him a place to sleep until we can get him set up on his own."

"Right away, Sir," Ringer said to Remenion. Once again, Ripley had been dismissed. He realized, however, that this time he didn't mind as much. Ringer placed his hand gently on the back of his neck and guided him down the hall and into the foyer. The doors opened mystically again, and they both stepped through. As they headed down the stairs, the opening closed with a soft whoosh.

"Follow me," Ringer said and dropped his hand from Ripley's neck. They walked down onto the boardwalk and headed back in the direction he and Whitemane had trod earlier. As he trotted next to Ringer, his mind swam with all the information Remenion had given him. Ripley was a *form bender? Why would someone want to make them all disappear?* He looked at the mottled array of people and animals on the busy street and wondered, *Are all of them form benders?* The horror of all of them being placed in cages or killed upset him deeply, and he wondered at that. He shook himself to shove the ugly thoughts away from him as he followed Ringer obediently. How odd…the more questions he asked, the more questions he seemed to have…funny how that worked.

Chapter Five

When they arrived, the Johns greeted Ripley warmly. "Come in, come in," Papa said to Ripley. "We've been expecting you!" His cherubic face and kind eyes sparkled. As Ringer stepped back and turned to go he added, "Won't you come in and join us, Ringer? There will be plenty of food in about fifteen minutes. We would be honored if you would stay."

Ringer smiled at Papa Johns and said, "Why I would love to, Papa...especially if Mama has made some of her delicious pumpkin pudding!" Mama smiled and blushed prettily.

"Oh, you two, stop it!" Her musical laughter floated to them from the kitchen, and Ripley felt himself warm to these two jovial people.

Since Ripley had met Ringer he'd been very serious in his demeanor; now he became quite animated. His gentle, quiet manner became ever-so-slightly more outgoing. He was glad Ringer would be staying, if for no other reason than he liked the boy's company. Something about him was gentle and kind.

"Then come and join us." He removed the pipe which seemed to be an extension of his mouth, and hugged the boy warmly.

Papa Johns smiled and stepped back so he and Ripley could enter the dwelling. Low to the ground, the earthen structure was solid and well lit; yet when he entered, the room was airy. The dwelling was dug at least four feet into the ground, so even though it appeared small from the outside, the ceilings were actually high once inside. Round windows sat at the top of the walls around the living space and gave a glow to the immaculate interior. Though the floor was bare earth, the stones with which it was built were dust free and shiny. It was as if they had been touched many times during their cleanings, and worn even smoother by the loving hands that tended them. Braided, hand-made throw rugs littered the floor and a large mahogany table sat surrounded by eight chairs. A worn, but clean, crocheted tablecloth lay across its top. A horn of plenty, its contents spilling haphazardly across the center of the table, adorned it in a festive manner. Fresh squash, gourds and autumn fruits like apples and pears burdened the table as a centerpiece to this warm and inviting place.

Mama Johns wiped her hands on her apron and smiled as she turned from kneading dough on a wooden cutting board. A fine sheen of flour dusted her arms, the front of her body, and the very tip of her rosy nose. A warm fire burned cheerily in the fireplace, and the huge iron kettle hanging in it steamed an aromatic scent into the room. Ripley's mouth watered as the fragrance from the contents of the pot teased his snout.

"There's stew on the fire and I'm making cornbread. You, young man," she indicated Ripley, "shall have some cinnamon rolls for in the morning!" She looked disparagingly at the flour covering her ample frame and smiled in spite of herself at the mess she'd made. "I was never a 'clean' cook," she giggled engagingly. "Everything should be ready shortly. If you gentlemen would like to find a seat near the fire, I'll bring you all some tea." Lovely blue eyes twinkled as Mama guided them toward the crackling fire which gave the home its warm feeling. It was chilly outside, so it was nice to have somewhere to call home—even if it was temporary.

"Yes, let's sit." Papa went to an overstuffed chair which sat to the right of the fireplace and Ringer joined him in the smaller version—presumably Mama's chair when there weren't any visitors—to the left of the fireplace. Ripley smiled at the warm comfort emanating from these two. He lay down between them on the rug in front of the fire, and listened to snippets of conversation as the heat, the camaraderie, and the warm smells of home cooking worked their magic on him. He hadn't realized how exhausted he was from his journey, or how hungry he was! He was almost asleep when the door burst open and two boys and a girl came bounding into the room.

"Daddy, did you hear? He's here!" The petite girl launched herself at Papa and landed squarely in his lap. Papa's air came out of him with a loud *woof,* even as laughter spilled from him.

"Yes Angel, I heard..."

"And did you hear, Papa? He's already changed!" Papa cleared his throat and looked down at Ripley. The boys—being older—seemed to have caught on to Ripley being there sooner than Angel did. He grinned inwardly at the girl's obvious discomfort as she realized her mistake.

"Oh, I'm sorry!" Her little red cheeks took on an even deeper hue as she smiled politely at him, and dark brown ringlets framed her heart shaped face. She looked tousled and wind-blown from playing outside.

Ripley picked himself up from where he was resting, stretched, and then sat at attention. He looked at Angel, and then at the boys.

"Ripley, I would like you to meet my children. This is Angela." His love for his daughter emanated from him like a tangible thing as he introduced her. "We call her Angel; everyone does." Angel hopped off her father's lap and did a quick curtsy. She fell to her knees in front of Ripley, hesitantly reaching out to touch his fur. When he didn't object, she stroked his back for a moment. Ripley decided he liked the feeling of her hand running along his spine, causing tiny shock waves of delight as she straightened out his fur. His head swung in the direction of the two boys and they stood watching him quietly, mouths agape, while their father continued.

Papa beamed as he stood and then walked over to the boys. He placed an arm around each of them and said with fatherly pride, "And these, are my sons...Ethan and Evan." He slipped a long forefinger under Evan's chin and gently shut his son's mouth. The other boy followed suit as if they frequently mimicked each other's moves. If there had been any doubt about the family resemblance, it ended when he looked into the duplicate pairs of eyes. They were the spitting image of each other. Both boys had identical haircuts and their laughing blue eyes told him Mama was part of their lineage. They had their father's dark hair and robust stature, too.

Mama headed for the door where the cool autumn air came into the room in bursts. "Have you forgotten your manners, Ethan...Evan?" She scolded them though there was no sting in her words as she closed the offending portal. "Shut the door when you come inside."

Both boys were immediately contrite. "Sorry Mama," they chorused.

"Go put your things away, and get cleaned up for supper. It's almost ready, boys."

The Form Benders – Janet Lee Carpenter

Mama shooed the boys from the room toward the back of the small abode. Ripley took in all the camaraderie and laughter in this home and realized what family should be. He felt his heart ache a little for the family he once had and would probably never have again. He closed his eyes briefly, and then opened them. Angel set the table, and even Papa was helping by getting the spoons to place at the side of each bowl. One place setting was strangely missing its utensil. He wondered briefly at it and then became distracted once again by the boys' chaotic entrance into the room (though they seemed a bit more subdued than they were during his first meeting with them).

Mama grabbed a metal hook with a long, well-worn wooden handle which looked as if it had been used for a very long time and walked to the fireplace. She levered the huge cast iron pot from the heat by latching it over the metal arm and pulling on it. The pot swung easily out of the fire. She handed her husband the oven mitt she held in her hand. He ceremoniously lifted the heavy container with the bubbling stew and set it in the center of the table. At some point, Mama Johns must have moved the centerpiece, because now it sat to each end of the table instead of the center. Accompanied by the mouth-watering aroma of vegetables in the thick broth, the heavy chunks of cornbread and the pot of honey were now making their way to the table in Angel's small, but capable, hands. He drooled in anticipation.

"Everyone join us at the table, please." Now he understood why there was one place set with no utensil; it was *his* spot and he couldn't use one. He was feeling embarrassed and touched at the same time at Mama's foresight and understanding. He smiled at her in his funny way—mouth open and tongue lolling to the side—with his eyes saying *thank you*. He moved to sit at the place directly opposite Papa. The children gathered 'round the table, each pulling out a chair. Ripley had the seat of honor at the head of the table and everyone, without exception, waited for him to sit before they sat in their places. When Ripley was seated comfortably on the footstool which resided near Papa's overstuffed chair, the family began their chatter as Mama dished up the stew with practiced hands.

Dinner was a noisy affair. The boys told of their day in the park, and Papa explained a little about the town. Ripley listened as he ate his food in comfortable silence. Every once in a while he would interject, but for the most part he just listened. He felt awkward lapping up his food from his bowl, but no one seemed to notice or pay it any mind. He began to relax and relish his meal with unaccustomed joy. This was quite possibly the most food he'd consumed in one meal in the last few years. The cornbread and honey was amazing, and he told Mama so.

"I believe, Mama, this is the best cornbread I've ever eaten!" Ripley said audibly to her as the gooey sweet honey dripped from his chin.

"Awww…you're just saying that, Ripley." He thought he saw her blush as she brushed the compliment away.

"No, really, it is. I've never had better!" He licked his muzzle again and enjoyed the sweet taste as it melted onto his tongue.

"Well, that's awfully kind of you. I am glad you like this simple meal."

Evan leaned toward Ripley and said softly, "She's been working on it all day."

"Oh *hush now*, Evan!" Angel and the twins broke into peals of laughter at the look on their mother's face when her secret was revealed. Her pleasure was evident on her face when the laughter finally died down. Even Ringer enjoyed the gentle ribbing Mama received.

"So, what is school like, Ripley?" Ethan asked him and then leaned forward intently to hear his answer. Ripley suddenly realized these boys probably had never been to school…he couldn't recall having seen one in town. He thought their story might be more interesting than his was, but ever mindful of his manners, he answered them before attempting to ask any questions of his own. "School is a lot of work," Ripley tried his best to explain. The twins looked at each other and smiled.

"Go on," they spoke in unison. Angel studiously watched her spoon as it made the journey to her mouth. Ripley wanted to laugh as he watched her "oh-so-intent" face. She was so focused on the spoon he doubted she even heard a word he'd said so far. Ripley smiled inwardly and continued.

"Well, I have six periods I go to, which allows me to learn a bunch of different things. I spend time in each class, and then I go home and do homework. I get graded on a lot of things…"

The Form Benders - Janet Lee Carpenter

"What are grades?" Evan was the one to ask this question. Papa and Mama watched them as they all interacted with each other, clearly pleased with the fact that they were getting along so well.

"Well, we have a teacher. Someone who has gone to school for several years to learn how to teach us, and they look at your homework to make sure you've done the work. Then, they test you on the information to make certain you know the material. If you did well, then you get a good grade. There are A's, B's, C's, D's and F's. A's are the best, of course!"

Ripley watched as their eager interest waned into perplexed frowns on their identical faces. "What's wrong, guys? You look confused."

The twins looked at each other again, and Evan was the one to address their confusion. "We don't understand why you would need a grade in each class. Don't you just learn it?"

Peals of laughter poured from Ripley, in spite of himself, and then he tried to control his laughter when he saw the boys' smiles. They seem halfhearted, at best, as they tried to join in on the private joke they clearly didn't understand. He calmed himself so he could give them an earnest answer. "Some people in my school learn the information, and some of them just blow off class to mess around with girls and do all kinds of things, rather than what they should be doing. They end up not passing the class and some of them even end up not graduating from school."

This seemed genuinely to amuse the boys as they grinned at each other. It was Ripley's turn to be confused by *their* reaction. "What's so funny?" he questioned the twins; his brows drew down over his eyes, making him look rather ferocious.

"Oh, sorry," Evan responded quickly. "It's just that we have something called mentors, not teachers. If we don't learn what they teach us, like our Life Skills class, then we don't get to forage in the woods with the others our age. Our classes are more intense, and the situations we face in the woods can mean life or death. We need to know what to do to protect ourselves, and maybe even save our lives and the lives of those who depend on us."

"Do these 'mentors' go to school?"

The Form Benders – Janet Lee Carpenter

The boys, genuinely amused, attempted to answer the question as best they could. "Well, if you mean—do they go to a building somewhere and learn stuff? No, not really...the community chooses our mentors. The Elders know which of us knows our trade well, and these form benders are chosen to share their knowledge with us. They serve for two years, and then they go back to their chosen profession," Evan finished.

"What happens during the time they mentor you guys?"

Ethan spoke this time, "The village takes care of them."

"Takes care of them? How do you mean?" Now Ripley was the curious one.

"The village shares its forage feasts and helps with clothing and things like that. The Miller family donates wool and cloth to be made into clothing. Mama helps sew clothes for the families during their time of mentorship." Evan spoke with obvious pride at his mother's contribution to the community.

Ripley thought it clearly made sense, seeing how they all would need different skills according to their different form bending gifts. He was quite certain the owls would use entirely different skills in the forest than, say, a wolf. He nodded to the boys and wondered what they meant by *foraging*. Was this something all of them did? He thought it might be impolite to ask, so he changed the tack of the conversation instead.

"I see. How long are your studies then?" Ripley's curiosity about people and things drove him to ask.

This time Ethan answered, "Our studies start when we are six weeks old with our parents, and then we begin our formal education at around three months old. It lasts until we are two."

Ripley was intrigued. "What do you do after you're two?"

"Then we begin to forage for ourselves. We have a 'Forage Quest' at the age of ten, where we go into the forest for three days and three nights and we forage for food for the entire village. We shape bend much sooner than those awakened ones on the outside. They don't shift until their sixteenth birthday." Ripley was fascinated. "When we have completed our mission, we return to the village with our kills and there is a great celebration and feast. There are games. We spend days

The Form Benders - Janet Lee Carpenter

celebrating our coming of age." The boys laughed at the memory of their celebration.

"And there are prizes for the winners!" Evan piped in. "It's all quite fun!"

"All right, boys, that's enough now. Ripley has only just joined us. Give him a rest!" Papa chimed in before the boys could begin bombarding him with more questions. Ripley had only seen the Johns in their human form; he was dying to know what they could bend their forms into. Something just made him think of bears when he looked at their family. He wondered if they were indeed bears.

The delicious meal was complete, even down to the pumpkin pudding. Angel was the first to stand from the meal as she snuck a shy peek at Ripley. She picked up her bowl and turned from the table so no one could see her blush. Then she went to the sink in the small kitchen and rinsed it. Mama saw her blush, and so did Ripley, but neither one of them mentioned it as they smiled conspiratorially at each other. Mama picked up Papa's bowl and utensil, expertly stacking them in her hands. She picked up Ripley's and Ringer's dishes, and then moved to take the boys' bowls from them but Papa's voice stopped her.

"They can do that, Mama," Papa said with firm conviction.

"All right, then I want you boys to go to your room and clean up. Ripley will be staying with you tonight."

"Woot!" both boys chorused with a high five in the air.

"Thank you for the delicious meal." Ringer smiled at Mama as he stood and stretched, scooting the heavy footstool back under the table.

Ripley nodded and said internally, *"Yes, it was the best meal I've had in years, Mama."* He was starting to get the hang of switching between speaking audibly and in his mind. Apparently, everyone had this ability to read his mind or hear his thoughts, whatever it was. He smiled inwardly. It was rather nice to give his vocal chords a rest.

"Now, boys," Mama said firmly and scooted them out of the room after they'd cleared the table. She washed down the old table with a damp rag and readjusted the centerpiece, arranging the fruits and vegetables at their usual places in the center of the table.

The Form Benders – Janet Lee Carpenter

"Ringer, you and Ripley come over here by the fire for your tea. We'll chat for a bit."

Both young men did as Papa asked and moved to the place where the fire had burned down during their late afternoon meal. Apparently Papa had some questions for Ripley himself, because he started right in as soon as they were all situated. Ripley declined the tea; and with a full belly for the first time in so long he couldn't remember he found himself wont to doze near the warm fire. Papa leaned forward, picked up a log, and tossed it gently into the fireplace. The flames licked eagerly at the wood, dancing about as they enjoyed their supper, snapping and crackling contentedly in the quiet room.

"So tell me, Ripley, did you find your way here all right?" Papa sat back and picked up his tea from the small-end table next to his armchair. He looked so content, with one hand firmly holding his tea and the other grasping an oddly curved pipe hanging from the corner of his mouth. A random thought occurred to Ripley as he watched Papa. He found himself thinking he wouldn't have much room left in his mouth for anything else with that pipe hanging from it. He watched as Papa sipped his tea, and then replaced the pipe to take a puff. He repeated this process several times. The thought made Ripley smile.

"I did, Sir. Though I have to tell you—when I started out, I had no idea where I was going—it just seemed as though my feet found their way here."

Papa rolled his eyes toward the ceiling as if remembering something and smiled at some private thought. "It's odd how everyone who is supposed to be here finds this place."

Ripley countered with a question of his own. "What do you call this place?"

"We call it Haven's Rest, and though it goes by many names, that's the formal one. A lot of folks call it Sanctuary, but Haven started this place." Papa set his cup of tea down. He tapped the contents of his pipe into the ashtray which sat beside his armchair on the small side table. He refilled the bowl, tamped it down with his thumb, and lit the contents, dragging on it several times to get it to light before he said more. When he finally spoke again he leaned back in the chair, closed his eyes, and smiled absently. "I'm sure you will meet her one of these days. The Elders will surely introduce you, since you two are one of a kind.

She's pretty reclusive these days, but I'm sure she will come to meet you soon. She is our leader for now..." he finished cryptically.

"Who is she? What form does she turn into?" Ripley's questions shot in rapid-fire succession as he grabbed onto Papa saying there might be another of his kind.

"All in good time, Son, all in good time. For now, I believe I am ready for bed. Ahh, Mama, you've done your magic again. I find myself utterly unable to stay awake." He smiled fondly at his wife who was just finishing drying the bowls on the drain board next to the sink.

It was still light outside! Ripley wondered if Papa was being politely evasive as he stood. Ringer followed his example. Papa reached out a hand to the boy and shook it, "Good to have you here, Ringer. You must stop by more often."

"Thank you so much for inviting me. It's been a pleasure." He turned to Mama who had just dried her hands on the wash towel. "Thank you for a wonderful meal. You are a fine cook, Mama." He leaned into her for a big bear hug, and then stepped back to follow Papa as he ambled to the door to let him out. He said something to the older man Ripley didn't quite catch, and then clasped his hand and leaned in for another hug and a lot of back slapping. Ringer peered around Papa and said, "Good night, Ripley. It was a pleasure, as well. Take care of yourself. I will be here bright and early tomorrow; Remenion has requested I return with you on the morrow for another meeting."

"What kind of meeting?" he questioned Ringer.

"I have no idea, Ripley. Sorry, he didn't make me privy to his thoughts."

"Ahh...okay, I see." Ripley wasn't sure if he should offer a hug, so when he got up and went to the door, he felt awkward as he stood on his hind paws, placed his front ones on Ringer's shoulders, and then laid his head on Ringer's chest. Ringer patted his side and scratched his fur. Ripley decided it was okay to hug at that moment, simply because it felt good and he liked it. Ringer continued to stroke his soft fur as Ripley's four feet were planted firmly on the ground once again. "Thanks again Mama, Papa...tell the twins I'll see them later."

"Will do." Mama joined Papa and slid an arm around his waist as he agreed to do just that. They stood in the doorway together until Ringer was far down the road.

"Nice boy, that Ringer." Papa smiled to himself and continued, "I'll go see what's holding up the twins. Where did Angel get off to?" He closed the door quietly and started toward the boys' room.

"She said to say goodnight to Ripley, she was very tired." Mama smiled apologetically at Ripley who shrugged in response.

"It's fine. She's awful quiet…," he commented, referring to her lack of chatting after their initial visit. "As a matter of fact, so is Ringer."

"Yes, she's curious, but she doesn't want to ask too many questions." She looked to her husband as they moved out of their one armed embrace. "As for Ringer, there is a reason for him being shy, but you will learn these things as you come to know us all better." She smiled at Ripley, and then turned to her husband, "She wants you to come and tuck her in." Then she turned back to Ripley.

"All right…I'll do that and go see what those boys are up to."

Papa headed off into the hall, and Ripley headed back to the rug near the fireplace. He lay down on the rug before the fire again, letting his thoughts drift. He wondered about today's events and all he'd learned. The warmth of the fire, the fullness of his belly, and the safety he felt here all conspired to make him relax. Before he knew it, he drifted off to sleep. From a long way away, Ripley heard a disembodied voice.

"Let him sleep. Better the twins are disappointed, than to wake him from his slumber…"

Papa's voice trailed off in the night. Exhaustion filled Ripley deep in his bones, and he would not dream this night. All was silent except for the sounds of the crickets outside. Familiar soothing noises lulled him and he slept.

Chapter Six

It was six fifteen in the morning according to the clock on the living room wall, and the scent of cinnamon and vanilla teased Ripley's nostrils, bringing him fully awake. The soft shuffle of Mama's slippers on the floor was soothing. As she hummed a wordless tune quietly to herself, she expertly rolled out dough and sprinkled cinnamon sugar over it. Papa stepped through the front door, removed his long, hand-knitted red scarf from around his neck, and hung it on the hat rack next to the portal. He removed his hat, hung it next to his scarf, and went into the kitchen. He slid his arms around his wife from behind.

"Oh..." she exclaimed in delight. "Your cheek is cold, Papa!" Her musical laughter trilled through the room as her husband laid his head next to hers and rested his chin on her shoulder. Mama reached up to touch his nose with a well-floured finger.

"Woman, you have marked me for life," he chuckled.

"Yes I have, and don't you forget it, Papa."

Ripley watched the couple and realized he was watching love in action. That warm, contented feeling filled him again. He lay on the rug near the fire, still feeling lazy after yesterday's business. At that moment, Papa turned to see his eyes studying them. He dropped his arms from around his wife's waist and smiled.

"Good morning, there, Ripley!"

There was no hope for it. He'd been found out, but he didn't mind. Deciding it was time to get up, Ripley stood and stretched his body. With his tail and hindquarters high in the air, his front paws stretched out in front of him, his head was only inches from the floor. He felt his spine pop. "Good morning, Papa...Mama. Something smells wonderful," he commented and shook himself. Ahh...that felt good!

"Cinnamon rolls are ready whenever you are, Ripley."

He could feel the saliva in his mouth starting to form, and he was certain he would start drooling at any moment. To save him the embarrassment, he licked his chops and smiled at Mama as he spoke in his mind, "I was born ready for these, Mama."

"I think I'll join you Ripley. I believe Mama made some scrambled eggs as well."

At Mama's nod of assent, Ripley eagerly moved toward the table, which was set with bowls once again. However, this morning the centerpiece still lined the middle of the table. When they sat down for breakfast, Ripley asked, "Where are the twins, and Angel?"

"Oh, they were gone at first light," Mama volunteered.

"Headed out to the lake with their fishing poles," Papa added. "I think they were talking about a fish feast for supper tonight. They tried terribly hard not to wake you. I see they succeeded."

Ripley was disappointed. He would have loved to go with the children to the lake to watch them fish, even if he couldn't join in. He sat down at the table in front of a bowl of scrambled eggs and a huge cinnamon roll. He waited for Papa and Mama to sit and begin their meal before he bit into the lightest, fluffiest eggs he'd ever eaten. "You'll have to show me how you cooked these eggs, Mama. They are really good." At that moment, he was thinking of home; of the times Ms. Schaeffer brought him eggs, and he'd cooked them in a pan. They stuck to the skillet because he didn't have any butter and they were drier than anyone could have imagined. Still, they were wonderful and he had eaten every forkful of them. These were *so* much better than *those!*

Pleasure filled her smile as she looked at him. "I'd be happy to, Ripley."

Ripley bent to his pleasurable task of finishing off the delicious meal while Papa and Mama spoke of the twins and shared adventures of all the children with him. Just as he was finishing the last of his cinnamon roll—his jowls grappled with the oversized bite and it seemed to want to fall to the floor—there was a knock on the door. Papa removed his napkin from his lap and got up to answer it in one fluid motion, while Mama began to clear the morning's dishes from the table.

"That was wonderful, Mama. Thank you," he said as he finally swallowed the last morsel of cinnamon roll.

The Form Benders – Janet Lee Carpenter

"Why, Ringer—*do* come in." Papa's jovial greeting echoed in the room.

"I'm glad you enjoyed it, Ripley. We'll have you all fat and sassy by the time they've found you a permanent home."

A shadow crossed Ripley's features at the reminder that he was just a visitor here. He liked it here. He didn't want to leave. It was nice to be part of a family, he realized.

"Can I take your coat and scarf there, Ringer?" Papa asked as he shut the door behind Ringer to keep the chilly air from entering their abode.

"No, Papa, thank you. I've got an urgent message for Master Ripley from Remenion. We must leave at once for the Town Hall. Whitemane has gone missing," the young boy blurted out.

Ripley was instantly on his feet. All the warm coziness he felt only moments before was replaced with a chill at the words Ringer uttered.

"No!" Papa cried in denial.

"Whatever is to be done?" Mama asked worriedly, still clinging to the empty bowls as if they were Whitemane herself.

"That is what Remenion wants to speak to Ripley about. Quickly, Master R, we must hurry."

"Wait!" Mama ran to the oven and pulled a pan of cinnamon rolls from it. "These are done. Take some to the Elders and tell them if we can do anything—anything at all—to please let us know."

Papa nodded his agreement as Ripley looked to the hat rack and realized he didn't need anything else. He already had a fur coat on, he just needed to high tail it to the meeting. The pun amused him…*high tail it*. Mama dumped the pan of cinnamon rolls into a towel-lined wicker basket. She flipped the edges of the towel over the steamy rolls and handed them to Ringer. He took them from her as Papa opened the door for them to walk out into the crisp autumn morning.

"Godspeed," was all he said as the two left the warmth of the home and headed toward the meeting place.

The Form Benders – Janet Lee Carpenter

They walked hurriedly down the path and back toward town, both lost in deep thought as they made their way to the Town Hall. Frosty puffs issued from them both as the warm breath they exhaled met the crispness of the morning air. Neither of them noticed the cold. Their thoughts were entirely consumed by the news that Whitemane was missing.

The imposing structure never looked as daunting as it did at that moment. As they approached it, thoughts ran through Ripley's head. *What happened to Whitemane? What could he do about it? Could he find her by himself?* He tried to get his jumbled thoughts under control so he could better communicate with the Elders.

As the door opened, Ripley realized all three of the Elders were there, standing by the fireplace. When Oren moved closer to the fire, Ripley saw someone he hadn't noticed before…a black wolf with sea-green eyes, who was staring intently at him. He never flinched or looked away. He made Ripley feel incredibly uncomfortable. He was…*intense,* Ripley decided. It was the only word that came to mind. He felt this other wolf was probing him, measuring him…against a yardstick of which he was unaware. Ripley wished he could be more silent and dignified, but his toenails clicked loudly on the slate as he neared where they were talking in hushed whispers.

Ringer moved to a table set with refreshments and put down the cinnamon rolls Mama had sent. As he turned to leave, he spoke clearly to the Elders and remarked, "Mama made some cinnamon rolls for you should you want them. They are still warm," he finished.

"Thank you Ringer, they smell delectable—as always!" Remenion replied graciously.

"If you require nothing more, I will leave you now."

"Good…good, Ringer. We shall call if we need anything further. Thank you." Ringer went back out the double doors into the morning chill. Ripley, fear and nervous energy coursing through him, moved forward toward the podium. Oren went to the table and chose a large cinnamon roll before joining them back on the stage. He licked his paw as he enjoyed the pastry in a total of *two* bites.

Remenion was the first to speak after Oren returned and Ripley came closer. "Master Ripley, we have a problem," he began.

The Form Benders – Janet Lee Carpenter

"Yes, Remenion, I have heard. Is there any news of Whitemane?" Ripley waited anxiously for him to speak.

At the mention of Whitemane's name, the older black wolf with the scar over his right eye, growled deep in his chest.

"That's enough, Malador. Give us a moment to explain what has happened."

So *this* was the famous *Malador*, the legendary wolf born with the keenest sense of smell ever…at least, that's what he had heard from Papa. Some called him the *Ghost Wolf*. He wondered who this Malador really was, and what interest he had in Whitemane. Ripley felt the hair on the scruff of his neck and all along his spine stand on end as he stood ready to meet the challenge Malador was so obviously issuing.

"*Enough,* you two." Remenion's voice brooked no disobedience and Ripley stood down first, though he kept a watchful eye on Malador as he acknowledged Remenion's order. "This is not about either of you!" he snapped. "You will need all your wits about you if you are to ferret out what happened to Whitemane. Speak to the sprites at the lake…perhaps they have seen something. If not, the Nymphs at the Crest of Clearing will know something. You must find her, and you must find her fast; if Kestler has found her and taken her, the FBEF could do anything they please, for they know of our fondness for her. There is no time to waste, you two must go together and find her…and bring her home," he added quietly.

Malador's scruff was still up, but he didn't make another outburst as he nodded to the wise owl.

Ripley questioned Remenion, *"Who is Kestler?"*

"She goes by many names," he began, "I believe you know her as Ms. Washington. She is the head of the FBEF, as I told you before. Even worse, she has crimes on her list of accomplishments I will not detail for you here. Suffice it to say, the woman is pure evil. If Whitemane is with her, she is in grave danger."

At the mention of Ms. Washington, pieces of the puzzle started to fit into place and Ripley felt himself growing chilled at the thought. He had *known* she couldn't be trusted. Something in her eyes was cold and calculating. He saw it that day when she came to his apartment, but he hadn't been sure what it was. Now, however, he knew. It was a steeliness he saw in her which allowed her to harm others. Ripley felt a shiver run down his spine and he looked at Malador. The realization hit him. Now he understood why she wanted to see his room that day. She'd wanted to know if he could escape through a window. She must have determined through a visual inspection that he wouldn't be able to make it out of the apartment to safety when she returned with those men the following day. She probably also knew he wouldn't risk his mother seeing him. *She couldn't have underestimated me more*, he thought derisively. He wondered what the Owl had in mind for him, because now that he was gone—*was his mother safe?*

Malador changed from the wolf Ripley had seen into a darkly handsome man. His deep voice filled the room as he spoke for the first time. His eyes shifted color—now they were green, he decided as he watched the transformation in disbelief. The same scar marked his forehead, but the strong jaw and the deep intense look in his eyes was unmistakable. Ripley couldn't look away. This man, even as a wolf, commanded respect and attention. *Who was this man to Whitemane? Why did he get upset when Ripley asked about her?*

"I would go and find Whitemane," he spoke like a man with strong convictions who would brook no opposition.

"You will take Master Ripley, here, with you," Remenion replied. It was more of an order, though he did not say as much.

"I don't need this wet-nosed tagalong to go with me," he argued. "I will find her myself, and bring her home."

Once again, Ripley's barely-relaxed strip of hair down his back rose again in anger; and, once again, Remenion spoke on his behalf.

"You will take him, Malador, because I have asked it of you. You must trust my wisdom and judgment. I will accept no argument here—this is how it will be. It is your destiny to mentor him. Teach him well. Now *go*! You are wasting precious time!"

"Where are we going, Remenion?" Ripley piped up. Too late, he realized he had given Malador more ammunition with which to fight Remenion's decision.

However, much to his credit, Malador said nothing, though he looked at Remenion as if to say, "See what I *mean*?"

65

The Form Benders - Janet Lee Carpenter

Oren finally spoke, while he selected another roll from the basket and took a bite. "You will need to trust Malador. He knows the way. Follow your heart if you cannot follow your nose." Oren smiled at Ripley, licked the last of the frosting off his claws, and then nodded toward the door.

The Prince stood up then and said, "May the forest protect you from the evil lurking there. If you need the nymphs or sprites, you need only call them forth with this." He placed a metal medallion with the symbol of a cougar upon its face about Ripley's neck and smiled. Ripley noted it had leaves strung around the outer edge of the pendant. As soon as the medallion touched Ripley's chest, however, the image of the cougar mysteriously vanished and turned into a wolf. The image bore a striking resemblance to Ripley himself. "I must beg your understanding, for I must leave to attend to other matters. Go with Malador; trust in his great abilities and you will find her." The Prince nodded with confidence. He wanted to ask the Prince why the medallion's central image changed into a wolf. At this time, however, he felt there was something much more important he would need to know if he was to rescue Whitemane.

"How do I call the sprites and the nymphs?" he questioned before his opportunity was lost.

"Why, just ask for them, Master Ripley. They will come." The Elders turned and left through a secret door Ripley hadn't noticed until now. He and Malador stood staring at one another for a moment, and then Malador swiftly returned to his wolf form and started for the door at a quick trot.

"Come quickly, Wet Nose, before I change my mind," he snarled ungraciously.

Ripley snarled right back, letting Malador know he wasn't going to back down and be bullied by him. He followed the older wolf in spite of his unruly behavior, quickly trotting out the automatic door and onto the boardwalk. They headed back out of town, the way he had come yesterday, and walked into the thick bushes and aspens marking the way in and out of the valley.

The two wolves slipped out of the wall and Malador began sniffing the ground and air. Ripley watched as the older wolf did his "thing" in an effort to pick up the scent. He looked about on the ground, noting that his tracks from yesterday had been wiped clean, but there was a roughed up place in the dirt a short distance from them. He interrupted Malador's ritual and pointed it out. Malador snarled again, but went to investigate Ripley's find. He sniffed around the area and seemed to get very excited.

"I have her scent. There were two men who took her."

"How can you tell?" Ripley tried hard to be disinterested in his comment, but his curiosity got the better of him.

Malador snorted at him, but chose to answer his question. "There are two distinct scents here...other than Whitemane's scent. Come...see if you can pick them out."

Ripley moved cautiously closer to the older wolf and sniffed the ground tentatively. He was so caught up in tracking he didn't realize Malador was watching him intently. The scent of pine and earth filled his nostrils. "I am picking up Whitemane's scent; but, I'm not sure about the other scents you are talking about."

Malador moved to a place further from him and said, "Here...smell here, Ripley."

Ripley did as Malador instructed and he picked up the scent of Old Spice. It was the same fragrance he remembered from years ago of his father's cologne. *That* was etched in his memory. There was also the lingering scent of a musky soap that stood out. *"I can smell it!"* he cried excitedly.

"Now, come here, Ripley."

Once again, he moved to where he'd been instructed and smelled the earth and the tree standing near the path. Ripley froze. "I *know* this scent." In fact, he swore he'd never forget it. It was the stench of cigars and sweat, and the odor of rotting apples.

"Yes," Malador nodded in agreement. "Most of us know that scent; it's associated with pure, unadulterated evil, Ripley," he said quietly, and then looked at the sun in the sky. He seemed to be gauging something, and then added, "Don't forget it, Wet Nose."

As if I could! Ripley thought sarcastically.

The Form Benders – Janet Lee Carpenter

Malador picked up a pine branch in his mouth and ran it over their tracks, effectively hiding any evidence they had been there. He turned and trotted off toward the south, following the aroma of Whitemane.

"Aren't we going to talk to the sprites and the nymphs?" Ripley called out to him as he loped forward without him.

"I don't need their help. I already know which direction they have taken her, and daylight is burning, Wet Nose. Let's get a move on!"

Ripley followed the wolf in silence, his ego still stinging from the nickname he'd been dubbed with by the older wolf. He didn't know why, but Malador's opinion was important to him for some reason. More importantly, he wanted him to stop looking at him as if he was a child. Maybe it was because his father left when he was nine and he missed a father and son relationship, he wasn't sure. However, he longed for it deep inside him. He didn't know whether he disliked this gruff wolf or not. He only knew he was learning a lot, and *fast!*

Now he realized why Malador had growled at him in the Town Hall as he watched him cover their tracks. It was his fault Whitemane had been taken! If only he had thought to cover his tracks when he'd come to Haven's Rest, she would have never been sent to cover them in the first place!

Ripley pushed the confusion from him and brought his mind back to the task of following Malador. Their footsteps were hushed on the pine-needled floor of the forest. Malador was quite a few strides ahead and Ripley quickened his step to catch up, when Malador stopped suddenly. He almost ran smack into him. The two of them had covered several miles and were now heading into the brush area, leaving the green woods behind. Ripley stopped just in time to see his companion raise his ears and flick them forward, listening. He was looking toward the edge of the forest. It appeared he was checking the perimeter of the woods, making certain there was no danger ahead. He lifted his massive head and sniffed at the air in several directions before he nodded at Ripley. Then he moved toward the edge of the forest and the tundra-like landscape they would cover next.

Ripley could see two huge cabins near the edge of the forest, but no one appeared to be milling about them. He realized whether he liked this black canine or not, he trusted him—and *that* was a good thing. He

The Form Benders – Janet Lee Carpenter

didn't have much choice one way or another, since he had been volunteered for this mission. Never mind that he would have insisted on going anyway—that was something Malador, in no way, *ever* needed to know. He had grown quite fond of Whitemane in the short time he'd known her. Now, he would have gone for another reason. He felt responsible for Whitemane's capture, and it made him feel as if he had a debt to pay to her and to the rest of the community of Haven's Rest. At this point, nothing could have stopped him from his mission.

Ripley's stomach was growling loudly, but he willed it to be quiet. Unfortunately for him, Malador heard the noise and looked at him. He said nothing, however. He just kept moving forward.

They left the safety of the forest behind and carefully picked their way down the steep embankment leading away from the highway. It was not lost on Ripley that Malador intentionally avoided the road. They had deliberately maneuvered around the curve at the top of the four-lane highway to end up making their way down the steep mountainside. He assumed Malador had good reason for keeping his distance from the busy thoroughfare and acted accordingly. After another half an hour at scrambling down the rocky hillside, Malador spoke up. "We'll stop up here a little ways…," he said quietly, "there is a small stream where we can drink."

The sun was high above their heads when they finally made it to the stream. Ripley hadn't wanted to say anything, but he was very tired, *extremely* hungry and wondering how much further they had to go. Malador lay down in a small patch of shade afforded by a scraggly Bull Pine and rested his head on his paws, closing his eyes for a moment. Ripley knew if *he* closed his eyes, he wouldn't wake up for several hours. *This must be how his mother felt when she tried to join him on hikes shortly after his father left*, Ripley thought. Panting and thirsty, he walked into the stream. Instead of taking a drink from it, he lay down in the water, lapping greedily at the gently rolling stream to quench his thirst. Then he got an idea! He opened his mouth and let the water flow into it. Suddenly, he felt as though he was choking and drowning all at once. He stood up and coughed, eyes tearing; he had practically inhaled a throat full of water. He gagged and spewed it all over the rocks and back into the offending stream. He heard Malador's deep mocking laughter behind him. Though lying in the cool stream had brought down his body heat from his exertion so far, he felt another kind of heat flush through

The Form Benders – Janet Lee Carpenter

his body as embarrassment flooded over him. Realizing how silly he must have looked, Ripley managed a self-deprecating laugh. His humiliation was complete! He stepped out of the stream and shook himself, sending droplets of water flying from his thick coat.

Malador composed himself enough to say, "Don't worry about it, Wet Nose. Everyone tries it sooner or later." He chuckled again.

In an effort to change the embarrassing subject, he took a different tack. "Why haven't you bent back into your human form?" Ripley asked curiously.

"A wolf in these parts wouldn't raise suspicion—however, a man walking around here and climbing all over the mountainside would have. Now, be still, Wet Nose. I am resting."

Ripley was satisfied with the answer and irritated at the nickname, but he held his silence. When he'd cooled down enough so he wasn't panting any longer, he got up, walked to a sparse bush, and attempted to get comfortable under it. He tried to use its tiny branches for his shade. This proved to be impossible since the bush had loads of prickly spines on it that poked through even *his* thick fur. He looked in Malador's direction to see if he'd noticed Ripley's plight—but he seemed to be blissfully unaware of his predicament. Gratefully, he noted another Bull Pine tree not too far from the place where Malador quietly slept. He made his way down the hill a little further, lay down in the shade, and closed his eyes. *"Just for a moment,"* he promised himself, but within minutes—he was sound asleep.

It seemed like only moments had passed since he'd closed his eyes, but now someone was annoyingly pushing at him with a cold nose...*a cold nose?* It all came rushing back to him...*Malador! Whitemane!* Ripley's eyes flew open as he jumped to his feet. He shook himself and looked about. The sun appeared to be going behind the mountains. The sky was turning a beautiful shade of azure and crimson, with buttery yellow, flame-like clouds scudding across a cerulean sky. A brilliant orange glow covered the landscape setting the valley into deep hues of amethyst and cadmium...of shadows and light.

"Let's go, Wet Nose. Can't loll about all day and night! We've lost the better part of the afternoon."

The Form Benders – Janet Lee Carpenter

Ripley's stomach growled loudly in protest. "I'm ready," he said, as he determinedly ignored his stomach for the second time that day.

"There are some berries here," Malador said as he moved toward an elderberry bush nearby. "They may not be much, but they'll fill your stomach and stop it from making that horrific noise."

Embarrassed once again, Ripley felt himself go on the defensive as he moved toward the bush. He grabbed a mouthful of the berries and got some leaves in with them. He started to chew on the tiny berries.

"I wouldn't eat the leaves," Malador said over his shoulder as he scoped out the valley below. "They are poisonous and will give you a mean case of…well…the 'trots'," he finished with a smirk.

Ripley immediately spit out the offending leaves as Malador snickered. He took another mouthful of the berries, this time careful to get only the sweet, ripe berries in his mouth. They were surprisingly good—sort of a cross between boysenberries and grapes. He liked the flavor. When he'd eaten several, Ripley joined Malador on the rock above the valley.

"Ready to go, *Wet Nose?*" he queried, still looking out over the deepening shadows which pressed their way across the valley floor.

"I'm ready," Ripley said, still utterly perturbed with the nickname he'd given him.

"Let's be on our way then," Malador said.

They made their way down the rest of the mountain without incident. Malador and Ripley trotted in companionable silence. It was after ten when they finally reached the outskirts of Fresno and both were looking for food and water by the time they arrived.

"*Stay here,*" Malador commanded Ripley as he moved toward the bright lights of a fast food restaurant. Ripley watched as he skirted the lit area, and then ducked around a corner and disappeared from view. In just a few minutes, he reappeared, carrying two boxes in his mouth. Malador opened one of them by nudging it with his snout; the other he left Ripley to figure out. He hungrily wolfed down the breaded chicken bites he found there, while Ripley opened his carton and binged on half a double-decked hamburger. He tried not to think about who had been chomping on his dinner only a while ago. Wow, it tasted like heaven!

The Form Benders – Janet Lee Carpenter

"I'm still hungry," Ripley complained when they had eaten the contents of the boxes. Once again, Malador disappeared around the corner—and once again, he reappeared with something in his mouth. This time, they feasted on French fries and small hamburgers. There was a stinky, fishy-smelling sandwich Malador passed on, but Ripley devoured it with delight. After they were finished, they made their way to the irrigation canal behind the restaurant and drank from it. When they were satiated, they took up their journey once again and headed to the downtown area of Fresno in pursuit of Whitemane.

Malador sniffed the unseasonably warm night air and began moving south again. Ripley followed suit and picked up the scent, as well. With his belly full, Ripley felt ready to take on the world. They walked down back alleys and dark streets, avoiding the bright lights of the city, creeping around in people's yards. The dogs barked at them until Malador hissed at them to be quiet. Then, everything went silent as they made their way downtown.

"Stay here," Malador ordered Ripley, and he obeyed.

Within minutes, Malador was back. They slithered down the alleyway to where a building with an entrance to it stood with one light aglow above a heavy metal door. They crouched in the shadows behind a dumpster—watching and waiting. Ripley picked up Whitemane's scent on a stray breeze, and became excited.

"I can smell her," he blurted.

Malador growled low in his throat in warning. "Silence boy, the shift change should be soon."

"Where are we?" Ripley spoke quietly.

"This is one of the FBEF headquarters based here in Fresno. There's one in Clovis as well, but that's not our objective. Whitemane is here."

A security light went on above a metal door across from where they hid. Ripley and Malador retreated further into the shadows as they watched two men step out of the building. The first one out was tall with blond hair; the other was short and balding. The first man lit a cigar, and then held the match out for his friend to light his smoke. They could hear the tall one talking and laughing—then something he said caught Ripley's attention.

"I'm guessing Kestler will keep her sedated until tomorrow at least. She'll probably interrogate her after that. Stupid b*ender*, she cleaned up the area and now *Kestler's* mad at *me* because I didn't mark the place! How the heck could I know she was *that smart?*"

They were talking about Whitemane! It *was* his fault she'd been taken! Now he understood what it meant to feel lower than a dog. He wanted to skulk away, to hide from everyone. He caught Malador watching him, and he hung his head in shame.

"You didn't know, Ripley," he offered in a soft voice, with what sounded dangerously like compassion. Then, without hesitation, he turned back to listen intently to the men's conversation.

Ripley didn't know how to react to Malador's unguarded comment to him. He turned his attention back to the men and realized he recognized the second man's voice from when he'd spoken outside of the aspen wall. It was the one who had baited the taller man yesterday when he succeeded in eluding their capture. There was no mistaking the scent of rotten apples emanating on the breeze from the blond man as the odor of cigar smoke permeated the air and almost made Ripley sneeze. He never would understand what people saw in those things!

"Well, you should have marked it, Steamer. Then she wouldn't have gotten so mad!"

The tall one named Steamer shoved the other man and he stumbled back against the building.

"Hey, now there's no call for that! I'm just sayin' 'at she wouldn't have been so mad if you'd 'a marked the area...heck, you stood there long enough!"

Ripley held in the sneeze that almost escaped as the two continued in their conversation.

"Shut up, Vinnie. I didn't see you marking anything, either!"

The one called Vinnie puffed up his chest and acted as if he was going to get in the other man's face. He seemed to think better of it, though. All Steamer did was look at him, and he backed down. There was more here than met the eye, Ripley realized. Vinnie was afraid of Steamer; he could smell it in the air...an acrid scent which burned in his nostrils.

The Form Benders – Janet Lee Carpenter

Malador was silent the entire time as he intently watched the two men. He stared at the top of the building across from them and visually investigated the surrounding area. Ripley was aware of the intensity of Malador's scrutiny as he sat perched on the edge of his seat, so to speak.

"You think the others will come looking for this one?" Vinnie asked Steamer.

"I don't know, but Kestler thinks they will. That's why she doubled the security around the place. There's no safe way in for them, except for the roof—but they can't get up there unless they can fly!" Steamer laughed…a deep, wicked sound which made Ripley feel as if he would need to take a nice long bath after this mission.

Steamer flicked his cigar into the alley, and Vinnie followed suit. Steamer lit another, while Vinnie moved to go back inside the building.

"You going back in?" Steamer questioned the bald man.

"You know she don't like it when we stay out here too long. Makes her anxious, ya know?"

"Pah!" he exclaimed. "Who cares what it does to her? I get anxious if I don't have my smoke."

Vinnie grinned, revealing a space one of his front teeth used to occupy. Then he slipped inside the door, leaving Steamer standing outside in the alley alone. Steamer took a long drag on his cigar and blew it out. Ripley was caught off guard and sneezed. Malador stiffened next to him, but a car passing by the alley on the street nearby must have muffled his sneeze because Steamer didn't appear to have heard him. He took another puff and leaned against the building. He stood there a few more moments and then flicked the half-smoked cigar into the alley. He seemed to adjust himself mentally, shrugged his shoulders, and stepped back into the building. The heavy metal door closed behind him with a clang.

Ripley sighed quietly when Malador swung around and turned on him.

"You could have gotten us killed right there, boy! What the heck did you think you were doing?" Malador's eyes burned like molten lava, and he snapped each word off as if it would break. "You can go back home right now. You are dangerous, boy!" He snarled this last comment.

The Form Benders – Janet Lee Carpenter

Ripley felt himself fill up with emotion as Malador brought him to task for his error. He wasn't a *boy*, he was a *man!* He was *sixteen* for heaven's sake! He'd been taking care of his mother for the past seven years! He wouldn't let Malador speak to him like this!

"I didn't do it on purpose," he defended himself. "It was just...the cigar smoke...it got to me!"

"Well, I can't have some Wet Nose, tag-along kid running around trying to do a wolf's job when he's ill prepared to do it. Nothing against you, kid—you just have no control over yourself."

Ripley'd had enough. He was sick and tired of everyone he knew treating him like a child. He wasn't a little kid! He'd taken care of both himself and his mother before all this happened, so he fought back. "Don't call me that!" he snapped. "I have a name! It's Ripley...R-I-P-L-E-Y," he quipped as he spelled it out succinctly for Malador. "I have control," he stammered. "It's not as if I did it on purpose. I want to find Whitemane as much as you do! I want her to come home, just like you! And more than ever, I want to help free her, JUST LIKE YOU!" The last few words came out in a rush; Ripley's eyes were blazing and tears streaked his muzzle as he stared down Malador.

Malador narrowed his sea-colored eyes at Ripley, silence filling the space between them. He stared at Ripley, and then said in a soft voice, "But you could get her killed son...are you prepared for that?"

Ripley blinked at Malador. He'd been ready for an all-out fight, and Malador's quiet rejoinder wasn't what he'd been expecting. Suddenly, realizing the truth of what he'd said, Ripley spoke in a small voice. "I'm sorry; I didn't mean to make a sound." He hung his head in shame. Why did he always seem to make mistakes these days? It was humiliating.

Malador's voice rolled over him like a soft blanket. "I know you didn't mean to, but that's what makes you so dangerous, son. You don't mean to do things, yet they happen. You will have to control yourself if you are to see this mission through."

Ripley fought the emotions threatening to spill out of him. He knew what Malador said was right; it was just hard to swallow. "I'll control myself. I will be extremely cautious in the future and I will wait for you to lead," he promised. Hope filled him.

The Form Benders – Janet Lee Carpenter

Malador searched his eyes for the truth of what he said. When satisfied, he nodded. "Very well, son…I will give you one more chance, but that's all. Should you fail me again, you will find your way back to Haven's Rest with no arguments. Understood?" He slipped into his human form as he waited for Ripley's answer.

Ripley nodded his assent eagerly. At Malador's frown, he nodded more somberly. "I understand." He didn't know why, but he was inordinately pleased Malador hadn't called him "Wet Nose" again, but had referred to him as "son." Not even his father called him that when they were still together…still a family. He smiled to himself as they snuck from behind the dumpster in the alley and began to search for a way up to the top of the building. That was their only way in; they would have to take advantage of it.

Chapter Seven

Malador and Ripley were still searching for a way onto the roof of the building where Whitemane was being held prisoner. They could see it from here, but were still unable to reach it. The sun began to turn the sky to deep amethyst—then lighter, until the day was awash with the sounds of birds greeting the new day. Even in Fresno, squirrels chirped their welcome to the sun as the trash trucks emptied dumpsters. The scent of bacon and eggs, along with maple syrup and coffee, mingled and filled the air with expectancy. Ripley's stomach rumbled in acknowledgement of the aromas filling the morning, and Malador looked at him. He didn't complain once and had followed Malador everywhere in their search for the way in.

"We'll find something to eat, and then we'll bed down until this evening. There's nothing more we can do here in the daylight. I want you to stay here. I'll be back shortly."

Ripley breathed a sigh of relief; he felt he'd somehow passed a test. He watched as Malador bent into his human form and left by way of the fire escape. Then he slipped behind a giant air conditioning unit atop the roof they were scouting, and lay down to wait. He was so tired after their trek here.

It seemed like only moments, but Malador had been gone for close to an hour when Ripley heard his feet hit the metal fire escape steps. He brought some day old donuts the donut shop owner gave him. He explained that the owner was going to throw them away, so he gave them to Malador for free. Ripley dug into the doughnuts ravenously, before he suddenly remembered his manners. He licked his chops and sat to allow Malador to eat his fill.

Malador chuckled. "Go ahead, son. I've eaten already. I have something else for you," he said. He placed the bag of donuts on the roof, disappeared around the air conditioning unit, and tromped down the fire escape stairs. When he reappeared, he had a bottle of water in one hand and a cup of coffee in the other. He opened the bottle with a flick of his strong fingers. He took the last few swallows of his coffee, and then poured the lukewarm water into it. Ripley lapped it up eagerly and watched with longing as Malador took a doughnut, and then handed Ripley another from the bag. *When would he be able to bend his form back to a human?*

He must have spoken his thoughts aloud because Malador looked at him thoughtfully before he said, "Has no one told you?"

"Told me what?"

"Your first form bend is the most difficult to master. However, you will not be able to shift back from your first form for three days, and then it is unpredictable when you will bend again. You won't be able to control it for at least a month or more. There are only three of you so far who are able to bend into other forms and there is only *one* who was able to master the bends sooner."

Ripley sensed the admiration in his tone and he wanted someone to feel that way about him. He asked, "Who was it and how long did it take him? And...what was his name?"

"*She* mastered it in a week. She is a very special bender. I'm sure you will meet her one of these days. In many ways, she's just like you," he commented. "Her name is Haven. Haven's Rest is named after her. She is our queen." Malador was refilling the cup he'd set out for Ripley, so he missed the look of utter amazement on his face.

"But I'm sure the Elders told you about her?" He let the question hang in the air.

Ripley didn't want to say anything to jeopardize hearing more about the form benders. He quickly filled his mouth with another doughnut to avoid answering Malador's question. Instead, he asked another question, talking around the food in his mouth, while Malador was in such a talkative mood.

"How is it that we can talk in our minds...I mean, how can I hear your thoughts and you hear mine?" Trying to swallow the dry pastry effectively distracted Malador from his line of questioning. Ripley choked on the too large morsel until he finally got it free from the place where it had lodged in his throat. He masticated the doughnut more thoroughly this time, swallowed, and waited patiently for him to answer. Malador turned from him and went to the edge of the rooftop to investigate. He seemed to ponder deeply what Ripley had asked him.

The Form Benders – Janet Lee Carpenter

One thought stuck in Ripley's mind: *He might be able to form bend within the week!* This was *terrific* news!

"All creatures, great and small," he began, "have the ability to communicate with each other. You simply have to be interested in understanding them. If you listen with your heart, Ripley, you can understand anyone. Thoughts, when shared, become words that warn or comfort. You can feel them from others. Thoughts are to your feelings as clothes are to your form. Without them, communication is difficult at best. As a form bender, you can speak to any being if you just focus on them—then concentrate on your message. The *impression* of the words drops into the other being's mind—and voila," he snapped his fingers, "you have communication."

Ripley wondered if he would ever understand the form of communication Malador spoke of. His confusion must have shown on his face because Malador reached over and patted him on the head.

"You will understand in time, Ripley. There is much to learn. Try focusing on the birds and animals around. Talk to them in your mind. The more you practice it, the more clearly the animals and people around you will respond to your thoughts. Some may not be aware they are responding, but for our intents and purposes, the practice will do for now."

Ripley watched as Malador moved closer to the edge of the roof where the fire escape was. "Are you leaving?" he questioned Malador.

"Since you can't bend right now, I'm going to leave you here. I'll be back in a little while. I can blend in with people, you know. I look like the norms down there, so I'll see what I can find out. I'll be back with more food around lunchtime. Stay low and don't come off this roof," he cautioned Ripley.

Once again, he was being treated as if he were a child, but at least this time he understood the precautions Malador was taking and said, "I'll wait here for you."

"All right then, I've poured you some more water; should be enough to get you through until I return. Stay out of sight and stay cool. There isn't much shade up here, so I won't leave you for long. Maybe I can find another safe spot for you to hide until tonight, and then we can both rest. We'll get Whitemane out, so get some sleep if you can. We'll

The Form Benders – Janet Lee Carpenter

be on our feet from the time we get her, until we return home. It's a long journey. Well," he chuckled, "I don't have to tell you that. You already know."

"Aren't you going to rest for this evening?"

"Not at the moment. I have other, more pressing matters, before I close my eyes."

"But won't you be tired?" Ripley asked, genuinely concerned.

Malador looked at Ripley probingly, and then smiled. "I'll be fine, son. I'll rest later when I return."

Ripley nodded and asked one last question before Malador left. "I have to know. I am very curious." Malador waited for Ripley to speak. "I realize this might be a little off the subject, but how is it you have clothes on when you bend into your human form, but you're not wearing any when you are in wolf form?"

Malador's eyes twinkled for the first time since they met. In a voice laced with laughter, he answered him, "Why…it's magic, of course." He turned from Ripley as if that explained everything and stepped on the first stair of the fire escape. As he made his way down the stairs, his dark head finally disappeared from view.

What magic? Was it the same magic that turned him from human to wolf? Had it changed the Prince from cougar to man, and even Oren from his massive bear form into the tall, well-muscled human into which he bent himself? Was it the same magic that protected them within the wall of aspens? *This was so confusing! How did they get the magic? Where did it come from?*

The medallion dangled against his throat, a comfort to him while he was alone in this strange place, though he had no idea how to use it. There had never been any money to come to Fresno. He had always been content with the apartment in Shaver Lake, and seeing some of the kids from Big Creek on the weekends. He heard the tales from the other kids in town about going to the mall and having hot pretzels and corn dogs. It sounded like a huge treat, indeed! He wondered if someday he would see this mall and what it held within its four walls.

With his tummy full once again, Ripley curled up in a ball, facing the direction he thought danger might come from—the fire escape at the south end of the building—and closed his eyes to rest. There was nothing else for him to do. He needed to build up his stamina if he was going to run this gauntlet with Whitemane.

Ripley found himself too excited to rest, however. He heard the laughter of children below him, so he got up to investigate. He went to the west side of the building. When he peered over the two-foot wall surrounding the rooftop like a fortress, he saw several boys playing basketball on a court in the park below. He gazed longingly at them and wished—more than ever—that he could join their ranks and play ball. It would help to ease the tension coursing through him; running and playing hard had always done that for him.

He wondered about Whitemane. *Would she still be drugged? Would they be able to get her out of the FBEF building? Would Kestler be gone, or would they have to fight their way out?* He had so many questions that deserved to be answered, but he knew the solution would not be found until they were in the middle of rescuing Whitemane. Realizing that, Ripley finally slept fitfully, whining in his sleep and awaiting Malador's return. He was dreaming about practicing his new communication skills in his mind with people. Even in his dream, the thought of being able to speak with other creatures excited him. *This might be great fun!*

Ripley awoke to darkening clouds billowing above him and the first few drops of rain. Heat waves emanated upward from the hot asphalt rooftop as the rain pelted its rapidly cooling surface. Ripley swore he could almost hear the hiss of the cool drops as they struck the graveled and tar-papered roof. Loud cracks of thunder boomed across the unforgiving sky as the rain fell in ever-increasing torrents. With no shelter to speak of, Ripley leaned against the air conditioning unit in an attempt to stay somewhat dry. The roof was holding some of the rain and giant puddles were starting to form. *If this kept up, how would they get the flat skylight open? They needed to lower themselves into the FBEF building. How could they do that if the rooftop was flooded?* Ripley wondered. Another peal of thunder followed close on the heels of a brilliant finger of lightning in the sky above him as he tried to make himself smaller to hide from the punishing downpour.

The Form Benders - Janet Lee Carpenter

"Ripley?" a deep voice broke apart from the cacophony of noise from the storm, becoming intelligible words.

"Here," Ripley cried. "I'm here..."

"Come quickly," Malador said as he moved back to the staircase once again and motioned for him to come. Ripley dashed to the spot where Malador stood near the fire escape. Malador held an overcoat over his head in a vain effort to protect him from the rain as they quickly tramped down the old fire escape steps. He led Ripley down the same alleyway where they had sequestered themselves last night near the FBEF building. They turned left at the end of the alley, staying close to the buildings, and then another left-hand turn led them into a smaller alley with several seedy looking doors. Malador rushed down the block, looking back to make certain Ripley was close behind. He needn't have worried though; there was no way Ripley was going to be stuck in this storm for long!

"Here, Ripley...in here," he called as he opened a small door with bars on the tiny, wavy privacy glass window placed there to discourage break-ins. *Not that anyone could possibly be that small, or get up that high...it must be at least five feet above the ground and maybe nine by twelve inches in size!* Ripley thought. He didn't question Malador as he followed the directions he'd been given and stepped over the stoop and into a warm, dry room. It was filled with cleaning supplies and mops, along with towels and toilet paper against one wall. It appeared they were in a utility room of some sort. The aromas that assailed him, as well as the tinkle of glassware and dining utensils, told him he was in the supply room of a restaurant.

Malador spoke softly to him. "You will be safe and warm here," he said as Ripley vigorously shook himself to get the rain off. *I must look like a drowned rat*, he thought as his ears stuck straight out from his head and his fur was spiking out all over him. Malador took some towels off of the shelf, wiped Ripley down, and threw them into the laundry basket at the end of the room. He took several more towels and laid them out on the cement floor for Ripley to lie on, and then placed his finger to his lips to indicate silence.

Ripley nodded his head to let him know he understood, and watched as Malador opened the door a crack, glanced furtively around, and then slipped into the hallway beyond. Ripley ran his face along the

The Form Benders – Janet Lee Carpenter

nubby surface of the terrycloth towel in an attempt to dry himself. He scooted, running his body along the floor, attempting to remove more of the dampness on his coat. He was really getting into it, sliding his face and front paws along the floor, hind feet pushing and shoving while his tail made a series of wild arcs in the air like the propeller on an airplane. It was precisely in the middle of all of this that Malador knocked softly on the door, opened it without hesitation, stepped through the portal, and caught Ripley in the act. Embarrassed at having been caught in this abandoned moment, he stopped abruptly and looked sheepishly at Malador. A soft chuckle escaped Malador, and he smiled at him.

"Dry yet?" he queried. Only then did Ripley realize Malador was holding a steaming bowl of something that smelled delicious! He felt guilty and embarrassed at having been caught scrubbing his fur on the towels Malador left on the floor for him to rest upon; he looked down, hesitated…then stole a glance at Malador who seemed genuinely amused. A wicked grin split his features as he set the bowl of steaming stew near Ripley.

He was glad he wasn't human right now because he would have been blushing up to the tops of his pert ears!

Changing the subject, Malador encouraged Ripley to eat his fill. "Go ahead, son. You did well."

Ripley wasted no time in getting to the bowl. He was already salivating as he took his first bite of the delicious stew. It was hotter than he thought, and he burned his tongue. Ripley was starving. The donuts he'd eaten earlier hadn't stayed with him very long. So he pretended it didn't bother him that the food was too hot to eat immediately. "Yum, this is good," Ripley said approvingly.

"I know the owner here. She's a great cook," Malador quipped as he looked suspiciously like the cat that had eaten the proverbial canary.

Sensing there was more to this story than he was being told, Ripley asked, "Just how well do you know her, Malador?"

"Well, enough, Wet Nose." He brushed the question aside. "Now eat your meal and when you're done, I need you to stay here quietly. Don't make a sound. Someone will hear you. She said she can hide you here for the time being. As far as she knows, you're a stray I picked up—so, if she comes in here, act the part—all right?"

"I will," Ripley stated over another mouthful of stew.

"All right...no more sliding all over this floor. As it is, I'll probably have to mop it before we leave. I'll be back. She has a cot in the back room I'm going to avail myself of and get a little shut eye before we have to head out." Ripley growled playfully, and Malador's hearty laugh rumbled in his chest as he stepped through the door and closed it softly. He could hear the sounds of a jukebox playing some songs that sounded like old rock 'n roll. He thought he could pick out the words to *Love Me Tender*, by Elvis Presley, but he couldn't be certain.

If Ripley had to guess, he didn't think Malador would return until much later, so he was surprised when he heard voices outside the storeroom. Ripley tensed. The voices got louder, and then started to recede. They were moving away from his hiding place and he felt his tension ease. He resumed eating the last vestiges of his bowl of stew. With his snout, he scooted the towels Malador had so kindly and *neatly* placed on the floor for him and tried to neaten them up a bit from the haphazard mess he'd made of them such a short time ago. As he got them into a reasonable facsimile of a tidy pile he thought, *maybe he's not such a bad guy after all.* He mulled it over in his mind for a while as he circled the towels and lay down on them. He had sure done a lot for both him and Whitemane, though she would probably never know how much.

He was beginning to like Malador, and he thought Malador just might be starting to like him too. The sting was gone from the name "Wet Nose," so perhaps there would be a truce between them, and they would be friends after all this was over. Ripley wanted to move and run; it was hard doing all this resting. His feet ached to feel the uneven earth beneath them as he ran through the woods at home. He sighed contentedly. His belly was full, and he was warm and almost dry.

Funny, already I think of Haven's Rest as home, Ripley thought as he closed his eyes.

A couple of hours later, Ripley's prayers were answered as the restaurant became silent except for a few voices in the background. Then it went still as he heard footsteps drawing near the door. He quickly

The Form Benders – Janet Lee Carpenter

backed into the corner in an effort to hide himself should it be anyone other than Malador and his elusive cook. The door creaked open slowly and the light came on. Ripley blinked furiously as the blinding radiance pooled around him. The contrast from total darkness to light momentarily kept him from seeing. As his eyes adjusted to the light, he saw a beautiful young woman—probably in her mid-twenties—with dark hair and soft brown eyes. When she spotted him, her delicate hands went to her face and her eyes widened and sparkled with delight!

"Oh, he's *beautiful!*" she exclaimed as she bent on one knee to invite him to come closer. Ripley wasn't sure what he should do, so he looked to Malador for guidance. Malador nodded imperceptibly and Ripley moved cautiously forward—head low—all the while sniffing the air, remembering Malador's warning about acting the part of a dog. She smelled nice…like coffee and vanilla…and spring flowers.

"This is no ordinary dog, Mal. This is a *wolf!*" she exclaimed. "Or he's at least part wolf. Look how huge his paws are!" She held the paw he'd offered to her as he sat patiently, waiting while she looked him over and stroked those kind hands over his almost dry coat. "He feels like satin," she cooed. "Oh, and look at this medallion," she cried. "Someone loves this animal very much. You need to find out where he belongs," she spoke softly now, barely above a whisper as she said, "Get him home, Mal."

"I will, Lacey. For the moment, though, I'll have to wait on that. He's coming with me tonight."

"Well, at least it's stopped pouring rain!" she said as she continued to run her tiny hands all over his fur, stroking him. Ripley was thoroughly enjoying this.

"Yes, that is exceptionally good…" and, as he realized he might have said too much, he distracted Lacey by saying, "I don't even think the weatherman talked of rain in the forecast for today." She smiled at him then and reached down to stroke Ripley's soft fur again and scratch him behind his ears.

"*Ohhhh, that's NICE!*" he thought as her fingernails scratched in all the right places. Ripley was in heaven as he sat and let her rub and scratch him, his tongue lolling to one side as he enjoyed the massage.

The Form Benders – Janet Lee Carpenter

"Silly, they are *never* wrong anymore...they said there would be rain but you—as usual—didn't listen to the news this morning!" Her tinkling laughter filled the tiny room. "He's really beautiful. Someone must miss him a lot. He's probably got some boy out there who is just sick that he can't find him."

"Ah...he's just an ordinary, wet-nosed dog, Lacey." Ripley snapped out of his trance long enough to shoot a glance at Malador. He saw the wicked grin splitting his face and realized he was being teased. It lightened his mood considerably. They would need to get to the roof soon to find Whitemane, and it had been weighing heavily on his mind all this time while he awaited Malador's return.

"Mal, look at him. He is no ordinary animal! It's kind of creepy really; he looks as though he understands every word we're saying."

"Whatever you say, Lacey," came his quick rejoinder.

Ripley didn't know what to make of Malador's quick acquiescence to her judgment of him. Of course, he didn't know him that well, but in his experience, he'd never seen him be so...so...*pliable!*

"Do you two have somewhere to go?" she asked Malador, standing up while loosely encircling his waist with her arms. "I mean...somewhere to stay tonight?" Ripley was suddenly bereft as the warm massaging hands disappeared and his heavenly lady stood up.

"Yep...we have a few errands to run tonight first, and then we'll go to my place..." Malador said as he slid his arm around her and squeezed her.

His "*place*"...*Malador had a "place" in Fresno?* This interested Ripley.

"But we'll come back and visit soon," he said, evading her question. She didn't seem to notice, or she didn't mind—Ripley wasn't sure which.

"Promise?" she whispered.

"Promise," he swore as he leaned in and gave her a light kiss on the forehead.

Ripley watched the couple in fascination, but the moment Malador turned toward him he looked off into the corner, studying the pattern of the bricks with extreme interest. They had been painted so many times the thick coating on the wall looked like congealed buttermilk.

Amused, rather than annoyed, Malador spoke to him, "Come on, boy—let's get going and let this pretty lady close up shop." He squeezed her one more time and released her.

"Come on," she spoke softly, "I'll walk you to the door."

True to his word, it had indeed stopped raining. The air was crisp and clean, and the streets held the evidence of the recent deluge. Puddles on the sidewalk and street echoed the street lamps' luminescence in shimmering ribbons on their still damp surface. The sloshing sound of tires wheeling through puddles marred the night's stark stillness. The sound of the distant train whistle pierced the dark—and then went still as Malador waved goodbye to Lacey and signaled for Ripley to join him. They walked together in silence until they were far enough away from the building and well concealed within the darkness of the alley.

"We're almost there," Malador spoke softly in the shadows.

Ripley still said nothing as they made their way closer to the alley where they had overheard Steamer and Vinnie talking last night. He could feel the excitement coursing through him as they neared their destination, and his nerves felt like coiled springs which would snap at any moment, hurtling him through the night and into…into what? It felt like an abyss, but it also felt like a gigantic adventure—like something he'd read about and dreamed about—but thought would never happen to him.

Malador reached down and touched the back of his neck and Ripley felt the electric energy leave him; the tension he'd felt all day just dissipated into *nothingness*.

"What did you do to me?" Ripley asked with amazement, not understanding how or why he had drained the surging energy from him.

"Shhh…," he quieted him as they approached the door in the back alley.

"I thought we were going in off the roof top," Ripley whispered back intensely, immediately distracted…more intent than ever on finding out what was going on.

The Form Benders – Janet Lee Carpenter

"No, that's what they wanted us to hear. A friend of mine, a *good friend* I trust," he added, "told me they are expecting us. To confirm it, we are to stay here and watch what happens."

Within minutes, Vinnie and Steamer emerged from the emergency exit door and lit their respective cigar and cigarette. To Ripley's utter amazement, they replayed the scene from the night before, down to the smallest detail. Steamer even remained behind to smoke another cigar before he pelted it into the alleyway and stepped back inside the door. It was like watching an instant replay.

Not certain what this meant Ripley asked, "Why did they do that?"

"They are actors, Ripley, playing a scene. A scene, I might add, for our benefit alone. They are expecting us to be standing out here. Not knowing when we'll come, they play this scene for us at odd intervals every evening, trying to trick us and get us to come in the rooftop entrance. "But," he added, "We're not going in that way...we're going in the back door."

Ripley stared at Malador in disbelief and whirled on him. "They are waiting for us behind that door."

"Don't you see, Wet Nose? That is what they *want* us to think. We're going in the back door, and I have it on good authority that she is downstairs, to the right of the doorway. So, we're going inside, turning right and heading down the flight of stairs...together. And when we find her, we're going to bring her out of there and take her home."

Ripley watched as Malador bent his form into the dark and mysterious wolf he had come to know. The denial died on his lips, and he fell silent. Instead, he followed him as he made his way toward the back door cautiously. *What was in store for them now? If only he had realized what he'd meant, instead of having Malador have to point it out to him.* Once again, he had shown how young he truly was—and it made him angry with himself. He had given his word he would follow Malador, no matter how much he balked at the orders. He had promised, so he followed as Malador led them up the stairs to the door which was left ajar, feeling as if he'd been put in his place once again through no fault of Malador's.

The Form Benders – Janet Lee Carpenter

They entered the warehouse, and Ripley was surprised it didn't have better lighting. Then again, *a dark place for dark deeds* the unbidden thought came to him—and he shivered. He followed Malador into the facility; boxes and crates lined the first floor. There was nothing terribly menacing here. Every once in a while, he noticed the lights would dim as they made their way into the bowels of the warehouse. They crept down two short flights of stairs and into a cavernous room filled with cages of all sizes and shapes shoved up against the wall—making a wide corridor of sorts. Men were sitting at a table at the far end of the corridor, playing cards. Above them was the skylight they'd been prepared to enter before they'd been tipped off by Malador's friend. There was a bottle of Meyer's Rum sitting on the table and every once in a while, one of the guards would grab it, fill a double shot glass and eye the others as he drank from his glass. They were too far away to make out what was being said, but the men were loud already and getting louder by the second. *That might work in their favor*, Ripley admitted to himself. The two wolves sat quietly and watched them for some time, trying to ascertain how to get to Whitemane.

Malador spoke in his mind to Ripley. *"Stay here—I'm going to see if I can find her. Keep to the shadows and talk to me only in your mind, they cannot hear us then,"* he warned. *"They are filled with liquor and are numb to their own senses."*

Ripley nodded and crouched low on the stairs behind the first row of empty cages lining the walls. He watched as Malador silently jumped to the top of the cage nearest them and slinked his way to the wall. He hugged the wall and moved soundlessly closer to the men. Ripley hoped Malador would go undetected. The men seemed overly preoccupied with their game and the booze, so perhaps Malador *was* all he was cracked up to be and could sneak in unobserved. Papa Johns had spoken of Malador's extraordinary abilities and told Ripley some of the fantastic stories about him. Now he would see if he could live up to his reputation. Ripley barely breathed as he waited for Malador to return. After what seemed like hours, with cat-like grace, Malador landed silently behind him.

"Well?" The question fairly burst from Ripley's mind.

"I found her," Malador said, but he didn't seem happy about it. *"She's at the far end of the room, behind those men at the card table. She appears to be unconscious. There is a cabinet with drugs in it in a glass*

The Form Benders – Janet Lee Carpenter

room to the side. I can get in there and get the drugs to wake her, but the problem will be administering them to her to before anyone notices. We'll be seen." He directed Ripley to look at the men at the end of the cages. *"Off to the right, there is another set of cages."* He hesitated here. Ripley watched Malador—and from the look on his face, knew he didn't want to hear what Malador was about to say. *"There are others here. I know them. I don't know if we can free them all, but if we can find a way, we must."*

Ripley's jaw dropped at this disclosure. There were more form benders...here in this place? *"We must get them out!"* Ripley urged in his mind. *"How many are there?"*

"Whitemane is the priority here, Wet Nose. She's first..." Malador stared hard at Ripley and, as if by the sheer force of his will, would imprint the importance of getting Whitemane out of here first.

"Ok...but how many...?" his thought trailed off when Ripley noticed the intensity in his eyes. Satisfied he understood what he was being told, Malador spoke to him again.

"There are two in the cages across from where Whitemane is being held. If we can, we'll release them. If not, well, we'll have to get the others and come back here to set them free."

Ripley nodded, following his lead against his own better judgment. All he could think about were the others he knew in his heart would be punished if they left them behind. He'd made Malador a promise. *"Ok, so what do we do?"*

Malador looked at Ripley, and then deep inside himself. Ripley could tell by the glazed look in the leader's eyes that his mentor had come up with an idea.

Eager for him to share his plan, he urged him, *"What?...Tell me."*

"Well," he started reluctantly, *"there is a way. We'll have to split up, though."*

Ripley frowned. He could tell Malador didn't like the plan, but was unable to find another solution to their problem. Undaunted he said, *"Go ahead...what is this plan of yours?"*

"We can follow the path I just took, but it would put all of us in danger," he said in his mind, and then stopped.

"Ok, so that won't work," he said distractedly, and then frowned. Ripley's mind was forming alternative plans even as Malador chose his next thoughts carefully.

"What may work—and I want you to understand, Wet Nose—I'm not certain this will work, but it appears to be the only viable choice we have..."

"Go on!" he insisted, impatience getting the best of him.

"Well, you would have to go down the other side. When I get to the glass room, you will have to provide a distraction while I go in there, get the antidote, and administer it to Whitemane. It should awaken her enough to get her in shape for the long run home...or at least to the wood nymphs and aid."

"All right—I'm ready," Ripley replied in his thoughts and steeled himself for the task ahead.

"This may be dangerous, Ripley, I'm warning you. These people are no lightweights."

He swallowed hard and nodded, pulling courage from a place inside of him he hadn't known existed. *"I'm ready. What do you want me to do?"*

Chapter Eight

Soundlessly jumping up onto the crates at the right side of the warehouse, Malador indicated that Ripley should follow suit across the aisle with a toss of his head. Ripley swallowed hard and gauged the distance from where he stood to the top of the crates, wondering if he too, could make the jump without a sound.

"*Go!*" Malador hissed in his mind.

Ripley looked quickly at Malador and wondered how he was going to do as he asked...every fiber of his body was on edge. He crouched low to the floor and commanded his muscles to spring into action. Nothing happened. He was frozen in place by the fear of what was to come.

"*Come on, Ripley...you can do this!*"

Ripley slanted a glance at Malador again, gaining courage from his support. Once again, he readied himself for the jump. Inside the corridor, Ripley heard the sounds from outside which told him they were no longer alone. The footsteps and voices of two men carried hollowly in the otherwise empty hallway. Ripley almost panicked when he realized they were coming in the door behind him. Malador whirled, ready to leap onto the men who were about to enter the warehouse.

Ripley's nerves sprang into action, his muscles bunched as they prepared for the leap; suddenly he was airborne. He lit silently on top of the cages. Immediately, he lay flat on the crates as the men walked from the well-lit corridor into the dingy warehouse light. Ripley's heart was pumping so fast he thought it might burst. He could see the tops of the men's heads as they started down the aisle. One of them laughed at something the other man said. With his ears pricked forward, Ripley listened.

"Hey, Vinnie!" one of them called out to the men sitting at the table.

"Max! Come on in!"

The Form Benders – Janet Lee Carpenter

Ripley looked at Malador—who was counting the steadily growing group of adversaries—and wondered if the plan was still on. Malador locked gazes with Ripley and spoke to him in his thoughts.

"Move quietly, Wet Nose. Take your time, and keep low to the crates. We can do this. We just have to be cautious when we get to the end of the crates."

Ripley nodded in acknowledgment and began to creep forward, stopping in the shadows to watch and listen. It took quite a while for them to reach the other end, but they made it there in tense silence.

"Now what?" he asked Malador through his thoughts.

"Just a minute...I'm thinking."

Ripley wished he could hear *those* thoughts, especially since it involved him; but he wasn't privy to them. *How was it they could hide their thoughts from him, but he was unable to hide his thoughts from them?* Malador's thoughts broke into his as he began to explain the plan.

"I am going to jump down and head for that glass enclosure—there," he nodded, indicating the small room across the hall, adjacent to where he crouched against the crates. *"When I do, I want you to watch the men below. Warn me if they head in my direction."* Malador looked across the room at Ripley, and he nodded in response to what the elder said to him.

"What should I do if they are?"

"Let me know. I'm not sure—but, if I can do this right, they won't even know we're here. I can get across the hall. Whitemane is in the closest enclosure...right there." He looked directly at the occupied pen and indicated Ripley should follow his gaze.

Ripley glanced across the hall and squinted until his wolf-eyes adjusted to see in the poorly lit warehouse. The entire room was lit with one lone, eerie light bulb. He saw Whitemane's head and tail against the cage, her sleeping features lovely. Relief flooded him until he looked down the row of cages and saw the other two benders Malador had spoken of. Horror gripped him as he realized there were tubes and IV's leading to one of the benders' bodies. He apparently had needles shoved into his veins. The other, like himself and Malador, was already bent into the form of a wolf, while the bear bender looked as if he had just started

The Form Benders – Janet Lee Carpenter

to bend. He appeared to be not quite half-human, half-bear from where Ripley stood. Both were lying in filthy cages. It was then that their scent assailed him, and he almost gagged at the stench.

"*Ripley...Ripley!*" Impatience laced Malador's thoughts as he brought him abruptly back to the task at hand. "*I need you to focus! Stay with me here. We'll come back for them later! Right now we have to get Whitemane out of here!*"

Ripley tore his eyes from the pathetic sight of the once proud form benders who filled those two cages. He forced himself to focus on Whitemane and what Malador was telling him.

"*If they should come, let me know. Then create a distraction so I can administer the antidote—all right? I need you to buy me some time. Do you think you can handle that?*"

He swallowed hard and nodded to Malador. "*Yes, I can do it.*"

Ripley looked around to see if he could find something to distract the men from Malador and Whitemane should he need to. However, there was nothing lying on top of the cages or anywhere in sight. *He would have to use himself as bait,* he decided.

"*Ready, Wet Nose?*" he questioned Ripley.

"*I'm ready,*" he whispered in his mind.

"*Here goes...*" Malador landed lightly on his feet and slinked directly to the glass enclosure. He bent his form into that of a human and fiddled with the lock for a moment before he was able to open the door. Suddenly, as the door swung open, an alarm went off. The men at the table scrambled in their stupors to pick up some strange looking sticks. Ripley hadn't seen them until that moment. Suddenly, there was pandemonium as the guards began running toward the glass enclosure. Ripley had to think fast! *What to do?* How to gain their attention? Suddenly, it hit him. Quickly dashing across the tops of the cages where he had lain hidden, he willed his muscles to bunch and release. They sent him flying over the open space in between them, narrowly missing the head of one of the guards. He lit on the side of one of the cages on the opposite side of the warehouse and grasped the wire mesh with his toenails in a desperate attempt to get to the top of the cages.

The Form Benders – Janet Lee Carpenter

The neatly stacked cages began to tumble like dominoes as he grappled with righting himself. The guards began yelling and Ripley kept grabbing at the top of each of the cages. Just as he would pull himself on top, the cage would begin to tumble, and then he would scramble up the side to the next one, leaping from one falling crate to the next. He finally made his way back to the corridor where they had entered, leaving cages strewn haphazardly across the floor. The men were trying to shove the crates out of the way, shouting at one another in the mayhem which ensued. In the meantime, Malador was working furiously to get Whitemane free.

"*I've got her,*" Malador's voice boomed inside his head.

Ripley didn't think he'd ever heard anything so wonderful!

"Wait, Vinnie...Steamer...*they've released her!*" The urgency in the guard's voice was unmistakable. Ripley looked back in time to see the men turning around and heading toward Malador and Whitemane. He had to do something! Ripley ran through different options in his quick mind, sifting through the ones that wouldn't work in a split second. There was no time! He leapt over the cages, digging his toenails into their mesh to propel him forward. He landed on the one nearest him and pounced on two more before he got to the men. The one they called Vinnie was right ahead of him. Ripley jumped onto him and sank his teeth deep into the man's arm.

"Ow!" he howled in pain. "Help me...Steamer...Don, *get this thing off me!*" The man was pounding on Ripley with his good fist, but Ripley held on tight with his jaws locked in place like a vise grip as he ignored the pain.

The two men stopped again and turned toward the new threat, giving Malador and Whitemane the precious time they needed to get to the other side of the warehouse and head out toward the corridor and freedom!

Ripley was wrestling with Vinnie. However, he released him when he saw Steamer. He assumed the one called Don was approaching him, along with Steamer. Both men had those giant sticks in their hands. He released the arm, and Vinnie grabbed just above the teeth marks as blood spurted from the wound. Ripley stepped back slowly against the fallen cages—head down and teeth bared—as a low growl came from deep in his chest, warning the men to keep their distance. Ripley checked both directions to see if he had an escape route. When he couldn't readily identify a way out, he started backing up more, and the strip of hair on his back stood straight up in warning. Then he saw it! *There was a small opening in the warehouse wall...if only he could get to it, he would be safe!* He kept moving backwards trying to get past the crates and over to the hole in the wall which would allow him to reach safety. He had almost made it when he felt something behind him that wasn't a cage. He turned to see what it was—and at the same precise moment, he heard Steamer speak.

"*Do it...do it now!*" Steamer shouted the order to someone behind him. Ripley caught the flash of blue light in the corner of his eye before he fully understood what was happening.

Ripley suddenly lost all control of his muscles as a debilitating pain shot through him and rendered his muscles incapable of movement. Shards of electrical agony burst in tiny shock waves throughout his nervous system. Every nerve ending felt as if it were on fire. His muscles wouldn't obey his thoughts and Ripley's body collapsed to the floor in a shivering mass. *What just happened?*

Steamer and the other man came toward him with evil grins on their faces as he lay there helplessly, growling and convulsing in pain...wondering what they had done to him and why his muscles no longer obeyed him. Then Steamer reached out with the stick he was carrying and poked him. When Ripley didn't...no, *couldn't* respond...Steamer laughed evilly and pulled a trigger on the handle of the stick. Once again, the shooting pains crashed through his nervous system, his body twitching against the sudden onslaught of electricity as it poured through him. Ripley cried out in pain, the howl coming from deep within him, but Steamer wasn't through; he shoved the stick flush against him one more time, and waited. When Ripley realized he was going to do it again, his look hardened and he issued the challenge with a deep growl with his teeth still bared. Steamer's deep, evil chuckle echoed in the warehouse, making Ripley shiver.

"You don't like that, do you?" he questioned Ripley in a soft, menacing voice. "Gee, that's too bad," he said and shoved the stick hard against his neck. The pulsating energy blasted through him once more before Ripley lost consciousness.

The Form Benders – Janet Lee Carpenter

When he awoke, they had placed him in the same cage Whitemane occupied only a little while before. Every muscle in his body hurt, and it was torture to move his head to look around. As he suddenly became alert, Ripley decided it wasn't worth it to move. He wondered if Whitemane and Malador had escaped the treacherous guards.

He was so thirsty, but there was no bowl in sight. He eyed the two cages where the other benders were being kept…*no bowls of water for them, either.* Their silent pain was tangible in the room about him. They watched him curiously as he laid there unable to move.

"Who are you, boy?" queried the gigantic half-human, half-bear bender with a thin scar that ran from one side of his nose toward his left eye. The scar looked like it might have been old because it was almost lost in the fur on his snout and barely visible to the eye. At least he looked as if he might be part bear. His face had turned somewhat human, though his snout still occupied his human face. He looked like some travesty of a form bender who hadn't quite made the switch. Tubes hung from the outside of his cage, and he was held in place by several ropes which kept him from lying down.

It took him a few moments to answer him in the way all form benders do…silently. His voice seemed momentarily suspended. *"My name is Ripley."*

A sudden hush came over the two benders…an aura of respect emanated from them both.

"You are Master Ripley?" the bear questioned him with surprise.

He cleared his throat and spoke again. "Um…I am. But, you can just call me Ripley." His voice was raspy. He couldn't hide his surprise that these benders knew of him.

"We have heard of you. There has been talk for a very long time, Master Ripley, that you would come to us from the wakened world. We have been expecting you."

"Ripley, please," he said in a tone that corrected the bear. "It seems everyone has known about my arrival…except me."

The huge bear chuckled at his statement. "That is the way of it, isn't it, Ripley?"

The Form Benders – Janet Lee Carpenter

"So it seems." Ripley tried to get up twice before he was finally able to stand. Once he did, however, he groaned and stretched his muscles in an attempt to loosen them.

"You've been out for quite a while," the white wolf in the cage next to the bear finally spoke. His gentle voice was a surprise to Ripley.

Suddenly he remembered how he'd gotten here. "Oh no...did they get free?" He directed the question to both of the benders, looking frantically around for some evidence that Malador had escaped with Whitemane and they hadn't been captured.

"Yes, and thank you for freeing our Whitemane...Malador will get her home safely," the wolf answered.

"So they made it?" He felt the relief surging through him even as he heard the next words.

"Yes, Ripley, if the attitudes of the guards are any indication. Steamer was exceedingly angry they got away, I think, and even more so when he realized Kestler was going to punish him for their loss. I think they forget we can understand them when they speak." Again, the big bear chuckled to himself.

"So, who are you two?" Ripley questioned the benders in the other cages.

"I am Skerrin, younger brother of Oren Trueblood."

Then the wolf spoke, "I am Revelan, father of Whitemane."

Ripley's eyes were as big as saucers as he looked from one to the other. These were the two benders who had disappeared almost a month ago!

"I see you know Oren," Skerrin said with a smile.

"Oh yes!" He looked at the huge bear. "You don't look like his younger brother," Ripley commented, and then realized what he'd said. "I mean, you look older..." At Skerrin's frown, Ripley realized he was putting his foot in his mouth and stammered..."I mean...oh, I'm sorry...I don't know what I mean." He was thoroughly embarrassed he had alluded to Skerrin's misshapen form.

At that, Skerrin laughed aloud, enjoying Ripley's discomfort. "It doesn't matter, Ripley—I know what you mean."

The Form Benders – Janet Lee Carpenter

Relieved, Ripley grinned sheepishly, thankful Skerrin knew what he meant when he wasn't even sure himself what he was trying to say. "What happened to you, Skerrin—if you don't mind my asking?"

"They gave me some sort of drug which has me trapped in a state of suspended bend, leaving me part-bear, part-man. The drugs they are pumping into me keep me from shifting fully into human or bear. We've been in here over a month. The others from our tribe have tried to rescue us more than once, but no one has succeeded. No one, that is, until you Ripley."

"But...you're still here," he stammered, "I didn't rescue anyone." He hung his head in shame. He hadn't gotten *them* out either. He felt like such a failure! "It was mostly Malador." Ripley brushed the compliment aside, knowing that no matter how badly he wanted it, he was not really entitled to it. Then he continued, "Without him, we never could have gotten Whitemane out of here. I'm just sorry we didn't get you out as well..." His voice trailed off and he looked to the ground, clearly disappointed in himself.

"Don't you worry about that, Ripley. Mal is going to come and get us out just as soon as he gets Whitemane to safety." Skerrin's voice was sincere, which made it all the more difficult for Ripley to come to terms with the fact that he wasn't able to save any of them. Instead, he'd gotten himself caught by the FBEF. *What a child he'd been...again!* He would make this right somehow. He vowed he would get them all out. He just needed his muscles to work properly. Maybe if he rested for a little while longer, he would be able to come up with a plan that would work.

As soon as Ripley lay down in the cage, he heard voices coming from the end of the hall. He looked up from where he lay, his ears pricked forward in alert. The other two benders scurried to the backs of their cages and were trying to make themselves as unnoticeable as possible. In Skerrin's case, however, he was in a hoist which didn't allow him to lie down—but he still managed to make himself small and inconspicuous. His curiosity was piqued as he maneuvered himself so he could see the people coming toward him as they rounded the corner. In an effort to identify the voices, he dug into his memory of earlier that day. He recognized Steamer and Vinnie's voices, but there was one voice that needed no introduction. Ripley remembered it well.

The Form Benders – Janet Lee Carpenter

He looked up just in time to see Ms. Washington as she rolled around the corner of his cage. But no, it wasn't Ms. Washington...*it was Kestler*, he reminded himself! He was situated nearest the glass cubicle Malador broke into only hours before. Ripley immediately stood on all fours, unwilling to let them see his discomfort; he winced only slightly with the movement. The hair on the nape of his neck and all the way down his spine stood at attention, and his eyes narrowed as he raised his upper lip and growled menacingly at Ms. Washington—or Kestler—or *whatever* her name was! Once again, she was wearing that cloying perfume. However, if he'd thought it was pungent when he was in his human form, it was even more gagging to him in his wolf form. He coughed and choked at the scent, and then once again took up his menacing pose. As his growl turned into snapping jaws and sharp teeth, Kestler smiled wickedly at him.

"Ahh...I see you remember me, Ripley."

Ripley lunged at the cage door, but it held fast. He ignored the pain in his muscles as he jumped up on the door of the wire cage and ineffectively barked and snapped at her. *If only he could get out of this cage!*

She laughed at him now with a deep, guttural excuse for laughter that held no humor—only bitterness and disdain. "Show him who the boss is, Steamer," she snapped out the order.

Before Ripley could react, the long stick was shoved through the wire mesh, and he felt it up alongside his chest. He moved just in time to avoid the full measure of electricity which issued from its metal head. He slumped over and didn't let on that they hadn't fully charged him with the stick. He couldn't believe how wily he'd become in the last few days! The evil laugh that came from Kestler was nauseating. He noted with satisfaction that Vinnie wore several layers of gauze around the wound in his arm. Perhaps he would think twice the next time he tangled with Ripley!

"Guess you won't forget that, huh, Ripley?"

Ripley weakly lifted his head from the bottom of the cage, and then let it drop back to the cement floor. This was by far the best acting job he'd *ever* done. He only wished Miss Fitzgerald, his drama teacher, could see him now. She would be so proud!

The Form Benders – Janet Lee Carpenter

She didn't look in the direction of Revelan or Skerrin's cages, and he meant to keep it that way. He didn't know what was in the I.V. they planted in Skerrin's vein, but he didn't want her pumping any of her diabolical concoctions into him before he could get them out of there.

"I suppose you'll do in Whitemane's stead." She seemed preoccupied by her thoughts and Ripley was quiet as he watched her from the corner of his eye, gauging her thoughts from her body language. She pursed her lips and tapped a puffy finger to her mouth as she contemplated *who* knew *what*. She must have come to some decision because she looked at Steamer, Vinnie, and the one he thought they called Max.

"We'll get the room ready, and then we'll come back and get him. You'll have to sedate him, of course, but we'll bring him to before we begin.

Or...," she paused here for effect, "we could always go and get his mother if he doesn't behave..." She left the threat dangling in the air between them as her eyes narrowed and she watched Ripley carefully to see the effect her words had on him. Satisfied they had met their mark when Ripley's eyes registered alarm, she nodded, and then teetered and toddled as she went back the way they came, all three men following her.

Then he heard her say, "Oh, I almost forgot..."

Now what? he wondered. *I have to get out of this cage and get to my mother, no matter what form I'm in! She's in danger!* Ripley thought she was coming back for Skerrin or Revelan—but instead she directed the men to get each of them some water.

"Stay here until they drink their fill, and then empty those dishes!" She barked out the order, and then continued down the hall and out of sight.

The three men got water for the benders, and then sat down to wait. Within moments, Max said, "I've got to go to the bathroom. She makes me so nervous sometimes."

Steamer laughed and said, "Go ahead. We can handle this."

"Thanks," Max said, and wasted no time as he sprinted down the hallway behind Kestler.

Steamer looked at Vinnie. "Man, I want a smoke..."

The Form Benders - Janet Lee Carpenter

Vinnie grinned, "She won't know. Let's go...we'll be back before she knows it."

Steamer eyed the cages. Ripley lay where they'd left him a few moments ago and tried not to give away that he was fully aware and able to move. He tossed a glance at Skerrin and Revelan, his mind made up. "Can't have a long one...let's go before she finds out."

With that, the two men jumped up from the bench lining the glass enclosure on one side and headed out the way Ripley remembered coming in...through the warehouse.

Precious water...he was so thirsty! Ripley jumped up as soon as the men rounded the corner of the warehouse and could no longer be seen. Suddenly, Ripley had an idea! If only he could somehow get their cages unlocked, they could make a break for it. He remembered they left the door ajar when they went to have a smoke. They could all be free soon if he could only figure out how to get the doors unlocked!

He drank some water, leaving a little for later. As soon as he stood up, the others began speaking to him.

"Thank goodness you're all right," Revelan said. His voice was soft and gentle. "You gave us quite a scare!"

"Can you call the water sprites?" Skerrin asked in a quiet whisper.

"I don't know how," Ripley replied. The pieces of the puzzle started to fall into place as he realized if he could call them—then perhaps they would know how to unlock these doors.

"You have the medallion. I'm not sure how it works, but you must know how to use it."

"There was no time. All the Prince told me was that I could call them if I ever needed them."

"You must know how it works, Ripley. Think, boy...think about what he said. There must have been something."

"Well," Ripley began.

"Yes, what is it?" the two benders questioned in unison.

"Well, it was something I just sort of understood in my mind. It was nothing the Prince said to me."

The Form Benders – Janet Lee Carpenter

"What was it, Ripley?"

"I got the feeling you had to be near water to call the sprites forth, and near wood to call the wood nymphs."

"Well...try it," they both urged.

"But we're not near the lake," Ripley hedged.

"This is true," Revelan said, and then seemed to give up hope.

"Wait...maybe I can use the water bowl instead?"

"We certainly have nothing to lose," Skerrin stated with conviction.

"Do you have any idea how I call them?" Ripley looked at his companions and hoped they knew something he didn't when it came to the water sprites.

Revelan spoke quietly, "I believe I saw the Prince use it once, many years ago. He closed his eyes and concentrated on them," he began, "then called them forth by summoning their leader, Arapham. See if that works...," he replied as his voice trailed off and Ripley moved closer to the water bowl in his cage.

Ripley closed his eyes and began concentrating on the name Arapham. He could feel a breeze begin to blow about him, and he heard the water rippling in his bowl. Spooked...he lost his train of thought, and the wind died down.

"What happened?" Revelan asked.

"I think you were doing it," Skerrin said. "Try again."

Ripley swallowed hard and closed his eyes again. He began to think about Arapham, repeating the name over and over again in his mind. The wind began once more; he could feel the air swirl around him as he concentrated on the water sprite's name.

"That's right," Skerrin said urgently. "Focus...don't let your mind wander..."

Ripley felt his thoughts gain momentum as a vortex of energy came swirling around him. He could feel the essence of water and its power to flow around everything. Its power was its ability to move around, and flow between and beneath all things, and eventually to wear them down over time. Suddenly, he knew he wasn't alone.

He began to call the sprite. "Come, Arapham. Come to us in our time of need. Prince Valiantheart has decreed this is so! Come Arapham, the children of Haven's Rest need you!"

The wind died down, and there was a peace pervading the small area in the warehouse.

"By God, boy, *you've done it!*"

Ripley opened his eyes and saw a small army of tiny water sprites. Some flew about him as he blinked and tried to focus on them. They were beings of great light. They had tiny wings, and their features were as near perfect as they could be. They could almost pass for fairies, but their bodies seemed to be made of water. They were translucent.

A hush fell over the room as the eldest of the sprites spoke. "Who summons me to serve?" He had a long gray beard and stern features. When his eyes landed on Ripley, he frowned deeply, concentrating.

"Um...," Ripley stammered. "I did," he confessed.

"And by what authority have you summoned us to your side?"

His voice got stronger as he began to explain. "Prince Valiantheart of Haven's Rest has given me the right to summon you in his stead, by the authority of the medallion which hangs about my neck."

The sprite moved closer to him and lifted a minuscule monocle, and then he inspected the shimmering medallion hanging from Ripley's neck. He touched it, and a *ping* rang through the still and silent room.

"As you say..." He seemed satisfied at the ringing tone filling the area. "Then what shall be your need of us?"

Ripley quickly told the ancient sprite what happened and how he came to find himself in this predicament. He told of Whitemane's capture and his responsibility in the matter, as well as her escape only a few hours before. Skerrin and Revelan nodded in agreement as he finished his tale.

"And what is it you desire of my army, then, young Master Ripley?"

There he went with that "Master" thing again. "It's just Ripley, Arapham," he continued without missing a beat. "We need you to help us get out of here…"

"Well," he said jovially, "What are we waiting for? Let's get a move on."

With that pronouncement, Ripley watched in astonishment as the sprites quickly set to work on the locks. One let its watery body slide into the keyhole, and then turned itself into ice. The other sprites would turn him like a key, releasing each of them in turn. Skerrin used his mouth to snatch the I.V. from his vein—and for the first time since Ripley joined them, he seemed excited to be going home. The sprites freed him from the ties that kept him from lying down as if they had never been there. The latches to their prisons snapped open, one by one. They were free; but for his idea to work, they would have to go back through the warehouse and out the alley door. Ripley only hoped he remembered the way back to Haven's Rest as the sprites waited for their orders.

"Follow me," Ripley spoke quietly in his mind, directing them all. *"Be very quiet, and stay close together. We're gonna get out of here."*

Skerrin and Revelan bunched in closer to Ripley, and the sprites flew upward to the ceiling, trying to gauge the distance between them and the door. Ripley called out to Arapham.

"Can you tone down your light a bit?" Ripley sent his thoughts to him. He could see he'd offended Arapham because he puffed out his rather enormous chest; well, it was enormous for a sprite anyway, so he tried to smooth the sprite's ruffled feathers. *"I don't mean to upset you, it's just that any light in this dark place will stand out, and we don't want to be seen."*

Still somewhat disgruntled, Arapham nodded. The sprites took a black overcoat from a coat rack at the end of the hall, and they all hid beneath its folds. No light shone from under the coat as they moved toward the cages he and Malador had worked their way over and around earlier in the day. Satisfied they could stay to the shadows and remain undetected, Ripley began the longest walk of his life toward the metal door on the other side of the warehouse and freedom.

The Form Benders – Janet Lee Carpenter

Someone had cleaned up the mess they'd made of the cages earlier that day and they stood, once again, in neat rows against the warehouse wall. Since Skerrin was too big to get on top of the cages, they chose to walk the distance down the center aisle. It left them vulnerable should someone open the door and come in. They squeaked by the empty table where the men had played poker; the same deck of cards and a few rings on the table were the only evidence left to show they had ever been there. When they reached the end of the aisle, Ripley stopped the entourage and said silently in his mind, *"Stay here."*

He snuck down the stairs to the door which, to his relief, stood ajar just as he thought it would. He nudged the door with his nose and peered into the empty corridor beyond. His nerves were on edge as he motioned for the others to follow him. At that moment, a door at the other end of the hall opened and two men stepped through it into the well-lit corridor. Vinnie and Max were finished with their smoke.

It's too soon, Ripley thought in panic, but he pulled himself together.

Ripley backed up quickly, motioning for the others to come back into the shadows behind the door. They all held their breath and waited as the two men approached the door, and then moved on past it to another one at the opposite end of the hall. Ripley breathed a sigh of relief, and then checked the hallway again. He nodded his head and stepped out into the lighted corridor. If they were going to get caught, it would be here. They moved quickly through the hall, while the giant, dark overcoat hiding the army of sprites floated eerily along the hallway behind them. Trails of water and light seeped from under its folds.

They made it to the door, but when Ripley tried it, the handle didn't budge. He tried again.

"Can you open this lock too?" he questioned Arapham in his thoughts.

"At your service," he answered in kind, and left the relative safety of the coat to unlock the door. Arapham slid the bottom half of his body into the keyhole. Ripley watched in fascination as the lower half of Arapham's body turned to ice, forming itself into a key. He simply twisted, and the door unlocked. Ripley didn't think he would ever tire of meeting all the astonishing inhabitants of Haven's Rest. When the latch gave way, Arapham turned back into water as Ripley pulled down on the

handle with his paw. *"Too late,"* he thought as he noticed the box on the wall with tiny buttons numbered zero through nine. Immediately, an alarm went off on the other side of the building!

The sprites dropped the coat—*their hiding place*—and turned to face the attackers who seemed to stream from every doorway into the hall.

"Go...get them to safety!" Arapham cried urgently; the need for silent communication was past. When Ripley hesitated he said again, *"Go!* We'll be fine!"

Men were soon filling the corridor armed with the sticks they'd used on him earlier, along with anything else they'd been able to pick up on the way. Ripley blinked at the suddenly bright noonday sun as he slammed the door shut and left the sprites to fend off their attackers. Hopefully, it would buy them enough time to get away. He hoped Arapham and his newly found friends, the water sprites, would indeed be fine. *Had he made the right decision?* He wasn't sure. He was only certain that these two benders were in his charge, and he must get them to safety...to Haven's Rest.

Chapter Nine

He hadn't bargained for daylight outside when they made their escape. Unfortunately, all the windows in the warehouse were blacked out so there was no sense of day or night, especially after he'd been knocked unconscious for hours. His sense of time was all out of whack. He would have preferred the cover of darkness to the daylight, but there was no going back now. He must find them a way out of this town. Both benders seemed a bit disoriented as Ripley took the lead and they followed him. They slunk around in the alleyways. Ripley picked up Malador's scent every once in a while, so it told him they were going the right way.

He passed the restaurant where he and Malador had stopped. He remembered how the young woman gave him refuge for a while. They had to get out of the daylight. He wondered if she would help him again. He really didn't have a choice. Ripley saw a black van cruise past the alley more than once. He instinctively knew it was the FBEF, and they had ducked into doorways and behind dumpsters twice already. So far, they were safe, but he wasn't willing to place them all in harm's way before nightfall.

He turned around and headed back to the door of the restaurant. He scratched at the back door, hoping the young woman would come to see who it was. He spent several agonizing minutes waiting before he scratched again, and then finally howled low in his throat, hoping she would hear him and the FBEF would not. He was just about to give up when the door opened a crack. Lacey's familiar face peered out the slit in the door. She opened it fully when she saw Ripley.

"Well, hello there, handsome," she said as she smiled and bent to give his scruff a rub. "What are you doing out here? Is Mal around?" she questioned him as she poked her head out the door and looked down the alley. "Are you in trouble, boy?"

If only he could have changed forms, this conversation would have been different. He would have been able to tell her what was happening. Instead, he had to make do with acting like a dog and hoping she would invite him in.

"You hungry, boy? Well, come on in, then," she smiled invitingly.

Ripley sat on the street, wagging his tail, hoping she would be okay with his friends. When she turned around and he hadn't moved, she hesitated. He tried talking to her heart, as Malador had taught him, hoping she would understand. When she did, he was pleasantly surprised.

"What is it, boy? Is something wrong?"

If she only knew how wrong it was! He called to Revelan and Skerrin in his mind, telling them to come out from their hiding place behind the dumpster. No matter how serious this all was, he had to admit it was rather comical when Skerrin was trying to hide behind the dumpster. The drugs had worked their way out of his system fast, and he'd returned to his full-on bear form. When Ripley made the request for them to hide it was quite obvious to him Skerrin was much too big to hide behind anything of that size. When he finally asked Ripley if he was hidden well enough, it was all he could do to keep from laughing. Though Skerrin's head and most of his body were hidden, his huge backside hung out from his hiding place for the entire world to see. He hadn't had the heart to tell him, though.

Slowly Skerrin and Revelan came into full view. Her eyes flew open wide, and her hands fluttered to her mouth as she breathed the single word, "Oh!"

She looked from Ripley to the other white wolf and the huge bear and must have noted they all seemed nervous. "Come on, bring your friends," she said in a no nonsense tone. "Any friend of Mal's and Ripley's is a friend of mine!" She held the door open, and the benders filed into the small storage room. Funny, it seemed much larger the last time Ripley was in there.

Skerrin went in and sat down almost immediately, aware that his girth was much too large for him to move around in the confined space. Lacey cautioned them to be quiet, and then slowly and quietly closed the door behind her as she headed back into the restaurant. Within moments, she returned with bowls of simmering stew.

"Be careful," she cautioned them as if she were speaking to humans, "it's hot."

She set the bowls down on the floor and left the way she came in—but not before she gave Ripley's soft fur one more generous pat. They all eyed their bowls of stew longingly, but heeded Lacey's warning. Each let it set for a bit to cool. As soon as she left, Skerrin spoke up.

"Who is she? How did you meet her…and how did you know we could come here and be safe?"

"Her name is Lacey. She's a friend of Malador's. She gave Malador and me sanctuary from the storm on our way to rescue Whitemane. We had no idea you two were there as well."

Ripley nudged his bowl, and then tasted a sample of Lacey's cooking. Once again, it was delicious as he began to eat gingerly. The other two took their lead from him and dug in to the delicious meal. The lapping up of the food and the guttural sounds of enjoyment were the only sounds filling the room for a while, as they each ate their bowls of stew in silence. Ripley finished first, and then lay down on the linoleum flooring to lick his chops. He attempted to savor any remaining bits of food which might be left clinging to his muzzle. Revelan finished his stew and licked his face also, relishing the tasty meal. He seemed to get sleepy then, and he closed his eyes. When he could stand it no more, Skerrin too lay down on the flooring. He looked at Ripley. It was obvious he had a question to ask him, but wasn't quite sure how.

"Spit it out," Ripley laughed.

"I was just thinking…"

"Yes?"

"You didn't answer my question earlier. How did you know we could come here and be safe?" Skerrin queried.

"Well, to be honest, I didn't. I just had to take the chance. The longer we stayed out there in broad daylight, the better chance there was of getting caught. Going back to the FBEF wasn't an option, so I chose here. It was a long shot, but it paid off."

"I see," Skerrin said thoughtfully. "When are we going to leave, then?"

The Form Benders – Janet Lee Carpenter

"Probably a little after sunset, I would imagine. I think she understands we're in trouble. She'll come and let us out when it's dark outside. So, for now, we need to get some rest. We'll need all the energy we can gather to make the journey home."

Skerrin nodded, obviously satisfied with the answer he'd been given, and looked to Revelan for confirmation, only to realize he was already fast asleep. "I guess he has the right idea," he chuckled, indicating Revelan's sleeping form with a toss of his head.

"Yeah," Ripley smiled inwardly. He knew it was a long way. He only hoped Revelan had the energy to get there. If he didn't, Ripley would have to come up with a way to get him home. Whitemane would never forgive him if he didn't bring her father home safely. He had to show *her*…he had to show them *all* he was grown up and could handle the challenges he was about to face.

It had been several hours since their meal when a commotion outside their hiding place forced Ripley awake. The others were awake already and he realized they were watching the door alertly. "How long have you been awake?" he questioned the other two.

"Not long. The noises just started a moment ago." Skerrin looked none the worse for wear; in fact, he looked ready to go. It pleased Ripley inordinately that Kestler wouldn't be able to use that drug to keep any of the form benders in the half form in which he'd found Skerrin in for long. He didn't think, however, that it would stop her from experimenting on whomever they could locate and kidnap.

They heard footsteps in the hall. As the footfalls got closer to their hiding place, Ripley felt his muscles bunch, ready to spring on whoever opened the door. A gentle rap on the door surprised them all as they exchanged glances.

"It's me." The soft melodious voice was unmistakable. Ripley felt the adrenalin drain from him as if someone pulled a plug. Lacey slowly opened the door, but she didn't flip on the light. "Quickly, you must go! There were two men here a few minutes ago looking for you three. I didn't tell them anything, but you *must go! Hurry!*" she said as she slipped a bandana over Ripley's head. "There is some food in there for all of you. I'm sorry, it's not much."

The Form Benders – Janet Lee Carpenter

She opened the door for them to exit the building, but not before she checked the alleyway to make certain it was safe. Ripley watched her, feeling love surge in him as she offered him and his two friends protection in so many ways. He understood why Malador chose her for his friend. She knelt quickly and slid her arms around Ripley's neck, giving him a squeeze.

"Hurry now," she said, urging them into the street. She gently touched each of them as they stepped out the door and into the anonymous night. "Go quickly. Follow this alley until you get to the end. It will take you to a one-way street. Go against the traffic until you find the underpass to the 180 freeway. Follow along it until you reach another freeway—the 41. You'll have to go a short distance until you arrive at the 168, and then stay on it until you reach home."

Ripley howled softly as she shooed them on their way. With one last look at their savior, the three disappeared into the night shadows, following the directions she gave them. They trotted along in silent camaraderie, each one knowing what was at stake. Ripley took the lead, and thought he picked up Malador's scent several times as they made their way from freeway to freeway, finally arriving at the 168. Many new homes were being built alongside the highway, which meant they would have to avoid them to keep from being found out. Homes meant dogs, and dogs meant barking. Travelling with Malador taught him that much, so they stuck to the shadows and made their way toward the foothills. At least there, they wouldn't have to be quite so careful. There was more cover there, and they could rest once they reached the orange groves.

Skerrin didn't complain once. Though he lagged behind a couple of times, he kept up with the other two. Revelan moved in the night like the wolf he was—all stealth and speed when he needed it. Ripley was surprised Skerrin was as agile as he was, given the ordeal he'd recently suffered. He thought a bear with such a bulky frame would be slow. Skerrin proved him wrong. They finally got to the aqueduct where the orange groves were. Ripley felt they could rest for just a few minutes, get a drink, and then move on. He remembered this was the place where he and Malador were only two days before. *Had it only been two days?* It seemed hard to believe they'd been here only two nights before, when Malador was calling him *Wet Nose* and leading them into danger without an ounce of fear. No wonder there were so many legends about Malador, the *Ghost Wolf*. Ripley's admiration for his mentor grew as they rested near the aqueduct, listening to the crickets, cicadas, and the gentle sounds of water flowing lazily down the cement confines of the river. It gave a cozy, yet deceptive, backdrop to their situation. Ripley knew they wouldn't be safe until they reached Haven's Rest. He remembered from his history lessons that this aqueduct contained water from the San Joaquin River. It wound its way through the Sierra Nevada Mountains looming in the distance. They could follow it home.

"*Let's go,*" Ripley spoke in his mind to the two benders who were already on their feet the moment he stood up. Skerrin bent into his human form for a moment, and then slipped back into his half-human/half-bear form again. He'd been doing that randomly since they'd left the FBEF. Concern furrowed Ripley's brow, but Skerrin assured him he was fine and he'd be even better if they could get home. Consequently, they began their journey again.

The trio headed through the remaining flatlands until they reached the foothills beyond Fresno. They stopped one more time as they kept to the stream following the highway into the mountains. Scrub oaks and dry grasses gave way to elderberry bushes and Bull Pines as they climbed the mountainside above the small town of Tollhouse. When they reached the stream where he and Malador rested on their way to Fresno, Ripley gave the go-ahead to rest once more. He opened the kerchief Lacey had placed around his neck and shared the chunks of cheese and turkey she'd slipped inside of it. They ate in companionable silence. Perhaps it was the memory of his expedition with Malador, or maybe just the lingering scent of him that played with Ripley's senses. Somehow, Ripley felt as if he was there with him, guiding their steps.

Within moments, however, it was clear his scent was strong for a reason. Malador stepped into the clearing—the quarter moon illuminating his form with eerie light—giving Ripley a start. How odd that he didn't hear Malador approach the small open area. He blinked to make certain his eyes were not deceiving him, and then realized Malador truly was there—in the flesh! Was this why they called him the *Ghost Wolf?* He was relieved to see him. They would not have to travel alone now. He wouldn't admit it, but he wasn't certain of his sense of direction and his ability to detect the scent of Malador.

"*Malador!*" Skerrin cried aloud at the sight of his old friend. "*You are here!*"

The Form Benders – Janet Lee Carpenter

Ripley's joy couldn't be contained at the sight of his mentor. His tail wagged and he jumped up to greet him. He nipped him playfully on the back of the neck as Whitemane had done with him when he first showed up at Haven's Rest. Suddenly, everyone stood still and there was a tense silence filling the other two. Ripley instantly regretted his unabashed reaction to Malador's presence. The awkward silence permeated his senses, and he realized he had committed another faux pas.

Malador shot a stern look at Ripley, who suddenly felt his joy fading. His tail slowed and tucked between his legs as his ears drooped. He looked at the ground and started to move away. He had done something wrong...*again*! Before he could apologize for revealing his feelings and losing control of himself, Malador's muzzle opened, and his eyes had a mischievous twinkle in them. He jumped and nipped Ripley on the back of the neck in return. The tense moment passed as Ripley felt the joy return; then, they all began talking at once.

"Wait...I've brought friends," Malador said as he turned. One by one, the others stepped out into view. First, there was the Prince; his stature and grace bearing the obvious signs of royalty as he bowed before Ripley. Next, Oren stepped out, thrilled that his brother was alive and well. Oren went to him, laying his head next to his brother's as they rubbed them together in an age-old dance of affection.

The Prince bent into his human form and began to speak, addressing Ripley. "I am in your debt, Master Ripley. For your heroism and bravery, I commend you. This medallion is but a token of your courage under fire." He lightly tapped the medallion hanging about Ripley's neck before he continued. "I make it a gift to you that you may follow it always in your heart and have power over the sprites and the nymphs of this world. For in true courage of the heart, leaders are born and as they serve the many, no help will ever be denied them."

Ripley bowed before the Prince, pondering what he was saying to him. He was delighted to accept the gift, and he had an inkling there was great responsibility which came with its acceptance. He knew the Prince was bestowing an honor upon him, and he swore he wouldn't take it lightly. Now that he knew how to call the sprites, they would be able to help them all in their fights against the FBEF and Kestler.

Whitemane was the last to enter the clearing. She tried to walk with dignified grace, but failed as she finally gave up and rushed to her father's side. "Are you well, Father? Are you hurt?" She inspected him from head to tail, checking to make certain her eyes did not deceive her.

"No…daughter…no," he laughed. "I am well, now that I've seen you with my own eyes and know you are safe."

"I am safe, Father," she assured him as she licked his face and nuzzled his neck with her snout. She reluctantly left her father once she was assured he was well. She looked toward Ripley longingly.

"Go, child," Revelan encouraged.

Whitemane looked at her father for understanding. She must have seen it in his eyes. She ran to Ripley and with much cavorting and sheer happiness to see him; she nipped him on the back of the neck, revealing her joy that they both were returned to her. Ripley's embarrassment at the unabashed attention quickly gave way to joy at seeing her safe and unharmed.

"Come, we must continue on. There is more ground to cover before we sleep this night," the Prince decreed. "We must leave this place and return home. The honor of leading our group shall fall to Ripley, as he has shown courage, creativity, and valor amongst all. Let us follow a leader who is worthy."

With his words, Ripley felt himself glow as he went to the front of the line with Malador beside him. The Prince shifted into his cougar form and fell in behind them, waiting for Ripley's signal to move ahead.

Malador also waited for Ripley to begin the journey home, but when he didn't move forward, he prodded him. *"Take us home, Wet Nose,"* he spoke quietly in Ripley's mind, so no one else would hear.

"Yes sir," he said in kind, feeling as if he'd finally achieved his mentor's approval as he headed up the hill, the entourage following closely behind. Malador hung back once they'd begun their journey, waiting until they all left the clearing. Ripley looked back and saw him pick up a broken, leaf-covered branch. He groomed the ground behind them, and then followed at a discreet distance.

Each of the others followed as Ripley led them through the woods, past the rocks and trees and headed unerringly toward Haven's

Rest. When the group reached the edge of the forest, one by one they slipped through the wall of aspens and elderberry bushes. Ripley waited for Malador to precede him, staying behind this time with a pine bough in his mouth to brush away any evidence from the ground. When he was through, Ripley returned to Haven's Rest.

He knew he was going to have to go after his mother; she wouldn't be safe as long as Kestler knew where they lived. Ripley didn't know what Kestler would do to her, but the threat she'd made at the FBEF building made him cringe with fear for her safety. He had some inkling of what Kestler was willing to do to get what she wanted after he saw what she'd done to Skerrin and Whitemane's father. The aching spot on his neck where Vinnie's poker came in contact with him was also a vivid reminder. That's what made him fear for his mother; the thought of what Kestler might do to retaliate. Ripley harbored a suspicion it was really *him* she was after, but if his mother got in the way, then Kestler wouldn't hesitate to harm her...or use her to get to him. Of *that*, he was certain.

Chapter Ten

"I have to go after her, Whitemane...she won't understand. If they get her, they'll be able to use her as leverage against us. Who knows what Kestler's evil plan is? All I know is...if I don't go after my mother, then we're going to have to pay a hefty price...*all* the form benders will." Ripley looked deep into Whitemane's azure eyes, hoping she would understand and help him.

"The Elders would not approve of you going off alone like this, especially since you have only just returned. Skerrin talks of your great heroism; there is a celebration planned, as well. The entire village has prepared a gift for you, too. My father is helping with the feast...you must be present to accept their accolades, if nothing else." Resigned, Whitemane sighed and looked toward the village. "If you will not listen to reason...at least talk to Malador and have him go with you."

Ripley shook his head. "No, I cannot have him there. He already thinks of me as a child. I would not have him think less of me for doing this. I can work this out and come back before dawn...before anyone knows I'm even gone. The celebration isn't for three days yet. No one will notice my absence this night, and I shall return by morning's first light. I know the paths...I know the way there and back."

"What if you can't persuade her to come? Remember, she won't be able to see past your form to who you really are."

Suddenly he realized the truth of her words; Ripley hesitated, and then countered with, "I read once that a mother always knows her children. It has something to do with scent—and you and I know plenty about that."

Whitemane looked away toward their village. "I don't know, Ripley. I have a foreboding about this that will not be denied..."

She spoke so softly he almost didn't hear her. "I understand," he replied urgently. "But, I must go," he pleaded for her understanding. "She is utterly defenseless against an organization like the FBEF—not to mention Kestler herself. Remember, she has no idea *who* that woman is...she still thinks she's part of the CPS." Ripley begged her with his eyes to understand what he couldn't bring himself to say after all the difficulties they'd been through. He loved his mother, no matter what she had done to him; to them *both*, he corrected himself...that fact remained. He must go get her, and he *must* leave soon. Kestler would never let the grass grow under *her* feet, so he, too, must not tarry if he wished to get to his mother before she did.

"All right...," Whitemane said reluctantly, and Ripley could see she wasn't convinced this was the only way to handle the situation. "Be safe, please? Take care of yourself and remember you have the power to call the nymphs and the sprites. Use it if the need arises. I will watch for you and your mother by dawn. If you do not return, I will raise the entire village to your side."

Neither of them said it, but Ripley knew their relationship was growing deeper. Her presence here and being so concerned proved she cared for him. If only he could declare how he felt about her. However, now was not the time to share his feelings with her. There was so much at stake, and there was a chance he might not return. He wouldn't want her to suffer because of his selfish need to declare himself. Better she not know anything just yet. Nevertheless, he couldn't resist giving her some sign. Ripley laid his head next to hers and rubbed his face on her cheek and muzzle. "I will return in no time. I give you my word I will be back before the sun rises on Haven's Rest. I swear it!" his impassioned declaration rang out. He licked her face gently and then tore himself away. Before he moved away from her, he heard her whisper in his mind, "Sally..."

Ripley turned again to look at her. Her sweet voice filled his mind again. *"Sally Brunswick."* Surprise must have reflected on his face, for she then looked away from him.

"*The* Sally Brunswick?" he uttered in fascination. *This is the Sally Brunswick who disappeared in the forest back home? The one the Mountain Press talked about? His Whitemane and Sally were one and the same? Wait...but, Revelan was her father...what did this all mean?* There was no time to talk to her right now, which is all he wanted to do at that very moment. He wondered if she had planned it, or if it was just an accident. He had so many questions, but evening had come. It was time, under cover of darkness, to make his way back to the apartment and figure out a way to get his mother to follow him.

The Form Benders – Janet Lee Carpenter

She turned back toward him then and urged, "Go. We'll talk later..." She left the promise dangling in the air between them.

How could he go...but worse...how could he stay? He was torn between duty and his heart; though if he were honest, they were one and the same where she was concerned. He took a few steps from her before he looked back.

"Go!"

Ripley looked into her stricken eyes and hesitated.

"Go on...," she spoke more gently this time. "Go...I will be here when you return."

Ripley trotted back to her and rubbed his face against hers once more, and then lingered for a moment before he turned and headed down the path leading to the wall, which separated one of his worlds from the other. Had she just thrown caution to the wind, declaring her affection for him? One quick glance over his shoulder told the story. She stood there on the small knoll they had occupied only moments before, watching him as the breeze ruffled her fur. Then he turned and was gone. *Yes*...he believed she *had* revealed her feelings. The picture of her standing there would be forever etched in his mind.

The aspens and elderberry bushes swallowed him, and then spit him out on the other side of the barrier of shrubs. He grabbed two aspen branches which lay nearby in the dirt clearing. He began to brush them lightly over the surface of the ground to erase any evidence that he had been there. He had no idea if Kestler would come here...but he wouldn't lead her to the benders twice! He made his way to the edge of the woods, turned around, and surveyed his handiwork. Satisfied no one would be the wiser that he had been here only a few moments before, he dropped the branches. Then he headed into the forest at a lope, sensing his way as if there was a marker every few feet.

He made the journey back to Shaver Lake without incident, and as if he'd done it a thousand times before; when in fact, it had only been once. Ripley stood at the forest's edge, thinking about how he would get his mother to come with him. He couldn't speak to her. He wondered if he'd learned enough to be able to speak to her mind, and then dismissed it almost as soon as it occurred to him. She wasn't a bender...and only benders could do that...*or could they? Hadn't Malador told him he could*

The Form Benders – Janet Lee Carpenter

communicate with all creatures? Maybe he *could* talk to her in his mind like he did with Lacey...*maybe she would hear him because she was his mother?* This new thought repeated itself over and over in his mind, becoming more plausible and believable as he mulled it over. Ripley watched the apartment, trying to see her. He was concerned about crossing the open ball field in this form. Assuming she was drunk, as usual, led his thoughts to a whole other problem...would she even be awake when he got inside?

Suddenly, the light on the porch came on, and the screen door slid open as his mother stepped into view. *Had his thinking of her called her out onto the porch?* Her hair was down and combed. She wore the bright red pullover sweater he'd given her two Christmases ago, and blue jeans. He blinked. She even had on a light coating of makeup. *What had happened? What was going on?* He hadn't seen his mother in makeup in over seven years, not since his father left. Ripley sat down on the forest floor and pondered this new development, while still trying to figure out how he would get her to come with him. He hadn't anticipated it would be quite this difficult coming up with an answer to his problem

Suddenly, Ripley jerked, his form shaking as he watched his mother on the balcony. Apparently she had come outside just to enjoy the early evening air. He felt the first twinges of that all-too-familiar pain as it coursed through him. *Oh no, this couldn't be happening!* The twisting agony began. *He was changing again!*

How could this be? He wasn't supposed to change for at least another few days—if at all! He crawled away from the sight of his mother and found an impression in the ground near the base of a tree made by years of other animals resting here...*perhaps even other form benders had lain here near this tree,* he thought absentmindedly. He crept into it and curled up before another spasm of pain hit him. He howled in anguish, feeling his body elongate and move, ever so slowly, into the old form of Ripley.

Ripley was confused. He didn't know whether to be happy about the change, or angry. He'd just become used to living in the form of the wolf...he'd accepted his new form, in fact...and now here he was, changing again! Even Haven hadn't turned this quickly. Something must be wrong! Maybe being back here near his home triggered his form change. He shouldn't have come without Malador. Whitemane was right! It no longer mattered what he *should* have done, however, as another

The Form Benders – Janet Lee Carpenter

wave of pain washed over him. He closed his eyes, willing the agony to stop. Would he spend another multitude of minutes, writhing in pain and sobbing like a child? He couldn't let this happen! He had to get to his mother and convince her to follow him to Haven's Rest. Kestler would be here soon. He must already have led his mother away from here before she arrived and found him trying to spirit her away!

He could see his mother moving about on the balcony of their apartment from where he lay. *So close, and yet so far! How could he get to her before Kestler came if he was lying incapacitated in the forest?* Another spasm hit him—he curled into a tight ball to stretch his muscles to relieve the pain. But, alas, it wasn't going to happen. He gritted his teeth and tried to stretch out in the other direction, allowing his elongated legs to flex as far as they would.

Ripley then tried, unsuccessfully, to raise himself from where he lay in the dirt, the pain rising into a crescendo of anguish as he closed his eyes and tried to cling to consciousness. Wave after wave of unbearable torment assaulted him. He kept opening and closing his eyes in an attempt to watch his mother only a few yards away on the veranda. Fixing his sights on his mother helped soothe his thoughts—because as long as he could see her, he knew she was safe. It gave the added benefit of distracting him from the suffering of his physical body. She stepped back into the apartment for a moment and returned carrying a glass in her hand. Ripley assumed it was wine. She was too far away for him to tell.

Another spasm struck him. His eyes rolled upward, and then back into his head as he tried to control the convulsions his body was experiencing. As the wave passed, he watched helplessly while an unmarked, dark van pulled up to the apartment and passed beneath the only streetlamp there. It had been attached to the telephone pole outside the apartments several years ago. Sometimes it worked, sometimes it didn't. Tonight, it was working.

"Oh God, no," he screamed in his mind, *"it can't be them!"* Ripley struggled to stand, sweat drenching him from every pore. He tried valiantly, but it felt as if his feet were resting on razor blades. Sharp stabs of pain traveled up his legs, making it impossible to maintain an upright position. He saw his mother turn toward the sliding glass door, and then step through it.

The Form Benders – Janet Lee Carpenter

"*NO!*" He was frantic now as he wished he could warn her and tell her not to answer the door. However, it was too late!

The form bending was almost complete. His arms had returned, as well as his legs. His face was still not back to normal...he reached a hand up and felt his muzzle still protruding. The pain continued to grip him, though it began to subside. He stumbled forward, trying to walk from the forest—mostly human yet still part wolf, while his whole body screamed in pain. He was unmindful now if anyone saw him. *He must get to her!*

He watched as Vinnie and Steamer came down the well-lit staircase of the apartment building, one on each side of his mother. Her arms were slung about their necks, and her feet dragged on the stairs as they got closer and closer to the van, and to him losing her. His steps faltered, and he dropped to one knee as he reached out to her limp form. Her head hung limply as her beautiful, silvery-blonde hair seemed lit from above as it flowed about her head. He struggled to stand again, and took another tentative step forward when he finally regained his footing. Ripley wondered if they'd drugged her...then knew they had, just as they had so many others before her. He could feel indignation rise in him as once again he stumbled and fell in an effort to make his way to her. It was no use—his legs wouldn't obey him, and the stabbing pains built to an intolerable intensity again.

Ripley watched helplessly as Steamer gathered up his mother while Vinnie opened the sliding door on the van for him. Then Vinnie took her legs and the two men laid her—none too gently—into the van and slammed the door behind her. Vinnie went around the van and Steamer opened the driver's door, hopped into the van, and started the engine before the door was even closed.

As the two men sped off into the night with his mother, Ripley finished his transformation, his fur replaced by damp clothes and his face still tingling from its return to normal. He sat there, stunned at the events that had just occurred. His mother...gone into the bowels of the FBEF...in the clutches of Kestler and *heaven knew* who else. His form, clad in damp jeans and a t-shirt, started to shiver. He was cold. *Gone* was his coat of fur to keep him warm. *Gone too* were the vestiges of the problem of how he would get his mother to know it was him in the guise of a wolf. If only he'd gotten here sooner, or the form change had waited until he'd made it to his mother. *"If only...if only...if only* what?" he questioned, furious with himself and his fate.

Ripley broke down then. He collapsed on the cold damp ground, and for the second time in years, he cried. Heaving sobs wracked his entire body as years of torment, hurt, and loss filled him. He grieved for the loss of his father, for the double loss of his mother who had fallen into a bottle years ago and left him alone to fend for himself *and for her*...and for the loss of her now.

The physical torture stopped, but the emotional anguish bubbled up and flowed over him like hot lava, burning everywhere it touched on its path to acknowledgment. As he thought about his past, and everything that happened to him the last few days, he sobbed more deeply. *He couldn't control anything*! They had taken his mother, his father was nowhere to be found and here *he* was, sitting in the forest, *freezing!* He wasn't able to feel his feet or his fingers any longer. It would be so easy to lie down here and just let the cold and the night take him. A false sense of warmth infused him as he wallowed there in the woods toying with the idea of just going to sleep and not waking up.

Then came an unbidden thought. *He saw Whitemane...no...Sally,* he corrected himself, *standing on the knoll when she'd finally told him her name...said who she was. She was beautiful with her blue eyes shining and sad with unshed tears for him, and her glossy white coat all windblown and wild.* Of all the pictures he carried in his mind of her, this would be his favorite.

What was he thinking? He had to get up and move! He had to get to Sally, to Haven's Rest and warn the others. He had to go help for his mother, and he had to go now!

Ripley moved slowly at first, trying out his stiff muscles. Then, realizing they were ready to move, he went from a lope to a sprint as he bounded toward Haven's Rest and help. His body was warming with the movement. Quickly moving through the forest, Ripley made it to the stream and waterfall in a short time, amazed to find his normal ability to run enhanced. *Was it from having been a wolf?* he wondered. He didn't bother to stop and drink but continued on relentlessly as he neared the wall of bushes. When he reached it, he turned about and found the branch right where he'd left it earlier. Wiping away his tracks, he noticed another set of footprints near the hedge. Hoping he'd left no trace and that no one found the secret entrance, Ripley brushed the ground all the way through the hedge before dropping the branch. He headed into the village and directly to the Town Hall.

He had no idea if anyone was there, but he must try. He must warn Remenion and the Prince!

There were only a few lights on in the village. Most everyone was home near cozy fireplaces at this time of night. Ripley headed straight for the Town Hall, no question in his mind that Remenion would be there. It seemed the owl had nowhere else to go. When he reached the building, it was dark inside. He stepped up to the door, but it didn't open for him. *Where was everyone?* A sense of alarm ran through Ripley as he frantically searched his mind for any clue as to where Whitemane lived. He needed to rouse someone—and quickly.

Ripley decided to go to Mama and Papa Johns' place; it was the only place he knew of where he could get help. It didn't occur to him that, in his human form, they might not know him. Instead, he sprinted through town, getting curious looks from the townsfolk who were still out and about at this hour. He passed the bakery, where delicious aromas teased him. He realized he hadn't eaten since the makeshift meal Lacey prepared for the travelers hours ago. His stomach growled in protest. He couldn't stop now, though. He had to reach Papa Johns; he would know what to do.

When Ripley rounded the corner and came upon the cottage, he went directly to the door. A few lights were still burning in the home. He remembered Papa's tendency to go to bed early, so he prayed he would be awake as he pounded on the door. When the response wasn't immediate, Ripley banged on it again, calling out to Papa as he did so.

"Papa Johns, answer please...it's Ripley! We must talk!"

The porch light came on, and the door opened to a disheveled Papa standing in the doorway, rubbing his eyes. His robe was hastily donned and left open, the ties dangling about, and he was missing one bedroom slipper. He stepped back when he recognized Ripley.

"Ho, son, what brings you here at this time of night?"

The Form Benders – Janet Lee Carpenter

Ripley gasped as he tried to catch his breath. "My mother...," he began, taking another deep gulp of air so he could speak.

"Come in here, son, out of the cold and calm down. Tell me, what happened?"

Ripley stepped into the warmth of the cottage and bent over, hands on knees as he caught his breath. "The FBEF...*they took my mother*! I must get help...where are the Elders? No one is at the Town Hall!" The words came out of his mouth in a rush.

"Here son," Papa Johns said as he led him to the comfy overstuffed chair by the fire and indicated he should sit.

Ripley let himself be led to the chair; however, he didn't move to sit. "I have to speak to the Elders!"

"We'll have to get you to Remenion; however, he won't be there until much later tonight."

Ripley glanced at the clock on the wall. It was already after eleven. How much later could he be there?

"Here, let me get you a glass of water. We have some leftovers if you'd like something to eat," Papa said as he shuffled toward the kitchen just as Mama turned on the light from the hall.

Mama Johns shuffled into the living room then, obviously awakened by them talking in the kitchen. "Why Ripley, what are you doing coming here so late at night?" she questioned him, genuine concern lacing her tone.

"The FBEF took my mother from her apartment. I'm certain they mean her harm...Kestler said as much at their headquarters. I must find the Elders to tell them what happened. We have to retrieve her from them before they hurt her. She doesn't know anything, but they don't know that. I'm afraid of what they might do to her when she can't give them any information on my whereabouts."

"Ahh, I see," Papa said as Mama began heating something in a pot over the fire. Her hands flew as she made dough with flour, buttermilk and some other ingredients he didn't recognize. Within minutes, a delightful aroma filled the kitchen as the dumplings she dropped into the boiling stew released their scent. The soup pot bubbled and simmered; and in only moments, it seemed, she set a meal before him of vegetable stew and plump, light dumplings. Ripley gave up, sat down by the cheery fireplace, and devoured the meal. He smiled at her as she refilled his bowl, and though he'd shaken his head in denial, he polished off the rest of what she gave him with a contented sigh.

"Tell, me, Ripley, what else has happened? We heard of your great courage and heroism in returning our beloved Whitemane to us."

Not certain what Papa meant, Ripley ignored part of the question and replied, "I'm not sure what to say here, Papa." Now that his belly was fed, the concern for his mother which had been hovering in the back of his mind while was eating now took center stage. He continued, "I made Whitemane promise not to tell anyone about my leaving until tomorrow. As you can see, tomorrow didn't come. I saw them come to the apartment and take my mother in their van. She must have been drugged, though, because she appeared to be unconscious when they put her in it and sped off."

"Why didn't you try to stop them?" Papa asked with no accusation in his tone. Genuine curiosity came through in his voice.

"I would have, but my form started to bend..." The thought suddenly occurred to him that Mama and Papa knew who he was without him having to tell them. Though he'd identified himself when he'd pounded on the door only a little over a half an hour ago, they had never seen him in his human form, so how did they know he was who he said he was? Before he could ask, however, Papa answered his unspoken question.

"As a bender myself, I will always know you, no matter what form you are in at the time."

"That's neat!" he exclaimed.

Papa smiled and stood up to take Ripley's dishes. Ripley gently tugged them away as an implicit communication passed between them. Papa smiled. Then he let go of the earthenware bowl to return to his seat near the fire. Ripley went to the sink and rinsed his dish and spoon, and then set them on the kitchen counter to dry. *How could he hurry Papa along without seeming to be rude,* he wondered? He needn't have worried, though, as Papa continued to question him.

"We should call on Oren then, though I'm sure he is in bed as well."

Ripley nodded in agreement. "We must rouse someone, and soon. There is no telling what they will do. I realized that I didn't know where to go should I not be able to reach someone at the Town Hall. It never occurred to me that someone wouldn't be there."

"I understand, son." Papa stood then and headed out of the room to what Ripley assumed was their bedroom. Within minutes, he returned, fully dressed. "Let's head over to Oren's place, and see if we can get Remenion and the Prince together so you can tell them about this."

Ripley nodded as they walked over to the coat rack. Papa lifted his hat, coat and scarf from the pegs there. He handed Ripley an oversized coat and said, "Here, put this on. It's chilly outside."

Ripley gratefully took the coat, and Papa leaned over to kiss Mama before they left.

"Thank you, Mama, for the delicious meal." Ever mindful of his manners, Ripley smiled graciously as he shrugged into the heavy jacket Papa supplied. The huge coat engulfed him, but it was warm inside just from being in the house…and he was grateful for that.

She smiled at Ripley then. "You two go on, now…Papa, you come back as soon as you can. I'll wait up for you."

Papa smiled and pushed his hat further down on his head before stepping into the night. He led Ripley down the walkway to the lane beyond. They made a right turn at the road instead of the left turn he made with Ringer when the two of them had gone to the Town Hall that fateful morning. Then they proceeded to make their way to Oren's house.

Chapter Eleven

The evening was clear and crisp, and a million stars studded the velvet sky. The scent of pine and damp earth danced lightly on the frigid night air. Ripley watched the frosty clouds puff from their lips as they made their way along the hill to Oren's home. When they arrived, Oren was as surprised to see him as Papa had been. This was only the second time Ripley had seen him in his human form. He could only be described as a big bear of a man, towering over his own six feet. He had a barrel chest and long hair, which matched his rusty colored beard. His cinnamon colored eyes sparkled with intelligence and humor, though any laughter seemed to be stifled due to the lateness of the hour and hence the obvious gravity of their situation. Then, a random thought occurred to Ripley—Oren could have easily encompassed his head with one of those large, paw-like hands.

"I see you have changed forms already, Ripley. This is indeed unusual. We must speak to Remenion about this."

Reminded of their mission, Ripley quickly told Oren what happened at the apartment. "She is in danger, Oren...I know it," Ripley said passionately.

Oren grabbed his coat, and Skerrin came out of the back room in time to join them on their walk to the Town Hall. As the quartet set out and headed the opposite direction into town, each of them was silent, deep in their own thoughts. Oren broke the quiet for only a moment as he assured them on the way that Remenion was inside the building. Oren told them he had just shut down everything until morning, when preparations for the festivities were to begin. Besides, he will already know something is wrong. Ripley felt a brief twang of regret as he realized the celebration they had so painstakingly put together for him might have to be placed on hold indefinitely in the face of this new threat. It couldn't be helped.

Oren reached out and tapped the plate next to the door. Until this moment, Ripley hadn't even noticed it was there. The lights came on and the door opened automatically, allowing them entrance to the Hall itself.

The Form Benders – Janet Lee Carpenter

Remenion was sitting on his podium near the stage. He was the only one Ripley found this evening who seemed to be wide-awake.

"What happened?" Remenion questioned without preamble.

"My mother...she was taken," Ripley said just as succinctly, fear washing over him once again.

Agitated, Remenion began to bark orders at the group. "Quickly...there is no time to waste. Raise the alarm, Oren. Call the people to a meeting."

Without a second thought, Oren headed to the back of the stage where a hidden door lay. He reached the panel, touched it, and it slid open to reveal a staircase which wound upwards from the floor they occupied. Oren had to bend over to fit through the door, but then he started nimbly up the stairs, belying his size, and disappeared from view. After a few moments passed, the unexpected peals of a large brass bell could be heard for miles. It wasn't long until Ripley also heard the voices of villagers making their way to the Town Hall in the chilly night.

"We must awaken the Prince! Fill me in, young Master Ripley, while we wait for him," Remenion requested urgently. As Ripley began to tell Remenion of what transpired earlier that evening, Prince Valiantheart arrived with Malador close on his heels. It seemed no one let much time lapse before answering the alarm.

"We heard the bell. What is it?" the Prince questioned. "What has happened?" He bent from his cougar form, which Ripley was sure he traveled in, to his human form. Malador followed suit and his wolf form dissolved as his human counterpart took over.

Ripley recounted his story once again to the Elders, making certain to leave nothing out as he told the tale. When he was finished, Remenion and the others were visibly shaken. Remenion paced nervously from one end of the podium to the other, and then back again, a snowy feather here and there randomly dropping from him as he moved back and forth. He kept pacing...the only other sign he was agitated at the information Ripley gave him. The Prince tapped his finger to his mouth, deep in thought. Skerrin repeatedly changed out of his bear form to human and then back again. It might have had something to do with his capture and subsequent bondage at the FBEF, but Ripley wasn't certain why he was unable to maintain his form. Malador simply sat there quietly, pondering this new information. Ripley knew they were trying to come up with a plan. He was trying to come up with one, as well...

Finally, the Prince turned to him and spoke. "Have you left anything out?" he queried, making certain he had all the facts.

Ripley thought back over his story when suddenly he remembered the footprint outside of the wall of bushes. "Wait! There *was* something!"

All eyes turned to him. "There was a footprint outside of the bushes. I cleared the area...both when I left and came back, so the print must have gotten there while I was gone."

Remenion looked at the Prince and Malador, and then to Oren and Skerrin. "They have found the entrance! Whether they have been able to unlock its secret remains to be seen, but it is no longer safe here. Once they find it, they will infiltrate Haven's Rest. We must take precautions!"

The Prince looked thoughtful for a moment, and then declared, "We must call Haven. She will know what to do! I will send for her now."

A murmur of approval at the Prince's declaration hummed through the crowd of villagers in their various forms gathered in the Hall. The Prince called to Ringer, spoke softly to him and Ringer turned without a word, leaving through the main door.

Remenion told the villagers the shorthand version of what happened. Afterward, the Prince and Ringer spoke and urged them all to gather their children and whatever belongings they would need to survive in the high country. The crowd quickly dispersed as the Elders, Oren and Remenion, as well as the Prince, Skerrin, Malador, and Ripley awaited Haven's arrival. Silence loomed over the hall in an ugly distortion of peace. There was no tranquility here...not anymore...as they waited for Haven to make an entrance. The air was charged with anxiety as each of them anticipated the arrival of their Queen.

Ripley was excited about finally getting to meet the fabled Haven. He'd heard so much about her, and everyone was so kind when they spoke of her. He had to admit, despite the reason they were meeting this night, he looked forward to the encounter. She was the only other bender who was like him, or so they said. He wondered what she would be like; what she would look like. Anxiety ate at him as he realized she would probably know of his adventures into Fresno to find Whitemane, and his help with the return of Skerrin and Revelan. He hoped they had skipped the part where he'd gotten himself caught! He lifted his hand to stroke the amulet resting upon his chest when he realized it was gone! *Oh no!* He looked around the room. He would have heard it drop, if it fell in here! It must have fallen off him when he'd changed forms near the apartment. It would be horrible if the medallion fell into the hands of Kestler and her cohorts. He had to go back and find it!

Before he could slip out, Haven made her appearance. In the form of a silver tipped wolf, she stepped into the Town Hall, an air of greatness following her. Ripley's first impression was that of awe. Her white coat, tipped with silver, glinted and sparkled like so many diamonds in the lights of the Town Hall as she made her way slowly and regally toward the group. Her violet eyes and pink nose were damp from her night run through the village to reach them. She acknowledged them all, stopping in front of Ripley and looking him over.

Ripley felt himself blush as she stared deep into his eyes. Then, the hint of a smile crossed her features and he felt himself relax a little, momentarily forgetting the amulet. She turned and made her way to the podium where Remenion still shifted uncomfortably on his perch. "Remenion," she acknowledged softly.

"Prince, Malador, Oren," she acknowledged them each in turn. Her features lit up when they landed on Skerrin and Revelan. "Skerrin, Revelan, it is so good to have you returned to us, safe and sound."

Skerrin switched back into his human form as he bowed low in recognition of her acknowledgement. He was halfway through his bow when he switched again into his bear form. A light frown crossed her gentle but intelligent features. "Why, Skerrin, are you not well?"

"I am fine, Your Highness. I haven't been able to control the bending since my encounter with the FBEF."

"I trust it is not permanent, Skerrin. It would pain me greatly should it be something you must live with for the rest of your life."

At that moment, Ripley realized how dangerous that would be. Many of the Form Benders shifted into other forms as a protective cloaking device. If Skerrin couldn't control his bending, then it would endanger him should he need to leave the village...like now, he thought angrily to himself. Once again, he had put these beings in danger, and once again, they were nothing less than gracious.

The Prince retold the story, hopefully for the last time, leaving nothing out and adding the fact that Ripley had spotted a footprint near the entrance to Haven's Rest. Haven's brows drew together as she thought about the information given to her. She was the founder of this place—their Queen. The entire colony depended on her sound judgment, just as they did with her son's, the Prince. *She is probably thinking of where they would have to go, and there must be regret in her that she would have to leave the place she founded as a sanctuary for all these benders*, Ripley thought. This last thought saddened him. He stared at the beautiful wolf before him. For some reason, he felt responsible that they would have to leave this place of refuge and head out for the unknown. If he had never come here, none of these benders would be in danger now. It didn't matter that he took precautions when he'd left early this evening. Someone must have been watching, waiting for him to reveal the secret passage in his naiveté. He blamed no one but himself for the mess he'd gotten all of them into.

Haven's violet eyes perused the crowd, and they lit on Ripley for a second time. He shifted uncomfortably under her watchful gaze. "Would you lead us from this place, Ripley?"

Her quiet request caught Ripley unprepared for the kindness and respect in her tone. "I would be honored, but I don't really know the way. Perhaps Malador..."

She shook her head in denial before Ripley could finish his sentence. "I would have you lead us, Ripley, for you know your way about these woods. Though I have spent many years here, providing shelter for those benders who could find their way here, I do not know the forest beyond a few miles. I have not ventured far because I have seen what men can do to those of us who are not like them. You grew up here. You can take us where we will be safe. Malador has knowledge of the ways of the wakened ones, and of the city which lies below us. He also has knowledge of the surrounding forest, but not the high country, which is where I suspect we will have to travel."

The Form Benders – Janet Lee Carpenter

Malador remained silent through the entire exchange, but cleared his throat loudly as he stepped forward. "If I may, Your Highness..." At her nod he continued, "there is another way, but Ripley would have to call the Wood Nymphs to accomplish it."

Interest and intelligence shone from her lovely eyes as she spoke again, "Go on, Malador. What is it that must be done?"

Ripley felt himself switch from being a bit dazed at the attention she paid him, to unabashed embarrassment at what he must tell them now. *How could he tell them he lost the precious medallion the Prince bestowed upon him only two days ago...the one that quite possibly might save all of their lives?*

"We can create a false front that leads nowhere, if we have the help of the Wood Nymphs."

Deep in thought now, Haven seemed to stare into space as she thought about what Malador suggested. Ripley watched in fascination as the thoughts running through her mind were reflected in the expression of her eyes. He knew she had made a decision, almost before she made it.

"If it is as you say, Malador, then we must still ready the villagers if this doesn't work. They should be returning soon. In the meantime, Ripley...would you please call the Nymphs to our aid to see if they can indeed help us?"

Ripley wasn't sure how to answer this. He stuttered and stammered before he finally got out, "I...I'm not sure...um...I know how, Your Highness." Then, he bowed in his most courtly fashion. "Besides," he hung his head and mumbled barely above a whisper, "It seems I have lost the medallion."

"You have *what?*" Malador barked at him, each word getting a little louder until the last came out and could probably be heard for at least a mile. Ripley jumped as he tried to meet Malador's fierce gaze, but failed miserably.

Haven looked to Prince Valiantheart for an answer. "Did you not give the boy his charm?"

"Aye, Your Highness. I did."

The Form Benders – Janet Lee Carpenter

Ripley tried to clarify what had happened. "It must have come off my neck when I bent in the forest near the apartment. I must go there and get it back."

Malador issued a deep, guttural growl before he spoke slowly, in frustrated tones, "I can't believe it! Wet Nose, you have failed us all."

Haven's voice rang out in the hall. "That is *ENOUGH*, Malador. It was *NOT* his fault! I asked that someone stay with him at all times, and he was alone, and without help!" Her clear voice cracked like a whip in the still room. She turned then and looked at Ripley. Her voice was softer now, though her words were clearly meant for Malador. She spoke kindly, "I am certain it was not his intention to put any of us in harm's way."

Contrite, Malador looked at Ripley who was almost in tears. "Sorry, there, Wet Nose. I know you didn't mean anything by it…" Malador sounded sincere, in spite of his obvious disappointment in him.

"I know…but I could get us all killed…," his voice tapered off. The words Malador had spoken to him that night in the alley in Fresno still echoed in his mind. It was when they had almost been found out by Steamer. Those words still stung as Ripley turned from them and started toward the door.

"Wait, Wet Nose…I'll go with you to find the medallion," Malador offered.

"I don't need your help. I can find it on my own!" The pain in his voice was reflected in his words as he continued to the door.

Haven trotted to Ripley's side. "Malador and I shall go with you." Ripley slowed his pace. "We will find the medallion and return with it. We must make haste to find it, for I'm afraid there is little time to do what must be done to save the village. They may wait until morning's light, which will only give us a few precious hours to retrieve the medallion and call the Nymphs. As yet, we do not know if they can accomplish this. There is no time for petty squabbles and hurt feelings. Are you with me, Ripley?"

At his nod, she turned to Malador, "And you?" One brow arched daintily as she awaited his answer.

"Aye, as you say," Malador bowed and shifted back into the formidable black wolf Ripley had come to know.

"Then, let us be off!"

The trio stepped out of the Town Hall and into the night, heading west to the wall where they would find the entrance into the world Ripley had once called home. The trip was thankfully uneventful as they made their way back to the base of the huge pine where Ripley had lain helplessly only hours before. The two wolves searched the ground along with Ripley and finally found the amulet. It lay just outside of the bushes leading to the baseball diamond across the street from Ripley's old apartment. It was half buried beneath the damp, colorful oak leaves on the ground. Ripley hung the medallion around his neck, the familiar warmth of the object reassuring to him.

Malador's silence was more unnerving to Ripley than his yelling had been earlier. Though Haven hadn't allowed him to continue his tirade, Ripley felt there was still much that lay unspoken between them. One day they would have to talk about this…but not now. So much was at stake as they traversed the woods and made it to the tiny stream. When they reached the wall, Malador took it upon himself to brush away the evidence in the dirt near the entrance. *As if he doesn't trust me to do it,* Ripley thought sadly. After all this time, he appeared to be back at square one with Malador. As soon as they spoke to the Prince, he would learn how to call the nymphs. The thought excited him. Perhaps it was similar to when he called upon the sprites for help? He would have to wait and see. In the meantime, he would content himself with following Haven, who only treated him with respect and kindness. *No wonder everyone loves her,* he thought, *she is fair and kind.* Then Malador caught up, staying a few paces behind them, keeping himself separated from them.

Chapter Twelve

"So, how do I do it?" Ripley wanted to know. Curiosity and a sort of impatience laced his tone as he stood before the council, awaiting the Prince's answer.

"I cannot tell you that, Ripley." He held up his hand to stem the flow of questions he obviously knew would follow. Ripley opened his mouth to speak and closed it immediately at the Prince's declaration.

He continued, "I *gave* you the medallion. At the moment I did that, it became yours, following the rules of the gifting of magical items."

Ripley's confusion showed plainly on his face as he tried to grasp what the Prince was saying to him.

"Let me explain. When you give an item willingly to another, then it is called a gift." Ripley bowed his head and rolled his eyes. *As if I don't know what a gift is,* he thought to himself. The Prince turned away from him for a brief moment as he shared a glance with Remenion before he continued. He missed the look on Ripley's face.

"Where was I? Oh, yes...when the item holds magic within it, as does your medallion there, then the *law* is invoked and it cannot be returned to the giver except in extenuating circumstances, such as death or mental instability. The gift I gave to you contained many generations of love imbued in the talisman. Returning the amulet, permeated with the power of love from countless ancestors who vowed to keep the flame of magic alive, and to protect this place of enchantment and power we call Haven's Rest, would bring a force of ruin upon us so catastrophic we would certainly perish as a race. The FBEF would look mild in comparison to what I am speaking of."

"But I don't understand," Ripley queried as he struggled with what the Prince was telling him.

"Some of this you will have to take on faith alone, young Master Ripley, but I promise you—if the forces for good instilled in this charm are ever returned to the giver—the charm itself will become useless for the power of good. All creativity and love is meant to be shared with many, and there is always one in each generation who is capable of wielding the magic it possesses. When love, which is the creative force of the universe, is turned in upon itself, it becomes destructive. At that point, it can only be used for evil purposes until its loving energy is directed back through it in the process of gifting it to another. The power of this amulet can only be entrusted to one who has a purity of heart and the courage to face the magic and not run. *Your courage* has already been tested. This person I speak of, is *you*, Master Ripley."

"He is right, I have seen it is so," Remenion replied softly. "We have been waiting a long time for the one who would bring back the magic to this land, and heal the rifts which come to us from outside our world. Because you come from that world, and are part of this one as well, you will marry them both, that we may all live in peace with each other."

"I cannot perform miracles, Remenion…Prince." His denial was heartfelt as he begged the two Elders to understand his position.

"As I said," interrupted the Prince, "some of this you will have to take on faith, and believe that we, as Elders, know some things better than you know about yourself. Trust us and let us begin the ritual to call the nymphs. Reach deep inside you, Ripley—the answers are there, just as they were when you called the sprites; so too, will you know how to call the nymphs. But, we must hurry now; there is no more time…"

Ripley followed behind the Prince to the antechamber behind the stage where he had seen Oren go earlier today. He felt more bewildered than he ever recalled. He walked up the flight of circular stairs and entered a small chamber with books covering all the walls. It was somewhat like an inner sanctum, and Ripley marveled at the books lining the shelves; *there were so many!* The Prince smiled as he encouraged Ripley's curiosity.

His confusion forgotten for the moment, Ripley stared in wonderment. "There are so many here, and some look really old."

"Yes, there are. Now that you have been brought here, you may come and study any time you like. The doors here are always open to you. We only ask that you never remove a book from this room; for as long as they are here, they are protected. Knowledge is power and these books, though they do not contain complete knowledge, will lead one to it. Placed in the wrong hands, Ripley, they would be very dangerous."

The ceiling was made of glass, and when Ripley looked up, he could see that the winding staircase travelled up the walls to at least two more floors. It gave the illusion that it continued upwards into the sky. It was filled with books, but the most impressive thing of all was the large brass bell hanging from the center of the tower above. It appeared to be suspended in thin air. How strange it seemed. *If it ever fell, it would shatter the glass and make an amazing sound,* he thought.

The Prince's voice brought him back to the task at hand as they seated themselves comfortably in the over-stuffed, leather chairs. "Each person calls the sprites and the nymphs in his—or her—own special way," he began, "so I cannot tell you how this should be done. I can only tell you that somewhere, deep inside of you, are the words that will call them forth. You have met Arapham and now you will meet Narassian. He is the head of the nymphs. Close your eyes, and concentrate on his name. Let us see what happens."

Ripley obediently closed his eyes and almost immediately felt a drawing sensation between his eyes, just a little above and near the center of his forehead. The harder he concentrated on Narassian's name, the more intense the sensation became, until it was very uncomfortable. It made him feel as though he was going to jump out of his skin. He opened his eyes and looked directly at the Prince.

"I need some wood," Ripley requested. He didn't know *how* he knew this, only that he *felt* he needed the wood to call upon Narassian.

"I have just the thing," the Prince replied as he stood and went to the bookcase behind him. He reached up and after a moment of searching, pulled one of the books off the shelf. He tapped the spine of the tome and out dropped a stick about the size and shape of a chopstick, though it was obviously very old. It was the right length to be a chopstick, but upon closer inspection, he realized it was crooked and gnarled slightly like the branch of a tree. Its distinctive reddish brown hue was beautiful. The Prince returned and handed Ripley the stick he'd produced.

"What is this?" Ripley asked him as he twirled it slowly in his fingertips.

The Form Benders – Janet Lee Carpenter

"It is a wand a passing wizard left for Remenion years ago. He has not used it for a very long time, but I believe it is made of fine Manzanita, capable of defining and channeling the magic. It's enough wood for our purposes here, anyway."

Ahh, Manzanita, he thought. *That is what gives it the beautiful color!* Ripley didn't know whether to laugh or cry at the information the Prince imparted. Maybe a little of both, but right now he had to be strong. He closed his eyes again, focusing on the name Narassian. Again, he felt the intensity of the drawing sensation in the center of his forehead, but this time it wasn't unfamiliar, so he allowed it to flow without stopping it. The pulling became more and more intense until finally, he felt the words form in his mind and he spoke aloud, "Oh great Narassian, Ruler of the Forest and Nymph of the Wood, come unto us in our time of need. Come forth, I command you, in the name of the magic of Love and the Prince of Haven's Rest, that I may see you."

A stirring, ever so slightly, began to whirl in the room. Air, like a dust devil, formed and created a vortex in the center of the area and touched down directly in front of Ripley. With his eyes still closed, Ripley waited for the wind to subside before he opened them. When it finally died down, Ripley's eyes came open slowly to find the funniest little creature he had yet seen. Where the water sprites were made out of water, these tiny fellows looked a bit like stick bugs—much like the walking sticks he saw in some of his science books about insects and such. Yet each of these tiny beings wore green caps and clothing made from the leaves of the aspen trees, shimmering as they moved. They were actually quite beautiful.

"Did you call me, sire?" the tiny nymph addressed the Prince.

"No, it was not I, but rather the young Master Ripley, here."

It was then that the nymph looked askance at Ripley. Suddenly, out of nowhere, he produced a pair of wings and flew closer so he could inspect him. "I suppose you'll do," he said unceremoniously.

"I beg your pardon?" Ripley was taken aback by the nymph's bluntness.

"I am Narassian, and these are my friends," he said, indicating a small entourage of beings much like him. "I assume you did not call on me to perform circus tricks, or simply to chat. So...*what* do you want?"

The Form Benders – Janet Lee Carpenter

Ripley wasn't certain how to handle this situation. The nymph was quite matter of fact, and he felt intimidated by him in an odd way. He decided the best way to handle this was head-on, so he proceeded to tell him about the breach of the aspen wall and what Malador suggested they do about it. He asked if the nymphs would be able to help them.

He walked back and forth on his minute, spindly legs and rubbed his chin with what Ripley could only call his thumb and forefinger—though it looked more like a claw. Narassian appeared to be deep in thought. He called to the other nymphs who were close by, and they did an excellent impression of a football huddle. The Prince and Ripley looked at each other, and wondered what would happen next. Every once in a while, Narassian would look over his shoulder at Ripley, and then return his attention to the cluster of wood nymphs.

Narassian continued speaking in hushed whispers with the other nymphs. Then, he nodded and the group dispersed. "I believe we have come up with a solution to your dilemma, Master Ripley."

Ripley had given up trying to correct everyone about his name. Instead, he asked Narassian and his friends to tell him more about their answer.

"Here is what we are going to do. The townspeople will not have to move their belongings or their children to the high country. We shall create a false front—another illusion shall we say—one which will lead them to the lake, rather than to Haven's Rest. It is simply a matter of magic to create the illusion. We shall just build it in front of the existing wall, and they will be none the wiser until they end up…*nowhere*." The "Miniscule Marauder," as Ripley would forever think of him after this, laughed. It sounded like the wind in the aspen leaves, a rushing sound on a zephyr. It was lovely to hear. The other nymphs joined in. In no time, it was like a chorus of wind in the trees in the high country, where Ripley loved to spend his summers when he could.

"How long will it take?" Ripley's concern marred his youthful features.

Again, Narassian stopped—and then paced, deep in thought and mumbling to himself about some mathematical formulae Ripley was unable to understand. When he stopped his pacing, he looked right at Ripley and said, "Two or three…hmmm…maybe it's a miscalculation…maybe four…"

"Two or three *what?*" Ripley's annoyance with Narassian was starting to show.

"Weeks...might be a little less..."

"WHAT? It can't take *that* long! We have only a few hours to accomplish this before Kestler makes it through the hedge and destroys the village and all the benders in it!"

"Well, no need to get all huffy...we can make it a rush job."

"How long will that take?"

"We can have it done in a couple of hours; but, mind you...it won't hold up forever."

"Can you build another after that which can be permanent? We need a permanent solution as well as a temporary one. We're almost out of time."

"Well, actually, the simplest way would be merely to close the portal for a while and open a new one."

Ripley was exasperated. "Well...then let's *do that*. If closing that one will keep the FBEF from getting through the portal...that is what we wish to accomplish."

"Well, why didn't you say so? That's a piece of bark!" He rustled up the twigs once again and then they all disappeared as quickly as they had come.

Ripley sighed in frustration and looked at the Prince who seemed amused by their little communication. Apparently, he had spoken with Narassian before and knew him well. "Wait!" Ripley said too late. "We have no idea where the new portal will be," he spoke into thin air and looked to the Prince for an answer.

The Prince lost his battle trying to keep his amusement to himself. The chuckle that came out was infectious. Ripley began to laugh at the whole interchange.

"We'll probably spend weeks trying to find it. Last time he helped, he moved the dam for Shaver Lake and the hydroelectric project. They spent weeks trying to find the materials and blueprints for that one. They finally drew another set and left the old dam where it was, under the water there in the lake."

The Form Benders – Janet Lee Carpenter

"I've lost more fishing line and tackle on the old dam than I care to count!" Ripley laughed in spite of himself.

"Well, at least the village is safe, and that's what you really wanted to accomplish for now, Ripley. I thank you with all my heart. You believed in the magic, and it did not fail you. It will always be there for you, if only you look to find it."

Ripley smiled at the Prince as they stood to leave the room. They exited the chamber and walked down the stairs to the stage, side by side.

"What news?" Remenion looked from one face to the other anxiously.

"They will move the portal," Ripley announced to the entire council.

"Where are they moving it to?" Remenion questioned him with one raised eyebrow, looking as if he already suspected the answer he would receive.

Ripley shifted a bit uncomfortably before he answered. "Um…well, they didn't say *exactly*. But, it will be in a different place, which will keep the village safe. We'll just have to hunt it down." He paused here, and then jumped in. "There is only one more problem left that I can see."

"Stupid nymphs," Remenion muttered to himself as he turned his back to the group and began his ever present pacing, "never can get it right…capable of figuring it out, but *never* good at communicating! Bah!"

"What is it, Ripley?" Malador asked as he ignored Remenion's outburst. He spoke as Haven stepped away from the crowd and headed for the grassy area outside the building to inform the villagers who waited there that they were safe.

"My mother…Kestler has her. We must find her and bring her back. We know what they do to benders, Malador. What do you think they will do to *her* if given the chance?"

Malador looked uncomfortable at the single-minded passion Ripley exuded. "There is no way around this, son, and you're not going to like what I have to say."

The Form Benders – Janet Lee Carpenter

Ripley already surmised *that* by the look on Malador's handsome face. In his human form, for some reason, Ripley found him less intimidating. "What is it?"

"We are unable to locate her. I've spoken with my sources and, unfortunately, she seems to have vanished into thin air."

Ripley was visibly shaken. He was prepared for danger, problems, and roads fraught with potholes; but, he was *not* prepared for the jolt of sadness and fear that slammed through him at the possibility of never seeing his mother again. "We must find her, Mal," he spoke. His voice was so soft Malador almost didn't hear him.

"We will, son. My friends are looking for her now. If anyone can find her, *they* can. They found Whitemane and they will find Lily."

At the mention of Whitemane, Ripley turned to see her standing to the side of the stage near the door. He'd seen Ringer come through the same door in what seemed like years before; but in truth, it was only days. His eyes met hers, and she stepped forward. *They* had a lot to talk about. She came to stand beside him.

"Come, I'll walk with you to the Johns' place. I'm sure you're tired after all you've been through."

What he truly wanted was to talk with her, hear her soothing voice, and to lie down in the meadow with her and let the earth take his cares away—but that couldn't be…not yet. Soon though, he promised himself. He sighed and turned to the other council members.

"Go, son—you're exhausted. We can all see that." Malador spoke for them all as Remenion, Oren, Skerrin and the Prince nodded their agreement.

It didn't occur to Ripley until much later that Malador knew his mother's name. How extraordinarily peculiar that was. *Had he mentioned it?* He was too tired to worry about it now. He let Whitemane…no *Sally*, he corrected himself, lead him out of the building to the Johns' cottage where they greeted him, fed him a bowl of stew, and put him to rest in the boys' bedroom. Whitemane left him at the door, promising him she would see him soon.

The Johns assured him he wasn't taking over the room since both Ethan and Evan were staying at a friend's house for the weekend.

The Form Benders – Janet Lee Carpenter

Ripley's head no sooner hit the pillow than he was fast asleep. He dreamt of his mother when she was younger and beautiful. He could almost see his father—but not quite. It had been too long. Her laughter made him happy, and he sighed contentedly and snuggled deeper into the down pillow as gentle visions of sweeter times filled his head. They would find her; he *knew* Malador wouldn't let him down. His dreams led him to Sally and her gentle ways, and a smile filled his dreams. Tomorrow was another day…

The Form Benders – Janet Lee Carpenter

Chapter Thirteen

The crisp morning air seemed highly conducive to a flurry of activity, if for no other reason than it would keep Ripley warm. His faith in Malador apparently was not misplaced. There was an early morning knock on the door and Ringer's familiar voice filled the living room, which was next to where he'd slept last night. He gathered snippets of the conversation as he jumped from the bed and quickly pulled on the clothing Mama had thoughtfully placed at the foot of his bed. Jeans and a white turtleneck were quickly donned against the early morning chill as he dragged on socks and pulled on his tennies thinking how much work it was to be a human; so many things to put on, just to keep himself warm!

"Remenion and Malador want to speak to him," Ringer said to Papa just as Ripley poked his head out of the bedroom. He tucked the last bit of his white shirt into his jeans, pulled down the bottom of the sweater he wore, and then he smiled.

"Good morning," Ripley said as he quickly finger-combed his thick head of silver hair.

"Well," Papa began, "Good morning! I trust you slept well?"

"I did, thank you," he said. Ripley closed his eyes and smiled as the scent of warm cinnamon and eggs teased his senses, making his mouth water. In her kitchen, Mama was busily preparing the usual feast. Everyone *must* have loved cinnamon rolls, since their home was always filled with their aroma…that, and vanilla. Ripley knew one thing for sure, *he* certainly did!

"Good morning, Mama…Ringer. How's everyone this morning?"

Mama smiled and handed Ripley a steaming mug of chicory, which she explained was a roasted root that was ground into a powder and then brewed. It tasted similar to coffee, and she laced it liberally with both cream and honey. The welcome warmth of the liquid as it slid down his throat spread throughout his body. It chased the chill away and infused him with its heat. Even at this hour there was a cheery fire, crackling merrily in the fireplace to remove the late morning's chill.

Mama giggled and went back to her preparations for the noon meal. Ringer nodded at Ripley and said, "I'm good. Remenion and Malador wish to speak with you over at the Town Hall."

Ripley took another sip of his chicory beverage and peered over the rim of his cup at Ringer. He set it down on the saucer Mama had provided and smiled. "Did they say what they wanted?"

"I believe it has something to do with your mother, but don't quote me on it."

Excitement coursed through Ripley. *Mom...? Have they found her already?*

"Don't worry Ripley, we'll hold down the fort. You go and see what those two have found." Papa smiled as he handed Ripley a coat that hung on the peg by the door.

Grateful he didn't have to explain his anxiousness to get over to the Town Hall; he grinned as he slung the jacket around him and slid his arms into its sleeves.

"Oh, wait Ripley," Mama said as she busied herself in the kitchen. She pulled two cinnamon rolls from their pan, honey-frosting dripping from them, and placed them on a small plate. "Here, take these. You're going to need some sustenance if they've found your mother." She quickly put the rest of the warm rolls from the pan into a small basket and handed it to Ripley. At his questioning look she said, "For the others," by way of explanation.

Ripley smiled, tucked the basket under his arm, and strode toward the door with a bounce in his step. He offered one of the rolls to Ringer, who promptly downed the confection. *It can only be good news that Malador and Remenion want to speak with me,* he thought cheerily. He tried to keep himself from being overly optimistic, since Ringer wasn't certain *why* they wanted to speak with him, but it was terribly difficult. His mood was infectious.

"I'm sorry I'm going to miss breakfast, Mama. I'm sure it will be delicious." Sincere regret filled Ripley's eyes and voice as he cast a longing look at the large trenchers filled with eggs, rolls, and fresh apples she had either baked or cooked on the stove. He was certain, were he to eat it, he would find hints of cinnamon there, too. Ripley grinned and gave Mama a peck on the cheek, to which she promptly blushed and went all shy on him. "Thanks, Mama. I'm sure they'll all appreciate your efforts."

Mama plucked at her apron and grinned happily. "Get along with you, then," she said, and shooed him with her hands.

"Yes, ma'am," he said. He could hardly wait to hear what his mentor had to say to him. He stepped over to where Ringer and Papa stood waiting for him. He wanted to jump and shout, but contented himself with a little victory dance instead.

"We'll see you this evening, young man," Papa chuckled, and patted Ripley on the back. He opened the door then, and a gust of cold air struck Ripley, causing him to shiver. Ringer and Ripley stepped through the portal into the frigid October morning, the cold a distinct contrast to the warmth of the Johns' home.

Ripley acknowledged Papa's comment with a nod as the sticky, honey frosting dribbled down his chin and fingers. He took the final bite of the once gargantuan cinnamon roll, shoveling the remainder of it into his mouth. He licked his fingers and closed his eyes as if he'd died and gone to sugar heaven.

"Good?" Mama questioned with a smile.

In response, Ripley rolled his eyes and nodded his head. "You are a *marvelous* baker, Mama!"

Then around his last mouthful of the delectable pastry, he muttered, "I'll see you tonight." He handed Mama the empty plate, and the two young men waved to Mama and Papa from the end of the walkway. They stood together for warmth, Papa's arm encircling Mama as they stood in the doorway of their modest cottage, waved back, and then quickly retreated into the warmth of their abode.

The two young men made their way to the Town Hall. Ripley pulled the jacket closer about his thin frame and shivered slightly. *How I wish I had my fur coat now!* "How have you been, Ringer?" he asked through clenched teeth in an effort to keep them from chattering. The biting wind cut through the barrier of fabric as he pulled the collar of his coat up, and hunkered more deeply into the heavy jacket he wore. He pulled it tighter around him, hoping his body heat would quickly fill the space between the cold jacket lining and his body...*it didn't*.

"I've been good, Master Ripley." Ringer continued forward, drawing ever nearer the Town Hall.

"We've known each other for a while, Ringer. Just call me Ripley, that's fine." Ripley's excitement was barely containable.

Ringer shot him a dubious look but continued forward. *Why is it so hard to keep up a conversation with Ringer?* Ripley wondered. It seemed as if he had been friendlier to him when he was a wolf. Ringer rarely spoke, and when he did, he only answered the questions asked with the minimum amount of words. *Maybe it's my imagination, but I feel either Ringer doesn't like to talk much, or maybe he doesn't like me..* He decided the best way to find out would be simply to ask him why he was always so brief.

"Why is it you barely say anything when I speak to you, Ringer?"

"Oh," he frowned in concentration as he considered the question for a moment, and then shrugged. "What else would you have me say, sir?"

Why does he do that? He always answers questions with more questions. It isn't fair! Ripley thought to himself. "I don't know," Ripley began, "Do you ever just chat…I mean, just to get to know someone?"

Ringer seemed to think about the question for a moment before he answered, "No, sir. My folks raised me not to ask people personal questions that are none of my business." Ripley turned to look at Ringer then, because his matter-of-fact tone caught him off guard. It was more than that; however, because there was also a curious lack of emotion as he made his last comment. *I wonder what Ringer is all about*, he thought to himself. Ripley wanted to get to know Ringer, but Ringer was making it exceedingly difficult.

Ripley studied his eyes, and realized Ringer didn't mean anything more than what he'd said by it. Ripley was even more confused than he had been before. It was as if Ringer just stated facts—there didn't seem to be any ulterior motive to his comment. Before he could probe further, however, they arrived at the Town Hall. The door opened then, and the pair of teens stepped into the meeting place. Ripley could see

The Form Benders – Janet Lee Carpenter

Malador standing on the raised dais at the front of the hall, speaking quietly to Remenion and the Prince. His excitement grew when Malador turned to him with a smile on his face.

"Good news, Wet Nose," Malador's voice boomed through the meeting hall. His dark countenance still commanded respect as Ripley responded and returned his grin.

"Yes sir, what is it?" Ripley wanted to jump up and down.

"Well, son..." Malador frowned for the briefest of moments. "I guess I *should* say, there is good news...*and* bad."

It felt as if Ripley's heart dropped into his stomach. His face became serious as he stood there, waiting for Malador to continue.

"Which do you want to hear first, *the good...*or *the bad?*" Malador questioned as he moved closer to Ripley. Remenion paced nervously on his perch staring at both of them, waiting for Ripley to make a decision.

"I..." he stammered. What *did* he want to hear first...the good news? Maybe it would make the bad news go down more easily. He thought about it for a few moments, and then decided. "Tell me the bad news," he surprised himself as the words left his lips. Then he realized it was the right decision and steeled himself for whatever Malador was about to tell him.

Remenion seemed to approve of his choice, since he stopped pacing briefly and reduced his gaze to about fifty volts, instead of the 150-watt stare he had been directing at Ripley up until that moment. Ripley wondered why there was so much importance attached to his decision. Before he could ask, however, Malador spoke.

"Your mother is being held by Kestler," he stated boldly. It was obvious to Ripley that he wasn't happy to be the bearer of *this* news—if his frown and stern countenance were any indication.

Ripley groped for a nearby chair and sat down heavily in the seat. Why was Malador telling him something he already knew? "I *knew* they had her; I *saw* them take her. What are you *not* telling me...?"

"If you're honest son, until this moment, there was no way you could know whether or not the FBEF *still* has her; those men might have taken her elsewhere. You couldn't have known before now. In fact, that

The Form Benders - Janet Lee Carpenter

is what I feared had happened when we couldn't find her right away. The benders I sent, however, say Kestler and her cronies found a new area in which to conduct their experiments. I told you before, she may not be the only leader in the FBEF...there could be others. You need to keep that in mind. I'm not certain how high her rank is, but she must be fairly high up in the chain of command, since she has a *lot* of freedom to do as she pleases. I believe Remenion has spoken of the others to you, as well." He looked at Remenion then as he flew off the podium. The enormous owl landed on the back of Ripley's chair, and cocked his head to one side as he stared at him and spoke in Ripley's mind. Remenion, at that moment, seemed larger than life as Ripley had to lean back to look him in the eye.

"We spoke of this before, not too long after we first met. This organization, Master Ripley, is widespread. We don't know if Kestler is the head of the group, or if there are others who are higher up than she is. We need to discover this information, and we have not been able to determine the answer as of now. But, we will find out one of these days soon."

"How will you do that?" Ripley questioned him.

"We have benders within their group who are sympathetic to our dilemma, and feed us information when they can. We cannot compromise their positions, or their secrecy, and we certainly cannot bandy their names about. You must learn to hold secrets, Master Ripley, so those you have been charged to protect are not revealed in a careless moment of speech or action. It is part of your training."

Ripley listened intently to the elder Owl, and wondered why he needed to learn these things. He wasn't sure what plans the Elders had for him as a bender, nor was he certain he would be able to fulfill them.

Getting back to the subject of his mother, though, he questioned Malador, "Is she all right?"

"We're not sure of that, son. According to my reports, she isn't conscious at the moment. I'm afraid I don't know what they are pulling now, only that she will be much more difficult to rescue than Whitemane was..." Remenion's voice trailed off as he began to pace in front of the podium. "At least, the drug they used on Whitemane will be of no use on your mother. She isn't a bender..." Malador added, "Or, *is* she?" He asked. He raised a brow as his piercing gaze pinned Ripley and he waited for an answer.

The Form Benders – Janet Lee Carpenter

The hesitation in Malador's question wasn't lost on Ripley. *I wonder what that means...* he thought curiously.

Before he could ask, Malador quickly continued, "Well, *is she?*"

Ripley met his intense query. "No, she's not a bender." At Ripley's denial, Malador seemed preoccupied.

Remenion spoke for the first time. "Are you sure, boy? If she is, we'll need to know. The drugs they used on the other benders were a nasty combination, meant to keep them from ever bending again, which I don't have to tell *you* is terribly dangerous for them."

"I don't *think* so. She never *mentioned* she was any different from other people. I think she would have warned me I was a bender and what could happen to me, if she were." He considered how logical his argument sounded. He realized then that Remenion and Malador must've thought so as well, because they didn't question him for several more minutes, each lost in his own thoughts.

Finally, when Ripley couldn't stand the tense silence any longer, he blurted, "So, where is she? When can we leave to go get her?"

Brought back to the present, Malador answered him. "It's not that simple, son...I wish it were. We will need to get the shaman to come with us, in case *he* can determine what has caused her unconsciousness. Since you assure us she is not a bender, we will need help determining the best course of action with her. We'll also need to find a way to transport her if he can't help her. Once we get in there, we won't be able to leave her behind, so we'll need to make plans for that, as well. It's all quite complicated."

"*Leave her behind?* You *can't* mean to leave her *there...!*" Ripley sputtered, incredulous.

Remenion rushed to explain. "We don't want to leave her there; that is why preparations must be made, Master Ripley. We cannot just go in there, willy-nilly, and expect to rescue her. This is different from rescuing Whitemane; we will have to lay careful plans. If you wish to succeed at something, young Master, then provisions must be made for its success." Remenion did that one-eyed blink and turned his head 180 degrees to look at Malador who stood there, nodding his head in agreement with what he'd just said.

"OK, I can accept that." It was evident Ripley didn't like it, however. "But when can we go and get her?" Paramount on Ripley's mind was making sure his mother was safe from whatever Kestler was planning for her.

"We can leave at first light, tomorrow. I believe I can have everything in place by then," Malador spoke directly to Ripley.

Remenion nodded to them both. "I will leave you to your preparations, then..." At that point, Remenion flew to the door, which led to the upper chambers. Ripley caught a quick flash of a deep, royal purple robe, long white hair and an outstretched hand before the apparition disappeared behind the closed door. It all happened so quickly Ripley wasn't certain he had seen it at all. Then, suddenly he realized what he'd just witnessed was that Remenion *could* change forms! Ripley thought what he'd seen just now might be a rare glimpse of Remenion in his human form. He turned to Malador then and blurted, "He *can* change forms! I was wondering if he could..." his voice trailed off at Malador's look of surprise.

"You thought he couldn't?" Malador's chuckle filled the room with its deep, rich baritone.

"Well...yes...I mean I never *saw* him change before..." Ripley stammered as he defended himself.

"Just because you don't see it, son, it doesn't mean it doesn't exist. You have a lot to learn about life..."

"What do you mean?" Ripley couldn't keep the defensiveness out of his voice. Once again, Malador succeeded in making him feel incompetent.

"Just what I said, Wet Nose. Only a child would think that simply because a person acts one way with them at any given moment, they are like that *all the time*. You see an acquaintance for a moment in time, and since the nature of the mind is to extend it into forever...that is what you *think* you see. A moment, son, is a *moment*. That is *all* it is. People appear to change only because you expect them to be the same every time you meet them. When they aren't, for whatever reason, you think they've changed; when in fact, they are rarely—in *that moment*—the way you witnessed them being to begin with."

The Form Benders – Janet Lee Carpenter

Ripley sensed what Malador was telling him was important, but still, he wasn't sure he understood what he was trying to say. "Are you telling me people are different than what they appear to be, from one moment to the next?"

"In essence...yes. To meet the *soul* of a man is rare, son. It is only when your vision is clear and you have no pre-conceived notions of who those people *should be* that you see someone for who they *really are*."

Ripley felt Malador's words contained some underlying meaning he was unable to ascertain at the moment. "I see," he muttered, deep in thought when he honestly didn't see at all. But, he *would,* he promised himself. He would think on it until he understood what Malador was saying. He instinctively knew it was vital for him to grasp this idea—and that it was fundamental to his maturity—but he didn't have a clue as to what Malador meant.

"Good," Malador revealed his even, white teeth as he grinned at Ripley. It was obvious to Ripley that Malador didn't believe for one second he understood what he meant, however, more than likely, he also knew Ripley would turn it over in his mind until he did understand. Ripley would not be satisfied until he'd unraveled the mystery Malador had presented him with. It may take months for him to understand it, maybe even years—and *that* was okay with Ripley.

Chapter Fourteen

Ripley left the Town Hall alone after his interview with Remenion and Malador, with the understanding that he would need to be at the Hall early the next morning for their journey. He clasped the coat tightly against him to ward off the chill as he hurried toward the Johns' home. Ringer was nowhere in sight. Malador had explained that Ripley's mother was at the outskirts of Clovis in an old, abandoned fruit warehouse. The small party would meet and make their way down the mountain to where she was being held. The Shaman agreed to accompany them, and everything was set. Ripley was looking forward to meeting the Shaman. He had heard much about him from Papa, but so far, they had not met.

The twins convinced Ripley to join them for a picnic and some fishing at the lake when he returned to the Johns' home.

"Can I go too?" Angel wheedled.

"No, Angel, this is a *man* trip." Ethan said firmly, and then relented a bit when he saw her crestfallen expression. "You can go another time."

Hope flared in his sister's eyes. "When?" she questioned.

"Next time," he said, offering her the proverbial olive branch.

"Okay," her pretty brow furrowed as she talked to him sternly, "but, I'm gonna remember you said so!" She was a tiny replica of her mother, and Ripley stifled a laugh as he donned the coat that had somehow become his while he remained at the Johns' home.

"Okay, Angel." Evan piped up as he shot a glance at Ethan. "I'll remember too, sis...I promise." He leaned over and planted a kiss on top of her curls.

The boys quickly pulled on their jackets and grabbed the tackle boxes and fishing poles sitting by the door. Mama joined them with a picnic basket similar to the one Ripley took to the Town Hall earlier this morning.

The Form Benders – Janet Lee Carpenter

"Here you are, boys," she said as she handed Ethan the basket. "Don't stay too late. Ripley has an early morning tomorrow, and he'll need his rest." She made eye contact with each boy, to make certain they understood she meant what she said. At their nods, she seemed satisfied. Mama offered her cheek and the boys leaned over and kissed her. Then she reached up to adjust Ripley's collar, which was half tucked inside the jacket. She slid her thumb under the folded edge, pulled the collar out, and smoothed it on his shoulder.

"Have fun, boys. There are sandwiches and honey tea in the basket. There should be plenty."

Ethan and Evan simultaneously rolled their eyes and grinned. "There is *always* more than enough, mom. Don't worry…we'll be back this afternoon in time for supper."

Mama shooed them out of the house then. She pulled Angel in front of her, and rested her gentle hands on her daughter's shoulders as the boys stepped out into the late morning sun. The two females, their mannerisms carbon copies of one another, waved together as the boys joked, laughed, and made their way down the path. They turned right at the end of the lane as if they were headed for Oren's place, but veered left at the last moment and made for the lake.

For the first time since Ripley joined the benders, he was excited at the prospect of doing something with kids his age. Ethan and Evan both seemed to be enjoying themselves as they got closer to the lake.

They reached the water's edge with their gear within fifteen minutes.

Ripley was the first to have his hook baited and in the water. "You guys gonna fish or goof around?" Ripley called to the brothers who seemed bent on getting one another wet, never mind that it could be no more than forty degrees out. Even in the sun, the air was chilly.

"Come on and join us, Ripley…" Evan called to him.

"No thanks, I think I'll stay dry…" He chuckled as Ethan scrambled up on a pile of rocks nearby, lifted a giant boulder, and threw it in the water near Evan.

"*Eeek!*" Evan screeched as the cold water sprayed him. "I'm gonna *get you* for that," he called to his brother.

The Form Benders – Janet Lee Carpenter

Ripley laid back on the sandy beach, soaking up the sun's rays. It felt fantastic to be back at the lake, although the violet sky seemed at odds with his memories of this place. The sounds and feel of the lagoon were the same as they were at home. He was lulled by the slapping sound of the waves against the shoreline. He closed his eyes and thought about his mother. *Is she okay? What has Kestler done to her?* If Kestler was here right now, he knew what he would do to *her. Hah! Who am I kidding?* He knew what he'd *like* to do to her, but it would require more strength than he had to subdue her and pump her full of the drugs she was using against the benders, and quite possibly his mother. Her actions angered him and touched emotions he'd not been aware he had until now. His thoughts drifted to Whitemane. *Where is she?* he wondered. He missed her.

Ripley was drifting in that half-awake, half-asleep place where it felt as if he were floating, when he was doused with cold water. "What the...?" He sputtered as he sat up abruptly; holding his arms away from him, the frigid water sliding down him as the twins made their hasty retreat, laughter following in their wake.

It took only moments for Ripley to realize what happened before he took off after the boys. He chased them down the beach, "Come back here!" he called to them. "Just wait till I catch you..." he warned as he threw his head back and pulled out all the stops, gaining ground and coming closer to the boys. When he was close enough and had almost caught up to them, the boys quickly bent their forms into bears and headed out into the frigid water of the lake. Ripley stopped dead in his tracks. *"No fair!"* he called to them as a series of grunts issued from the two. Ripley assumed those would pass for laughter in *bear talk*.

Before he could utter any more, he heard the bell on his fishing pole go off. He sprinted back to the pole and suddenly realized that, after the chase and his subsequent return to the fishing poles, he wasn't even winded! He remembered the first run he'd made from the forest—which seemed like forever ago now—and how he'd had a stitch in his side from the exertion. Now, however, it didn't bother him much. He felt as if he could run forever and never tire, and it pleased him. With a smile on his face, he reeled his line in. When he got the fish to shore after a nice fight with it on the other end of the line, he was thrilled to see it was a beautiful Rainbow Trout. He estimated it weighed a little more than two pounds. *Mama will be overjoyed to fix this catch for supper*—he smiled

The Form Benders – Janet Lee Carpenter

at the thought. He slid the stringer through the fish's gill. He'd tied a small knot at one end of the line, leaving a loop. He now slid the untied end through the fish's mouth, the gill, and then through the loop at the other end of the stringer. He found a stick, shoved it deep into the sand, tied the line around the stick, and slid the fish back into the water once it was secured to shore. Being in the water would keep it alive until they were ready to head back to the village. Ripley looked up when he heard the boys whooping at his catch. They had returned to their human forms. He waved to them and smiled. He loved fishing!

He was getting hungry. Ripley took the last few steps to the picnic basket, reached in, and grabbed a sandwich and an apple. He munched on his lunch while he watched the twins having fun in the lake. Before long, however, they must have gotten hungry too, because they headed back over to where Ripley lay in the sand, just finishing up one of the sweet, crisp apples Mama had packed.

The boys pulled off their wet clothing down to their undergarments and lay on the beach in the sunshine, getting warm. Gooseflesh still appeared on the twins, but they didn't seem to be bothered by the cold. The boys rummaged through the basket, pulled out their honey tea and took generous gulps of the sweetened liquid. Then Evan grabbed two wrapped sandwiches, throwing one to his brother in a single fluid motion.

"Aren't you guys freezing?" Ripley asked, his curiosity getting the best of him.

The boys looked at each other and smiled. "Naw, the sun is warm…not like it is in the summer, but it feels good. Besides, when you start bending, the change causes your metabolism to speed up, keeping you warmer in different weathers and climates. At least, that's how Pop explained it to us."

"Is that why you changed forms out there in the water, then?"

"Yes, by doing it several times, we can rev up our metabolisms so we don't feel the cold like you do. When you have mastered your form, then you'll be able to switch back and forth."

"Hah, I don't think that will *ever* happen…" Ripley said mockingly. He sounded discouraged, even to himself.

"Oh, *trust* me," Evan said, "It will happen. You'll see."

The Form Benders – Janet Lee Carpenter

"How can I bend, if nobody wants to teach me how?"

"Have you *asked* anyone to teach you?" Ethan piped up.

"Well..." he thought for a moment, "no, I guess I haven't." Ripley was perplexed. "You mean I have to ask?"

"Well, *yes,* of course you do. How will the Elders know you're ready if you don't ask?" Ethan answered him matter-of-factly. He seemed surprised Ripley didn't know this.

"I realize this must be a terribly obvious answer to you guys, but I honestly never thought about it."

"Yeah, it *is* obvious. If we want to know something, we either ask Mama or Pops, or one of the Elders," Evan added simply.

"Can *you* teach me how to change my form?" Ripley asked the boys.

"No, *we* can't do that," the boys laughed heartily. "You'll have to ask your mentor, or Remenion." Ethan answered when he'd managed to subdue his laughter.

Ripley smiled at their well-meaning humor. He had to admit, the question seemed silly, even to him. He thought seriously about what the boys said. *Well, Remenion is definitely out, he makes me* way *too nervous. I could ask Malador, though; he'd probably teach me. He is my mentor, after all.* "Cool, I'll ask Malador then. Thanks!"

The boys nodded in unison. Ripley wondered if, no matter how long he knew the twins, he would ever get used to this *mirror image* thing they had going on. Sometimes they even answered in identical sentences! It was somewhat creepy, in a way.

Ripley put the apple core back in the picnic basket and tended to his pole. He baited his hook again, while the worm wriggled in his fingertips. He wondered if the worm felt pain as the hook pierced its flesh and he ran the sharp metal end up inside its body. Maybe that's why it squirmed so much, it *could* feel pain. He didn't like the way his thoughts were going. He would have to ask Malador if that were true. If it were, he would have to find another way to fish. Ripley sighed. It seemed he had become so much more aware of the world around him as a bender. He wasn't sure he liked it...it required him to give things up and work on himself, and that was sometimes tough. Like now...*if the worms feel pain, then I'll have to figure out how to fish differently.* He never intended to cause any*thing* or any*one* pain. *What a pain!* He chuckled to himself.

The twins had already baited their hooks and cast their lines into the water. They were resting again on the sand, their eyes closed as they soaked up the weak autumn rays. Ripley set his line, placed it back in the forked branch he'd found to rest his pole in, and laid back on the sand again in the early afternoon sun. He removed his shirt, and for the first time in a long while, looked at his stomach. His abdominal muscles were tight. He was surprised when he realized he had a nice *six-pack*, and it was well defined.

I wonder what Whitemane would think of this new body I have now? He grinned inwardly; she'd like it, he'd bet his first catch in Haven's Rest on it. The twins quieted now that they'd eaten, and were fishing exclusively. He closed his eyes and let his thoughts float to Whitemane, and how beautiful she was. He wondered if she liked him, as much as he liked her. He wondered what hope there could be for their relationship if he was stuck as a human, and she remained in her wolf form. He knew she could change between forms, but she remained in her wolf form—was it as *protection?* he wondered. *Protection from whom...? From him?* She didn't need to protect herself from him because he would *never* hurt her. Far from it, he was falling for her.

He laid there, questions floating around in his mind, until another bell sounded. He sat up quickly, however this time it was Ethan's pole. Ripley lay back down while Ethan pulled another Rainbow Trout from the lake, placed it on the stringer, baited his hook again, and set his pole. Within half an hour, each of the twins caught another fish, and so did Ripley. They had plenty of fish for dinner that night. It was time to head back; the sun was beginning to hang low on the horizon.

"We stayed later than we were supposed to. At least when Mama sees all the fish we caught, she won't be too mad," the boys laughed. They secured the hooks on the eyes of their fishing poles, picked up their tackle boxes, and headed back the way they'd come earlier. They chatted among themselves, rehashing the day's events and laughing at Ripley's attempt to capture them after they doused him with water. The boys used Ponderosa pine needles to draw lots and see who would carry the picnic basket home. Since Ripley lost the draw, he won the dubious honor of carrying the now-empty picnic basket, as well as his fishing pole and tackle box, back to the cottage.

Ripley wasn't sure how he felt about being drenched earlier, but since he was a good sport, he laughed with them. He'd enjoyed his time with the twins. Tomorrow he would have to be serious; he would be called upon to help with the rescue of his mother. Maybe even learn how to bend his form at will, which might help his mother, though Ripley wasn't sure how. But for now, it had been a fun day with the twins.

They reached the cottage. While Ethan and Evan cleaned the fish out behind the house, Ripley took their gear inside and returned it to where it belonged. He hung his jacket on its peg and called to Mama that they were back. "Where should I put the picnic basket?" Ripley called out to Mama.

"There's some hot cocoa on the drain board in the kitchen. Help yourself, just set it there. There's some for the boys, too, when they come in," she called to him from the fireplace where she was tending a pot of something which smelled delicious.

"They're cleaning the fish, and said they would be right in," Ripley said as he picked up his steaming mug of cocoa and tasted it. Mama had laced it with cinnamon; Ripley smiled and shook his head...*of course* it would have cinnamon in it! It seemed cinnamon found its way into almost *everything* Mama made. However, he had to admit it *tasted* sublime!

"Thank you, Ripley. Come on in and sit by the fire. Papa will be home any minute. He had to go into town for some supplies. How'd your fishing go?" She queried.

"Good, you should have plenty for the evening meal."

"*Oh*...not *tonight*," she spoke loud enough for it to carry to him. "We're having corn chowder, zucchini bread, and warm honey butter."

Ripley's mouth watered instantaneously at the mention of the menu for tonight. He loved corn chowder and zucchini bread! Mrs. Richardson loved to bake. She always told him there was too much for one person to eat, so she would frequently bring him some when she made it. On more than one occasion, she had brought him whatever she'd made that evening for her dinner too—soup, stew, or something else entirely. She never came in to the apartment; she just wanted to make sure Ripley and his mother were eating well. She was such a kind woman. He often felt as if she were his guardian angel. He smiled and realized several minutes had ticked by without him asking Mama what she wanted him to do with the fish. "That sounds wonderful, Mama. What do you want us to do with the fish, then?" Ripley asked as he entered the living area.

"I'll have the boys put them in the smoke house. That will give us fish later in the winter, when it's too cold *and* there's too much snow to go fishing. Though, I swear—those boys will find a way to make it out to the lake." She chuckled as she stirred the pot.

"Yes, it seems they love to fish as much as I do," Ripley said and smiled as he sat down in Mama's chair near the crackling fire in the fireplace, watching as she stirred the bubbling pot of chowder. "Is there anything I can do to help?"

"Thank you for asking," she replied as she smiled at him. "You just sit there. I'll ask for some help to set the table for dinner in a little while." Mama hummed softly to herself as she stirred the thick chowder.

Ripley nodded and said, "I'll be happy to help. Just let me know when." He snuggled deeper into the softly cushioned chair, sipped his cocoa, and watched the flames as they danced and snapped in the fireplace, letting the soothing sounds mesmerize him. Before long, he set his empty cup on the small end table next to him, stretched out his long legs, crossed them at the ankles, and folded his arms across his stomach. His eyes seemed to drift shut all on their own and his thoughts turned to Whitemane. *Where had she been today? He would find her tomorrow...or would he? Would he have time to see her before he left?* He thought, *perhaps not.* This brought a sense of sadness to him. *Was she staying away because he wasn't in his wolf form?* He would have to ask her. With that settled in his mind, he dozed off. He never heard the boys come in with their catch, nor mama call them for supper. He awoke in the middle of the night, with a blanket over him. He tiptoed into the room where the twins were asleep, undressed, and climbed into bed.

It was a blustery morning, bruised clouds hung low over the village, and the wind whipped the air into a frenzy. The scent of moisture hung heavily in the atmosphere. The sound of birds and small animals, as well as the villagers, were strangely absent as Ripley made his way through the town to the hall where he was supposed to meet everyone for their journey to Fresno. Ripley pulled the jacket more tightly about him, wishing he had some gloves to protect his stiff fingers from the biting cold. Since he didn't, he tucked them under his armpits and hoped to find any stray warmth that might still reside there.

He stepped inside the warm hall, where Malador, Prince Valiantheart, Remenion, and the person he assumed was the shaman stood waiting. They were speaking in soft undertones. He noted the newcomer's long, slightly wavy, blonde hair trailing down his back, but his most outstanding feature from the back was his height. Next to Remenion and Malador, both of whom matched or exceeded his six-foot plus height, the shaman looked as if he were a midget. He must have stood just shy of five feet tall, and when he turned to face him, Ripley inhaled sharply as he noted the features the shaman possessed. Ripley could only describe him as *beautiful*. Although he was deeply tanned, his gentle features seemed to remain in a perpetual state of calm. His eyes were deep-set and yellow, the color of molten gold. His lips seemed to be fused into a gentle smile as Ripley moved closer to the silent group. Standing with his feet spread slightly apart, his long, graceful fingers intertwined as they remained clasped in front of him, the shaman watched Ripley as he approached.

"Ripley," Malador's voice echoed throughout the room, "this is our Shaman, Eurythacles." Then he indicated Ripley to Eurythacles as he stood at the end of the podium. "This is Master Ripley."

Ripley started to object to the title of Master; then, studying the shaman's features, changed his mind and bowed slightly to him. "Eurythacles," he said by way of greeting.

"I have heard much about you, young Master. I shall enjoy this journey with you as we come to know one another. I am certain you have many questions which, in time, I will be happy to answer. For now, I believe the urgency to find your mother should take precedence. So, with your permission, Prince, my dear ones..." he held out a hand, gesturing for Malador to precede him, "shall we leave without further ado?"

"Are you coming with us, Prince?" Ripley asked surprised, thinking Eurythacles had indicated he was.

The Form Benders – Janet Lee Carpenter

"No, I must stay here. You have the medallion, do you not?" the Prince asked Ripley.

"Yes, I have it." Ripley touched his chest and felt the medallion's familiar warmth next to his skin.

"Then all will go well. The water sprites and wood nymphs will come to your aid, should you need them. Remember to call upon Narassian or Arapham and they will assist you in your desire to help your mother. May the Golden One light your path," the Prince said, and then he blessed them.

Within moments, the small trio of Ripley, Eurythacles, and Malador left the confines of Haven's Rest on another journey. It would be one of the most significant journeys of Ripley's young life. He kept casting looks about the area as they made their way to the wall, hoping to catch a glimpse of Whitemane. Disappointment flooded him when he realized he would not get to see her until he returned. With difficulty, he turned his thoughts back to the task at hand and followed Malador out of town.

How are we, as such a small group, going to rescue my mother if we cannot carry her? he wondered, but chose to keep his silence. His thoughts returned to Remenion and what he'd said about keeping secrets. He wondered if he would ever be able to do that. He also wondered how long he could control himself and *not* ask questions. It would be hard, but he thought he'd like to try. They stepped through the wall of brush and began their journey to Clovis.

As they walked, he wondered why he hadn't seen Whitemane recently. He thought she would be there this morning, but no...she wasn't, and he wanted to see her *so badly*. *We won't be gone long*, he thought. *Just long enough to get mom and bring her home.* Suddenly, he was confused. Was Haven's Rest going to be her new home? He wrestled with the idea in his mind. She couldn't return to Shaver Lake, since Kestler knew where she lived...she would no longer be safe there. He frowned. Ripley knew it was going to be an interesting and eventful journey to Clovis as he trailed behind the group...*I will* not *let these things worry me!* He mentally shook himself and smiled; they were going to find his mother, and he was in his human form! Life couldn't be better as far as he was concerned!

Chapter Fifteen

As they made their way through the forest, Eurythacles dropped back beside Ripley and let Malador take the lead.

"So, Master Ripley," he began, "tell me a little about you. I have heard *much* of the legend and *little* of the young man about whom it was written."

Ripley thought about what Eurythacles said. *Legend? What legend?* He chose not to ask what the legend was, at least, not yet. He decided, rather, to focus on answering the question the shaman asked. "Where do I begin?" he asked as he considered the dilemma.

"Well, how you came to find yourself here might be a good start."

Ripley remembered that day all too well. "Well, first it came in a dream," he said to the shaman. "It was the day before my sixteenth birthday. I decided to lay down for a nap. You see, some*thing* chased me in the woods that afternoon, and I was tired. When I came home I found Kestler there, posing as someone from the Child Protective Services."

Eurythacles listened intently as Ripley told the story of his dream, the form bend, and of his subsequent flight to Haven's Rest the next morning. He told of Whitemane's kidnapping, her rescue, and Kestler taking his mother from their home in Shaver Lake. He nodded frequently, but otherwise remained silent as Ripley spoke. When he'd finished his tale, Eurythacles asked him one simple question: "And so now, you are able to change your form at will? *Amazing!* It usually takes longer…"

Ripley rushed to explain, "Oh no, sir, I can't do *that*. I just bent the one time. I don't know how to bend my form." He searched his mind to think of what he'd said to make Eurythacles believe he had acquired the ability to change his form at will.

"I'm sorry; I just assumed you were able to change your form since you spoke of going after your mother and bending in the forest. Because you changed your form there, I assumed you could do it at will...my apologies, young Master. However, you do know how to change, Master Ripley. And if the legend is true, you will be able to take on all of the forms."

"This is the second time you have referred to *the legend*. What is this legend you speak of?" Ripley asked, genuinely wanting to know.

"The Legend says, one will come from the world of the Wakened Ones, and through many trials, he will prove to himself that he is worthy of the title of King. This title shall be held in high regard, higher than the title of Prince or Queen, as it has never been bestowed on anyone. He shall rule with a just hand, the mighty sword of Truth, and Wisdom beyond measure. This King shall have mastered the four forms of the realm, and the benders will unite under his rule. At this time, the world will become whole again."

Ripley stood silently, trying to absorb the import of The Legend. He tried earnestly to comprehend what it meant to him, and then shook his head. "I don't know if I am the one the legend talks about...I can't even change my form at the moment," he said quietly.

"You will, my friend, you will." Eurythacles reached out and touched his shoulder briefly.

He had been prepared to ask Malador to teach him how to change; however, it seemed this was the perfect opportunity to ask the shaman to teach him to bend his form at will.

"I honestly don't know how to change, Eurythacles. I have a friend..." Ripley began.

The shaman smiled knowingly at Ripley. "This friend, would he have a twin?" he questioned.

Inexplicably, Ripley looked away. It felt strange to have someone look into your life the way Eurythacles could. Moreover, he did it so effortlessly Ripley was constantly amazed at his ability, *and* discomfited.

"Never mind," Eurythacles waved away Ripley's discomfort.

"How did you know what I was going to ask you about?" he questioned when he finally got control of his thoughts, once again astounded at the depth of the shaman's insight into him. He probably

The Form Benders – Janet Lee Carpenter

knew, as well, that Ripley didn't know how to approach the subject of bending his form with Malador.

"It is easy to read your mind when it's written all over your face, young Master." He peered into Ripley's eyes for a moment. He changed tack then and responded to what he'd seen in Ripley's eyes. "Love will never steer you wrong, Ripley. If you follow it, your heart will lead you to all the right places in your life."

Ripley felt the creeping sensation of warmth burn up his neck into his silvery hair. *How can he do that? How much of his feelings for Sally had he revealed in that short exchange? How much did Eurythacles know?* he wondered.

Ripley thought he understood what Eurythacles meant, though. Sometimes he was able to tell what his mother was thinking—and what she felt—just by focusing on her. He had thought it was because he had these latent abilities as a form bender. Now, however, he wasn't so sure.

"How did you know what I was going to ask you? What do you know about Sally? Can you teach me how to master my wolf form?" He couldn't control the flow of questions as they popped up in his mind and flew out of his mouth.

Eurythacles, amused, ignored some of Ripley's questions for the moment, and shared his benevolent smile with him. "I believe there was another whom you wanted to ask that question. Shall we call him to us so you can ask him? Perhaps Malador would be a better choice for you, since he is a wolf himself—don't you think?"

"If you think it would be best, then of course, let's do that." Ripley started to call Malador over to join them when Eurythacles interrupted him.

"It is not what *I* think is best, Master Ripley," he corrected, "but rather, what *you* think would be best. You must learn to trust your instincts, and your heart. They will never lead you astray."

Confusion filled Ripley for a moment as he thought about what the shaman said to him. What *did* he think? Did he want Malador to teach him the way of the form benders? Yes…he believed he did. He had only asked Eurythacles out of fear. He realized now that he was *afraid* to ask Malador.

The Form Benders – Janet Lee Carpenter

"That's right, young Master," Eurythacles answered his unspoken thoughts, "conquer your fears by confronting them. The things in your life worth doing are the ones that are the hardest to do. I don't mean things that in all good conscience you know you shouldn't do, but rather, the ones that keep you from doing what you wish to accomplish. If you want to learn how to bend your form at will, then you must ask the person whom you believe to be the best suited to teach you. It is the only way to learn to trust yourself. Go on, son—follow your heart."

Ripley rolled the idea over in his mind. He *knew* what the shaman was saying was true—he could *feel* it. He smiled brightly at Eurythacles then. He sped up to catch Malador, who was winding his way into the clearing above the four-lane highway.

"Can I talk with you for a minute?" Ripley asked Malador.

"What's up, Wet Nose?" He cast a brief glance at Ripley, then turned back and kept moving forward.

"I went fishing yesterday with Ethan and Evan."

"Yes?"

Malador wasn't going to help him out with this; Ripley could see that. So he blurted it out before he could think about how ridiculous he might sound. "They told me I have to ask for training to master my wolf form, from my mentor. Would *you* teach me?" It all came out in a rush. Ripley felt winded from the request.

Malador stopped moving and looked directly into Ripley's eyes. Ripley stood his ground and allowed Malador to probe his thoughts without looking away. It was perhaps the most difficult thing he'd done in a long time.

Nodding, apparently satisfied with what he saw in Ripley's intentions, he said, "I will teach you, Wet Nose."

The exhilaration Ripley felt in those words could not be described. He felt as if he'd been given a wondrous gift, even better than the eggs Mrs. Richardson had shared with him. "When can we start?" he questioned excitedly.

"Well, now if you like, son."

"I would like *very much* to begin now. What do I need to do?"

The Form Benders – Janet Lee Carpenter

Malador began his trek again as Eurythacles and Ripley followed closely behind. They passed the four-lane highway and were getting close to where he and Malador had stopped and rested on their first trip to Fresno. He assumed this trip would be no different. He was wrong. Malador stopped briefly, only long enough for them to quench their thirst, and then they continued to move ahead before he began to teach him.

"First, you must clear your mind, son. You must guard your thoughts at all times, as that is the doorway to your forms. If you cannot hold them suspended, then at the worst, malformations can occur. In the best-case scenario, you will only be unable to bend at your will. Do you understand?"

Ripley nodded as he listened with rapt attention.

"Good. When you imagine yourself as your wolf form, you will hold it in your thoughts, unwavering. Remember what it is like to feel the wind in your fur, the earth beneath your paws, the feel of the sun on your back, and the elements in which you move."

Ripley could feel all those things, and more. He could feel the way he felt when Whitemane declared her name to him, the pain of his mother's kidnapping, and the hopelessness he'd felt when Kestler's thugs snatched her from beneath his nose. He remembered the odor of his tennis shoes that first night, and the feel of the wind in his fur as he'd run from what he thought was the CPS.

"Nice work, son," Malador said from somewhere far away. It brought him back to the moment with a jolt. He realized then that he had bent his form into that of his wolven counterpart.

Ripley was ecstatic! He'd done it! He hopped around joyously, pleased with himself and his ability to change into his wolf form. In that moment, however, he also realized he would need to be able to change back to his human form. *"How do I turn back?"* he asked Malador, speaking in his mind in the way of the benders.

"The same way you became your wolf form, silly. Just imagine it!"

Ripley settled down, cleared his mind, and remembered what it was like to have his human form. He felt the way his lungs heaved as he ran from the thing in the woods the day he'd met Kestler. He felt the spray of the shower in the bathroom at home against his skin. He remembered how it felt to fish with his best friend, Pete, and the times they laughed and played in the water during the summer.

"There you go, Wet Nose," Malador's voice interrupted his thoughts. "The more you practice your bends, the more quickly you will be able to achieve them. It's like a river." At Ripley's frown, Malador continued. "Each year a river flows, it becomes wider and deeper until it eventually forms great canyons. The power water embodies is that as it makes inroads into the earth, it leaves behind traces of its life. You can tell the years in which there was a drought by the width and nature of the walls of the canyon. Since the canyon was created by the river, it tells us the story of the river, not just the canyon itself. So also will your thoughts create inroads in your brain until your bends become instantaneous and immediate."

Ripley, back in his human form again, concentrated and bent into his wolf form. As the trio made their way down the hillside, Ripley couldn't help but be reminded of Skerrin and how he'd flipped back and forth between his forms as they'd made their way to Haven's Rest. He thought he must look like that right now, first as a wolf, and then human, and back to wolf again. If anyone saw him, what would he or she think? He chuckled to himself. They would think him odd, indeed!

"You must be careful, Wet Nose, so no one observes your bend." Malador counseled. "It is imperative that you keep these two lives separate and distinct, even though *you* experience them as united. It can bring great danger to the bender clan and to you as well. Do you understand?"

"Yes, I do...I think. If someone were to see me bend," he tried to explain what he thought Malador meant, "they could misunderstand what a bender is and be frightened, which may cause them to harm me, or themselves. Also, because I am only one part of a much larger group, I could bring the authorities down upon us due to some misunderstanding."

"That is correct, Wet Nose," Malador nodded approvingly. "I am glad to see you understand your responsibilities."

Ripley decided it was much easier to traverse the mountainside as a wolf, so he shifted into his wolf form and continued his downward

The Form Benders – Janet Lee Carpenter

path behind Malador. Eurythacles, who had remained silent for most of their exchange spoke up, "How much farther is it?"

Malador squinted up at the sun, noted the shadows from the bushes to determine the time, and then said, "Another twenty minutes should see us near the warehouse. We'll have to see, but I think we may wait until nightfall to approach; their security should be more lax then."

Eurythacles nodded and once they'd made it to the foothills, Ripley changed into his human form. Now the three of them looked like a couple of men walking with their dog off the mountain. Eurythacles altered his clothing to fit in with the people they might encounter. He wore work pants and a dark blue denim shirt whose sleeves were rolled up to reveal strong, but delicate, forearms. Malador remained in his wolf form so he could track the scent of Ripley's mother.

As they neared a small farm on the roadside in the foothills, Malador stopped suddenly and crouched low in a drainage ditch. He motioned for the others to join him. Eurythacles lay down on his stomach in the ditch and inched forward. Ripley followed suit. "What is it?" he queried.

Malador spoke in his mind and hushed him. *"Shh...she's nearby. Perhaps in that metal building over there,"* he said as his companions looked off into the distance toward where Malador was gazing.

Both pairs of eyes met, and a silent communication passed between Eurythacles and Ripley before Ripley spoke in his mind to Malador. *"What do you want us to do?"*

"Stay here. I'm going to go and check it out. If I'm not back in ten minutes, go around the back side—you'll have to go around the hill there—and make your way to the back of that building. I'll scout it out, and we can communicate in our minds, just like when we rescued Whitemane. Okay?" he looked directly at Ripley.

Ripley nodded. Next, Malador looked at Eurythacles questioningly. *"I understand, Malador."* He had that sublime smile plastered on his face once again, which Ripley was beginning to become quite familiar with. He seemed amused at Malador's lack of faith in his understanding.

Seemingly satisfied, Malador nodded and then crept through irrigation ditches, behind bushes, and ever nearer to the building where

The Form Benders – Janet Lee Carpenter

he thought Ripley's mother was housed. Ripley and Eurythacles watched in tense silence until they could see Malador no more as he slipped behind the building. Ripley listened intently, straining to hear any altercation that might be transpiring, however he heard nothing as the seconds turned to minutes in that desolate ditch.

It had been more than ten minutes when they watched Malador sneak away from the metal building, hiding once again behind bushes and in deep ravines as he made his way back to where they waited for him.

When he reached them, Ripley demanded, *"Well?"*

Keeping in mind that sound carried out here, Malador spoke in his mind as all benders do. *"She's in there. There are two guards outside and three inside. Steamer and Vinnie are there too. I think the other one they call Max is there, as well."* Malador looked directly at Eurythacles. *"They have her in a cell of sorts. She's lying on a mattress they've provided for her. I got close, and she appears to be sleeping. Her face is flushed, there is a rattle each time she draws a breath, and she has a strange scent about her; it smells like musk and mushrooms. It's very strange. I've smelled many odors in my lifetime, but there is nothing familiar about this scent."*

At the mention of mushrooms, the shaman's brows knit together into a frown. *"This isn't good,"* he spoke distractedly in his mind. Both Malador and Ripley waited in silence as Eurythacles seemed to ponder the facts. *"Did she have a fever? Were you able to determine that?"*

"When I saw her that is what I thought...I mean, since she was flushed and moaning in her sleep. I would guess she has a fever, simply based on those signs. I'm sorry I couldn't get close enough to touch her to make sure. Vinnie and Steamer are there, patrolling the confines."

Ripley queried, concern lacing his words, *"Why is it important whether my mother has a fever or not?"*

Eurythacles looked up at Ripley and shook his head. *"Well, if she does, it means her body is fighting the effects of the drugs they have given her, or,"* he paused here until Ripley urged him to go on. *"It's possible she's become ill, which could complicate matters."*

"What do we do?" Ripley questioned him earnestly.

The Form Benders – Janet Lee Carpenter

"I will need to see her. If what I think is happening is what's really going on, then I'm going to need some herbs from around here."

"What do you think is going on," Ripley's concern was a palpable thing as he waited for Eurythacles to answer.

"I believe she's not only been drugged, but is suffering the effects of the drug and perhaps pneumonia, which is prevalent in humans at this time of the year. She may have acquired it from one of the people she's been in close contact with, but the only way I will know is if I see whether there is anyone else who is ill in there." He looked to Malador then. *"Do you think I can approach without being seen?"*

Ripley thought this was an odd question for Eurythacles to ask Malador. After all, hadn't Malador just done as much? He watched Malador as he seemed to ponder the question before he finally answered the shaman.

"It would be better if you could wait until dark," Malador answered quickly.

What were they talking about? His mother was in there...she was sick, perhaps dying, and they wanted to wait three or four hours until nightfall? What were they thinking? Ripley couldn't remain silent. His thoughts came swiftly to Malador. *"What are we waiting for? She's sick..."*

Malador interrupted him before he could send any more thoughts. *"We need to be prepared to go in there. We have to wait until nightfall so Eurythacles will not be seen. You're just going to have to trust us on this one."*

Ripley countered with, *"But you just went in and came out without being seen..."*

"This is different, Wet Nose. You'll see what I mean later. For now, let's get to work."

Ripley didn't like it, but he agreed to wait. Eurythacles and Ripley went to gather herbs near the river. Ripley was sent to gather some daisy-like lavender flowers called Echinacea. He picked them with care, thinking of his mother and hoping she would be all right until dark. Malador stayed behind and kept watch on the building, to make certain they didn't move her. Eurythacles picked mushrooms. He'd also brought some gnarly looking roots with him, which he explained were called Goldenseal. This root would boost his mother's immune system and help her to heal if she were ill. He was going to make a tea from the root and the flowers, and administer it when he got close to her.

They were far enough away from the building now that they could speak to one another. They would have to go back to speaking in their minds once they returned to where Malador was, but for now they could use their voices. He called Ripley to him and said, "Look, Ripley, here is how to tell this plant from others. It grows wild in the forests near cedar trees, which we have in abundance near Haven's Rest." He scraped his thumbnail up and down on the root of the plant he held, revealing a deep, golden-colored woody structure beneath the brown root's surface. "This is how you can tell it's Goldenseal. There is another plant that looks similar in the woods up there," he said as he tossed his head in the direction from which they'd come earlier. "That plant would be the Thimbleberry. However, Goldenseal's leaves are deeper green and waxier looking than the Thimbleberry leaf. Their berries look similar. Where the Thimbleberry can be eaten, the Goldenseal berry is poisonous and should not be ingested."

Ripley nodded and smiled. "Interesting!" He was amazed at the shaman's knowledge of plants.

"We'll need to build a fire and brew it." Eurythacles looked toward where they'd left Malador.

"We can build a fire here; it will be too obvious anywhere else." Ripley started to look around for wood and tinder for the task.

"Good thinking, young Master." They gathered dry wood and made a small ring of stones in the dirt. Ripley realized they didn't have a pot in which to boil the tea.

"How are we going to boil the tea?"

The shaman smiled at Ripley then, that benevolent smile which seemed to say he was amused at the question. "We'll just use that pot over there," he pointed to an old pot Ripley was certain hadn't been there ten minutes ago when he was gathering the flowers. He frowned and wondered how it was accomplished, but went to get the pot for Eurythacles.

The Form Benders – Janet Lee Carpenter

Ripley rinsed it out, though it appeared to be clean, and filled it with water from the stream. Eurythacles then snapped his fingers near the dry firewood and a spark flew from his thumb and forefinger, which ignited the tinder he'd placed there only moments before.

"Wow! That was *cool!*" Ripley watched in amazement as the flames licked the dry wood and flared into a delightful little campfire.

The shaman smiled and began to pull the flowers from their stems. When he had enough, he placed them in the pot. He added the root from the Goldenseal plant, and dropped mushrooms into the pot as well. He let the concoction simmer over the fire while they sat in companionable silence, waiting for the medicine to be complete.

When the remedy was ready, almost thirty minutes later, Eurythacles lifted the pot from the fire and set it aside to let it cool. He handed Ripley some dried pine nuts and berries he'd brought with him from the forest. Ripley shoved a few in his mouth and chewed thoughtfully while the shaman went to deliver some of the dried treats to Malador. None of them had eaten anything on the way down, and Ripley was hungry—so chances were that Malador was, too.

Ripley watched the two benders a short distance away. Malador must have said something funny, because they both laughed quietly. *I wonder if I can light fires like Eurythacles can. That would be so cool! It's so quiet here,* he noted absently.

As always, when left to his devices, his thoughts turned to Whitemane: her gentle manner, her intelligence. He wondered if she would be as excited as he was about his ability to bend his form at will, and then knew without a doubt that she would be. If for no other reason than he was excited about it. They shared that kind of camaraderie. Ripley smiled as the daylight began to wane. Soon they would have his mother, and his world would be complete again. Well, almost complete. His father wasn't there, but then he hadn't been for some time. Ripley shrugged and leaned back against the trunk of a fallen oak which lay across the river near him. He closed his eyes and thought to rest for only a moment, but with his belly full and the warmth of the winter sun beating down on him, he drifted off to sleep.

Malador's insistent nudging awakened Ripley, "Whaaa…?"

The Form Benders – Janet Lee Carpenter

"Come on son, it's time."

The promise of rescuing his mother soon brought Ripley instantly awake as he noted that Eurythacles stood less than ten feet away. "I'm awake..." he muttered, shaking the last vestiges of sleep from him. The trio headed in the direction of the outbuilding where his mother was being held and once again, they fell into their silent communication. *"How are we all going to get close enough?"* Ripley asked Malador.

"We aren't. We're going to stay here, Wet Nose, while Eurythacles takes the medicine to see if he can help her. If he can, he'll signal us."

Ripley's brows drew together as he tried to understand what Malador was saying. *How is Eurythacles going to signal them? What plans were made while I slept?* he wondered. *"I don't understand,"* Ripley began in silent thought.

"You ready, Eurythacles?" Malador questioned.

"I am," he smiled benignly.

Then in a moment, Ripley understood what Malador meant earlier as the shaman bent his form into a magnificent shimmering owl. The moonlight danced on his feathers, like miniscule droplets of light on his body, glistening in billions of tiny, iridescent, rainbow-like colors. Ripley thought *this* was the most beautiful thing he'd ever seen. Each movement Eurythacles made caused the glint of undulating rainbows of light to cascade upon his feathery body, almost making him seem translucent.

"Close your mouth, son," Malador reminded him.

Ripley didn't even know his mouth was agape with awe. *"Sorry,"* he said soundlessly to no one in particular.

Malador smiled and nodded to Eurythacles who, in a soundless flurry of wings, lifted from the ground and headed toward the metal building. *No wonder he had to wait until nightfall,* Ripley thought. *He blended in with the velvet sky and twinkling stars above him.*

"He's truly beautiful," Ripley exclaimed as he watched the flickering of light cast upon Eurythacles as he neared the building. He was like the night, silent and deafening all at once. He disappeared

The Form Benders – Janet Lee Carpenter

behind the building. Malador and Ripley kept to their silent vigil, awaiting Eurythacles' signal. Neither one of them said anything as they watched, and waited.

They were getting antsy by the time they finally saw Eurythacles leave the building and return to where they lay hidden in the ravine. When he landed in a silent whoosh of air, Ripley was the first to question him, keeping to the discipline of speaking in his mind. *"Did you see her? Is she all right? Can we help her?"* He shot the questions out in rapid-fire succession.

"Let him gather himself, Wet Nose." Malador admonished him.

Ripley barely acknowledged Malador's caution as he looked to Eurythacles for answers.

He bent his form into the familiar shaman as he spoke, *"She is fine now. She's resting, but she's aware. I was right; she has pneumonia, so we'll need to get her out of there right away. One of us may need to stay behind until she is stronger. I don't think she'll be able to travel in the condition she's in. She's running a fever and is coughing a lot. Most of the men are staying away from her, which will work in our favor,"* he finished speaking.

Malador picked up his train of thought and said, *"Yes, it just might. If they are trying to avoid getting sick, then we may be able to get her as far as my friend's farm near here. If we can do that, she'll have a chance to recuperate before we drag her all the way to Haven's Rest. Ripley can stay with her while I go and get some supplies and return you to the safety of Haven's Rest. He can administer the medicine to her as well."*

"Why wouldn't you stay, Malador?" The shaman questioned. *"Ripley can go back to Sanctuary and bring some supplies back,"* he frowned.

Malador quickly jumped in to assure him Ripley would be the best choice to stay behind and administer to his mother's needs in their absence.

"As you wish Malador," Eurythacles frowned, reached into the sleeve of his robe, and produced a vial of dark brown liquid. *"This is quite concentrated, young Master,"* he said as he handed the vial to

The Form Benders – Janet Lee Carpenter

Ripley. *"Two drops on the tongue every couple of hours should do it. Do you understand?"*

What are they talking about? he wondered. *"Yes I understand,"* he answered distractedly in his mind. He felt an undercurrent of communication here he didn't fathom. *Of course, I will stay with her...why wouldn't I? After all, she is* my *mother! Why would Malador stay behind with her and, odder still, why would Eurythacles* think *Malador should?*

Within the hour, Ripley and Malador lay in the ravine just outside of the building where his mother was. Anticipation filled Ripley as he realized that within a few moments he would see his mother! Malador cautioned Ripley with a look and crawled a few more feet in the ravine. The most dangerous part would be when they had to leave the relative security of the ditch and run the last ten yards to the outbuilding. A small door stood ajar only a short distance away.

Malador had already briefed him as to what the interior of the building looked like. Just inside the doorway there were two desks, large enough for them to hide under should the patrol walk by. When Malador cleared them to get his mother, it would all have to happen fairly quickly. Ripley was to go to the cage and unlock the door while Malador distracted the men. The key was on the wall next to the desks. Once he'd gotten the door open, Malador was to turn into his human form, lift Ripley's mother and carry her in his arms from the building.

Ripley hoped all went according to their plan. Malador looked at Ripley and nodded. *"You ready, Wet Nose?"*

Ripley bent into his wolf form and nodded. *"I'm ready,"* his mouth was dry, and his heart beat a rapid staccato in his chest as the adrenalin pumped through him. Thank goodness he didn't actually have to speak, for he didn't think he'd be able to around the dry mouth he was experiencing.

"When I say...go..." Malador ordered, and kept his eyes trained on the door, *"go, Wet Nose!"*

Moments ticked by as Ripley's muscles bunched, ready to launch him toward the door.

The Form Benders – Janet Lee Carpenter

"*Go!*" Malador finally urged above the clambering of Ripley's heart.

On that word, Malador's voice became the gun at the beginning of a track meet. Ripley's body was propelled out of the ditch at breakneck speed. He ran toward the door, feeling each paw as it touched the earth briefly and forced him onward toward his destination. He didn't look back, but he could almost feel Malador's panting as he closed the distance between them. Ripley was first in the door, and directly to his right there was a desk, just as Malador said there would be. He scrambled under it, into the area where the chair would normally go, panting heavily. He was thankful when he realized it was an old metal desk with an enclosed area where your legs went beneath it. It would keep him hidden from view by the patrol.

Vinnie and Steamer walked near the desks just as Malador slid under the second one and hid himself from view. Ripley gagged when he smelled the odor of rotting apples, like vinegar, floating on the current of air as they passed them.

"I wish she'd leave," Steamer said. "She makes the men nervous."

"Yeah, well, that ain't gonna happen. She seems to think the only way to keep her 'pet project' safe is for her to be here." Vinnie sneered. "As if we can't take care of business; I have half a mind to walk off and let *her* deal with it."

Ripley's heart slammed into his chest. He spoke to Malador in his mind. "She's *here! Kestler is here. Now what?*"

Malador didn't say anything.

"*Mal?*" Ripley questioned anxiously.

"*I'm thinking Wet Nose. Give me a minute. Our plans will have to change. I'm going to wait until they're out of earshot, and then I'll step out and see what else I can find. Stay here and keep low,*" he said.

Ripley laughed, "*Like where am I gonna go?*"

Malador shot him a stern look. "*You know what I mean,*" he admonished. "*I'll be right back.*"

The Form Benders – Janet Lee Carpenter

Ripley was waiting for only a few brief moments before Malador returned and continued in their unspoken dialogue. *"Okay, here's the plan. The first part is going to be the same. You'll unlock the door and give her the medicine. Then I'll create a HUGE distraction which should get everyone on the other side of the building, including Kestler. I'll come back here as soon as I can, and we'll carry your mother out of here. Okay?"*

"What do you mean by huge?" Ripley wanted to know.

"There's no time to explain. There are some explosives here, so I'll need to make a run for it as soon as they are lit, all right?"

Alarmed, Ripley nodded.

"You just keep to your job, and I'll do mine, son. Now when I say 'go', grab the keys and head to the cell they're keeping her in. It's against the wall right behind you. You ready?"

"As ready as I'll ever be," Ripley stated.

"All right then," he waited for Vinnie and Steamer to make one more pass before he said, *"Go!"*

The moment Malador said, *"Go"*...Ripley jumped into action. He stepped out from under the desk, turned into his human form, and grabbed the keys. He crouched low and duck-walked his way to his mother's cage. He called to her and she lifted her head weakly. *"Ripley?"* her voice trailed off. Her head dropped heavily back onto the bare mattress. It was obvious to Ripley that she was terribly weak.

"It's me, Mom. Malador and I are going to get you out of here. Just be still, okay?"

"I'm sorry, Ripley, I didn't mean for them to…I'm such a failure…" she whispered miserably.

"Hush Mom, I'm okay. Shh, now…just rest." He lifted the vial to her lips and let two droplets of the medicine drip into her mouth. *She must be delirious,* he thought to himself. *What on earth was she talking about?* As soon as he'd administered the healing potion to her, he heard a ruckus on the other side of the building.

"Get him!" Kestler's voice rang out in the building, bouncing off the walls like a Ping-Pong ball.

"Don't let him near there! Hurry...*Stop* him!" Kestler's voice registered alarm.

Ripley looked up in time to see Malador lighting a match near some barrels in the far corner of the building. At least ten barrels and some crates were stacked neatly in the corner. Malador was in his human form as he smiled a rakish grin toward Kestler and dropped the match he was holding onto the floor. The straw caught on fire and seemed to be making a beeline for the crates.

"Put it out!" Kestler demanded, even as she headed for the large double barn doors close to her. The fire, however, was spreading too rapidly and the men scrambled to reach the fire extinguisher on the opposite side of that end of the building. "I'll have your heads if this thing blows!" Kestler snapped.

Within seconds, Malador lifted Ripley's mother in his arms, and she cradled her head against him as he hoisted her once to get a better grip and the three of them dashed out of the building. Malador ran for the ditch and fell headlong into it, covering Ripley's mother with his body to shield her just as the flame reached its target.

The explosion was tremendous. Chunks of metal and wood exploded from the building as it disintegrated. Ripley felt the concussion of the explosion in his body as his hair was blown forward into his face from the blast. It propelled him into the ditch that lay ahead of them. He lay in the ravine next to his mother and Malador, with his arms over his head to protect himself. A shower of shrapnel rained down on them until a piece of metal landed haphazardly over them, partially protecting them from the majority of the fallout.

Silence permeated the surrounding area for a few moments, as if nothing wished to disturb the concussive boom that had occurred only moments before. The seconds ticked by as Ripley waited for the scene to return to normal. A smaller blast came from the building where they had stood only moments before, and Ripley felt himself flinch at the unexpected sound.

Slowly, the world around him began to rouse from its stunned silence. First, the call of a Blue Heron signaled all was well. The song of sparrows and the cry of a lone Red-Tailed Hawk pierced the stillness. Ripley moved then, testing his body to make certain nothing had been

The Form Benders – Janet Lee Carpenter

broken during his flight and the consequent impact with the ravine wall. He groaned and pushed the piece of metal off Malador and his mother.

"Are you all right, Mal...Mom?" Ripley questioned aloud.

Malador's body half covered his mother in a protective manner. Ripley could see blood flowing from a wound in Malador's shoulder, but other than that he appeared to be unharmed as he, too, came alive and began to roll off Ripley's mother.

"Lily...?" he said softly as he brushed dirt and her hair away from her face. "Can you hear me?" he spoke to her gently.

Ripley's features drew into a frown as he watched Malador with his mother. The air was alive with electricity, a kind of energy with which he was unfamiliar. She started to come to, coughed, and then moaned. Malador moved off her fully and continued to stroke her long locks.

"Rafe...?" she questioned as she tried to open her eyes and look at him. It took a couple of tries, but she finally managed to get them open. She locked gazes with Malador and mumbled, "I couldn't keep him safe...I'm so sorry...I tried Rafe...they took him," her voice trailed off as a tear slid down her cheek forging a pink trail through the dust covering her face. At the mention of his human name, Malador went eerily still.

Rafe? This was Rafe? Suddenly, everything clarified and came into sharp focus for him. In the beat of a hummingbird's wing, Ripley shifted into his wolf form and turned from the scene. *Malador* was his *father?* Deep in his pain and his sense of betrayal, Ripley ran with no destination in mind—tears pouring unheeded down his muzzle. He heard Malador cry out to him in some small part of his brain, but he was too blinded by his own pain to heed the grief in Malador's voice...no, his *father, not* Malador!

"Ripley! Wait...son, we can explain!"

But Ripley's paws continued to pound the earth as he ran across the field unseeing, not caring where he ended up. His mind went over all the odd things he'd seen. The way people stopped speaking when he entered a room where Malador was. How Malador almost spoke over Eurythacles' suggestion that Malador remain behind to tend to his mother—and why Sally pushed him to tell Malador before he went to

The Form Benders – Janet Lee Carpenter

their apartment to rescue his mother. He remembered how Malador began to call him son on his first trip to Fresno. It seemed as if everyone, *except* him, knew what Malador's relationship to him was all along. However, to be fair...in a hidden place within his heart, he had known, as well...*hadn't he?* The pleasure he felt at Malador calling him *son*, and taking him with him when any other bender might not have been so congenial about it. In some ways, Ripley thought he'd known it all along. *"No!"* his mind cried out, but his heart knew the truth.

Within moments he heard, rather than saw, Malador pounding behind him. Ripley gained momentum; the sky was darkening, and lightning split the sky as his father bore down on him.

"Ripley...*wait!* Let us explain!"

Malador was gaining ground rapidly; his feet seemed to thunder in sync with the building storm. Fat raindrops began to fall as Ripley veered left around an outcropping of boulders. Malador was almost on him. Ripley flashed a look behind him, but he needn't have done so; he knew he was racing against his own inevitable capture.

Malador leapt and sailed through the air; as he did so, he turned from animal to human. His arms snaked out and closed upon Ripley's hind legs, drawing him to the ground. Ripley rolled, teeth snapping amidst growls, warning him to leave him alone. Malador grabbed the fur on each side of Ripley's neck to keep him from hurting him as he spoke.

"Stop it, son...I said, *STOP IT!*" He shook his head and held Ripley fast. Although Ripley had the strength of his youth to his advantage, Malador had the strength of his years and wisdom to draw upon. Ripley fought him for a few more minutes before he stopped altogether, realizing how futile it was to fight him. He returned to his human form and lay there beneath his father, chest heaving, tears streaming down his cheeks as the sky opened up and drenched the two of them.

"Let your mother and I explain..." Malador begged him. Ripley didn't think he'd ever seen Malador express remorse, but it was there now, in his eyes. Ripley steeled himself against the urge to forgive him. He turned away from the obvious pain in his father's eyes, saddened that they hadn't trusted him enough to tell him the truth.

The Form Benders – Janet Lee Carpenter

The pain and sense of betrayal Ripley felt was there in his expression for everyone to see. Whether he wanted to or not he couldn't hide how he felt from anyone. It pulsed violently through him. "I don't need for you to *explain* this." He spat out. "What *possible* explanation could there be for my *father* to abandon my mother and me for seven years...*seven years, Dad!*" he snarled the words. Bitterness coursed through him as he accused him, "You *left us,*" he cried out through his tears over the cacophony of the thunder as it rent the sky. "You didn't *care* for us...*not at all!* You were only thinking of *yourself!*" he accused.

Malador ignored the outburst of Ripley's pain and said instead, "Come back with me. Let us explain...*PLEASE?* There is much you don't know or understand. Your mother and I would be happy to explain, but you need to give us a chance, son."

"*Don't call me that!*" he snapped. Although Ripley had calmed down some and hadn't moved since his accusations of only moments before, he was still angry and hurt that they hadn't told him before this. They had led him to believe his father had left. At least, they hadn't lied about *that*.

Malador said, "If I let you go, will you promise not to run?"

Ripley nodded his assent. He was rapidly losing the battle with his desire not to let them explain. But the war was not yet over. "Very well," Malador said. However, as soon as he moved off him Ripley tried to run again. Malador grabbed his foot and held fast to him. Ripley kicked at him frantically, trying to get him to loosen his hold until Malador captured his other ankle and held on.

"*Stop!*" he commanded. "You gave me your *word!* Now *quit it!*" Malador ordered.

Ripley finally gave up. *I can't run...he'll catch me; he won't let me go, so I might as well hear what he has to say.* Ripley didn't like admitting defeat, but he resigned himself to listening to their tale.

Perhaps this is what Remenion meant when he said I wouldn't be able to hold on to my grievances in the face of new evidence. He stood then, brushed his clothes off and realized it had all turned to mud. Shaking his head, he followed his father back the way they'd come—rain beating against them every step of the way. He shivered from the damp and the cold as another crash of thunder boomed across the field. Ripley remembered what the twins had told him. As they walked in silence to where they'd left his mother and Eurythacles, he changed into his wolf form to warm himself. He did it twice before he finally felt his body begin to warm from the inside out.

When they returned to the ravine, Eurythacles had salvaged metal from the old building and created a small structure from the wreckage to keep his mother dry. It would only worsen her pneumonia if she were to get wet. The structure was big enough to house the four of them comfortably. He had built a fire and placed his mother near it to keep her warm. Near the structure, he had also placed several pieces of wood and tree limbs beneath a bush to keep it dry. His mother was sleeping again, exhausted from her ordeal and the pneumonia. "She's resting comfortably. She'll need her medication again within the hour," Eurythacles said looking at Ripley. He acted as if nothing had happened, though everyone knew it had.

"I'll make sure she gets it." Ripley nodded, still sad that his parents hadn't trusted him enough to tell him what happened.

Eurythacles noted the strained silence between father and son and said quietly. "I believe I shall go find some more mushrooms; they will help your mother rest. You two might as well get comfortable; it will take at least a week for her to be strong enough to return to Haven's Rest. Hopefully the rain will stop soon. I'll be back in a little while," he said, and then bent over and stepped out into the rainy afternoon.

Chapter Sixteen

On the third day of his mother's illness, she awoke and weakly accepted some broth the shaman prepared. Ripley and his father declared a shaky truce for the time being, until his mother was fit for travel. Malador refused to talk about what happened seven years ago until Lily was awake, so Ripley waited impatiently until she was able to talk with him. They fished without speaking. They performed daily rituals with a minimum of communication, and the strained silence was getting to them both. The intermittent thundershowers and gloomy days didn't help the situation either. They spoke to each other through Eurythacles, who seemed amused at their stubborn refusal to speak to one another. Whenever they needed something, it seemed to appear magically with Eurythacles around: fishing poles, pans, bait, eggs, and whatever else was needed by the small group while they waited for Lily to recuperate.

Ripley and Malador sifted through the rubble and found some bones, but nothing to indicate Kestler didn't make it out of the building alive. Of course, they couldn't prove she did, either. This seemed to add to Malador's frustration. Ripley personally felt Kestler was a goner, and until they had proof otherwise he, for one, would operate on that assumption. He was chomping at the bit, awaiting his mother's return to health so Malador and his mother could explain what happened seven years ago.

On the fourth day, the sun finally poked its head from behind the clouds and the day dawned bright and clear. Tiny droplets of dew clung stubbornly to the grass, and as the sun struck them, they reflected miniature rainbows over the entire valley floor as far as the eye could see. Lily awakened that morning seeming to be clear headed for the first time. She smiled at Malador and her son. She must have noted the strained relationship her loved ones shared because she frowned deeply and tried to speak. Her voice came out in a raspy whisper. Ripley was so lost in his own world that, until she reached for a cup of water nearby, he wasn't aware she was awake.

The Form Benders – Janet Lee Carpenter

"Mom!" he cried and scooted next to her. He reached for the cup and held it to her parched lips.

"Lily?" Malador was at her side, as well.

"I believe I must go get some more wood for our fire." Eurythacles stated as he stood within the structure. "Lily should be ready to move in a couple of days, and then we can head back to Haven's Rest." Ripley smiled in spite of the strain he felt. It seemed Eurythacles had drawn more than his fair share of the firewood-gathering chore than either he or Malador. Eurythacles excused himself, and before he ducked through the makeshift door, Malador and Ripley acknowledged his statement with a nod. When he was gone, they returned to Lily's care.

"How do you feel, Mom?" Ripley asked, concern etching his brow.

She nodded and turned her gaze to Malador. "Rafe, what's wrong?" she questioned him.

"I gave Ripley my word we would explain to him what happened seven years ago. But it is too early yet, you must rest."

"Help me," she asked as she tried to sit up.

Ripley moved to her side, slid his arm beneath his mother's arms, and helped her to sit upright. She patted his forearm gently and smiled reassuringly at him.

"I am strong enough now. Let's tell him." Lily smiled sweetly at her husband.

"Seven years ago," Rafe began, "your mother and I became aware that someone was trying to get to me. There were two attempts on my life. So I went to the Council of Elders and asked their advice."

So I was right! Everyone but me knows Malador is my father! His brows drew into a deep frown. Not wanting to interrupt now that he was talking, Ripley remained silent at this outrage instead, and let Rafe continue.

"They heard that one of the benders who fell from grace with the tribe left the area and was attempting to take over the race of benders. Since it had been determined by the Great One that your mother would conceive and give birth to the next leader of our race—they decided I should, by any means at my disposal, remove myself from my family so as not to endanger them."

Lily reached a hand out to her son and took hold of it. "When your father left," she looked at Rafe for support then continued, "I was so lonely. I tried for a while to take care of you, and to be strong, but it was so hard on my own. Sometimes I could sense your father in the forest behind our apartment, and it would tear me apart. He was so close, and yet so far from us at that time."

Rafe reached out and placed a comforting hand on his wife's thigh. He continued the story. "It was torture being away from your mother and you, son," he looked into Ripley's eyes. Ripley was beginning to understand what they had gone through to protect him.

"Go on," he urged his father.

"The agreement I made with the Elders was that I would return to Haven's Rest. Your mother would need to remain behind and live as a human, in the Wakened Ones' world. She would raise you as one of them so Kestler could not find you. You see," he added here, "if you weren't being raised as a bender, then she wouldn't be able to find you and set her minions on you. You would remain safe."

"I'm sorry I failed you, son," Lily said.

Ripley's denial came swiftly, "You didn't fail me, Mom." He tried to assuage her guilt. "You were there when I thought Dad left us for good. Why didn't you tell me?" He couldn't keep the hurt from his voice.

"I couldn't. If you were to think, for even one instant, that you weren't a human, then with Kestler's ability to read minds she would have found you and all would have been lost. It was urgent that you *not* know and that we maintain your ignorance to save you," Lily explained to him.

Rafe picked up the story once again. "The night before your sixteenth birthday, I waited for you out in the forest, hoping I could help you find Haven's Rest and keep you safe. However, I hadn't bargained on one of Kestler's minions being in the forest that night. When I sensed it, I knew I had to lead it away. I called for Whitemane to escort you instead. I saw the thing chase you earlier that afternoon in the forest, and tried to lure it away from you. However, it stayed on your scent, stalking you. It wasn't until the end, when I saw you were going to make it out of the forest that I went in the opposite direction. I went to the forest's edge and watched you run across the baseball field. I waited until you went up the stairs to your apartment. It was then that I thanked the Great One that you were safe."

Ripley realized it was his father's familiar scent he'd noted in the forest that night while he'd lain in his bed. This was all so *overwhelming!*

"Go on...there is more, isn't there?" Ripley urged his parents to continue. He could feel the hard knot of betrayal melting in his chest as he began to understand the sacrifices his father had made for him.

His mother spoke next. "I knew what was going to happen on your sixteenth birthday, and I needed to maintain my wits about me to be able to help you. I knew our time of being alone was almost over. The wine helped me to forget how lonely I was without your father there." Ripley's parents exchanged a glance before she continued. "But then, our song came on the radio," she looked deeply into her husband's eyes before she continued. "I was so sad, and lonely. I opened a bottle I'd hidden in the couch and drank the entire thing. It was wrong of me. I realized that the morning you ran from the apartment. I vowed at that moment never to drink again, Ripley. I didn't know what to do if Kestler came to the apartment; I'd never seen her before. All I knew was that she was evil and she wanted to hurt my baby," tears ran unheeded from her eyes as she looked at Ripley then. "I'm so sorry, son. I failed you when you needed me most."

Ripley shook his head, unable to speak for the tears threatening to choke him. When he finally got his emotions under control, he sputtered, "You didn't fail me mom. It's okay..." he hugged her as she cried on his shoulder.

She held him away from her. "Yes, Ripley, I did. I cannot change what happened in the past. I only know that when the CPS arrived at our door that morning I *knew* it was Kestler. When I saw you hit the screen door at a run and leap to freedom, I knew your father would find you and you would be safe." She smiled softly and whispered, "You were always *such* a good runner!"

Ripley grinned at the compliment. "Yeah...I love to run, Mom."

The Form Benders – Janet Lee Carpenter

"Whatever we did, son," his father said, "we did because we love you and had to put your safety and the safety of our tribe above our own. Family is all we have when everything is said and done. The lesson of the wolf is that of family, of the pack...and our responsibility to each other. Wolves everywhere are brothers and act accordingly, son. The Wakened Ones are a family too, but as yet, they don't understand their responsibilities to each other and the world as a whole. It is our destiny to show them the way."

Ripley understood now that his father hadn't abandoned him and his mom. That in truth, he couldn't. Rather, he'd protected them and kept them safe from harm in the only way he'd known how. He did something then he hadn't thought he'd ever be able to do again; he reached out and drew his father into his arms. Rafe clasped his son tightly to him and Ripley dissolved into tears. They were not of sadness, however, but of joy. He had found his home. His mother reached up and placed her arms around them both, and Ripley's arm encircled her as well.

After a few minutes, Ripley finally released them and looked at them both. He reached up with a shaky hand a wiped away the tears on his face. "Okay, you two...is there anything *else* I should know?" He shot them both a skeptical look.

"Oh, yes...there *is* one more thing," Lily smiled at her son and reached for Rafe to help her to her feet. Rafe bent and let her place her arm around his shoulders. She let her arm drop from him once she stood, and before his eyes—she turned into a *wolf*—a stunning, lovely, gentle gray wolf. His mother was a *wolf*, as well! She *was* a bender! He didn't know what he expected; only that he hadn't expected her to be one. He had never guessed she was.

Ripley's jaw dropped before he held up his hands, shook his head, and said, "That's *it! No more* secrets...from *either* of you, *ever!"*

Lily and her beloved Rafe dissolved into laughter, and Ripley had to smile. *It sure is good to be home!*

Epilogue

Two days later Ripley and his newfound family, along with Eurythacles, arrived in Haven's Rest. Remenion, Skerrin, Oren Trueblood, and Haven greeted them in town at the square, which was filled to capacity with the townsfolk. Ripley's disappointment at not seeing Sally was a palpable thing as he joined in the celebration in their honor. The Prince stood in the Town Square, raised his hand for silence, and when the crowd quieted, he began to speak.

"This day is one of *great rejoicing*. From this day forward, on this date there shall be a day of feasting and celebration for each and every bender within the clan. Forever onward shall the first day in November be known as the day when the sons and daughters of the bender clan have overcome the dangers of the FBEF." The crowd cheered, raising their arms and clapping. The Prince held up his hand again for silence, and the noise of the crowd lowered to hear the Prince's words.

"We shall call this day the *Day of the Hero*. It will be known to benders all over the globe that this was the day in which Kestler's organization was stopped, and the benders became safe from fear and the tyranny of our oppressors!" The cheers of the crowd swelled to a crescendo of sound in their little community.

Rafe, Lily, and Ripley stood at the forefront of the crowd of benders. As Haven stepped up to the podium in the square, the crowd knelt before their queen and once again became so silent you could have heard the beat of a butterfly's wings in the stillness. She stood there, regal, poised, and at home in her own world. She motioned for her people to stand, and sent a dazzling smile to Rafe and Ripley before she began to speak.

"Because our brothers have shown their fierce loyalty, kind hearts, and extraordinary courage; and have demonstrated the knowledge of what it is to be a bender, I hereby decree that the *Cottage in the Wood* becomes their own. In gratitude for their selfless service and deep empathy for the bender clan, this same cottage shall be forever bequeathed to them, and to their heirs, for all generations to come." The roar of approval from the crowd was deafening as Haven stepped down from the podium. She walked to the father and son who returned to their home as heroes, and bowed before them for a moment before she stood again.

"Thank you, Malador, Rafe Adams. May the Great One bless you and keep your family safe, now and forever more." She placed a medallion around Malador's neck, stepped back, and smiled. Malador reached behind him, and Lily took his outstretched hand and joined him as they stood before their queen.

She stepped over to Ripley then. He felt himself blush and grow warm when her kind and gentle eyes met his. "And Master Ripley Sean Adams," she winked at him then to disperse his tension and began, "In light of your recent arrival in Haven's Rest and your subsequent selfless service to its inhabitants, I honor you with the title of Page of Learning. This title allows you to command the elements with the wisdom, caring and devotion afforded to our beloved and sacred elementals." Haven removed the medallion from around Ripley's neck, held it to the moon, and beams of light flashed as they touched the medallion's surface. When she returned it to Ripley, it had become the color of liquid silver, and shimmering upon its surface was the light of the moon.

She hugged Ripley and then stepped away from him. Then, she addressed the crowd. "Let the celebration begin!" she commanded.

Music burst from the platform at the center of the square, and people began singing and laughing, dancing and sharing a mug of ale between them. Ripley's joy would have been complete, except one thing was missing—Whitemane.

He walked across the square, away from the festivities and toward the road that would lead him to the Johns'. In a way, he was saddened that he would no longer reside with them, but he knew the twins and he would have many more adventures. He passed the small pipe shop and barbershop, but before he could go any further, he turned to look over his shoulder. He saw his mother and father dancing. Lily's face was flushed as she smiled at Rafe.

He turned back to watch where he was going, and there she stood. Her shimmering white hair cascading down her body, blue eyes soft and luminescent, she smiled shyly at him.

The Form Benders – Janet Lee Carpenter

"Sally..." he breathed. Ripley's heart was beating so fast he felt as if he'd run miles.

"Ripley," she spoke his name in a soft whisper.

"Where have you been?" he asked her.

"In here," she smiled and tapped him with a forefinger on his chest.

Ripley knew what she meant. She was right. She had never been far away from his thoughts, and had somehow found her way into his heart as well. He opened his arms and Sally stepped into them. "There is no replacement for this," he said, indicating the place in his arms she now occupied.

"No, there isn't," she agreed. "It feels like home." She smiled as Ripley pulled her against his chest.

He held her away from him and looked seriously into her eyes. "Why didn't you tell me he was my father?" Ripley asked quietly.

"It was not my place to say, Ripley. I knew your history, where you came from, and who you were when I met you. I tried my best not to fall for you, because I knew it would be some time before we could ever be together. I also knew it would take a great deal of adjustment for you when you did find out Malador and Rafe were one and the same. I knew I would have to give you time to adjust, and come to terms with who you are and who your parents really are."

"I see," he said. "I just have one more question," he whispered.

"What's that?" she asked him.

"How did you do on the 'not falling for me' part?" he questioned teasingly.

She laughed sweetly in the night. "Not very well," she said, and then countered, "How about you?"

Ripley chuckled. "I'm afraid I failed miserably. I must say, though, it was the most pleasurable failure I've ever experienced. I'm glad I'm not alone though," he grinned.

I don't think either of us will ever be alone again," she smiled gently and reached up to touch his beloved face. Her fingers traced the lines of his cheek and lips before her hand dropped back to her side.

The Form Benders – Janet Lee Carpenter

Sally slipped back into his embrace as he opened his arms again, his chin resting gently on top of her head as he inhaled deeply of her scent. She smelled of flowers, earth, and water. "This is where you belong, Sally…in my arms. Don't ever believe you don't."

She tilted her face up into the moonlight; her delicate features were bathed in the moon's glow and love. The luminescence from the moon, however, was nothing compared to the glow Ripley saw within her. He bent and gently brushed her lips with his, and then pulled her against his body once again.

The soft strains of music floated on the frigid night breeze and he felt her shiver against him. "Shall we dance?" he asked her. She didn't need to answer him as he began to sway with her. He broke away after only a few moments, and then grabbed her hand and pulled her toward the celebrants and the warmth of the bonfires that raged around the square.

If home is where the heart is, Ripley thought, *then I have found my first* real *home in Sally and in Haven's Rest.* He smiled contentedly. He twirled Sally out onto the dance floor, and then crossed his hands over each other and grabbed both of hers as they whirled about in circles. She threw her head back in pure abandon and laughed lightly. *It sure is awesome to be home,* he thought. *Home…* he liked the sound of it.

The Form Benders – Janet Lee Carpenter

✐ About the Author ✑

Born and raised in Los Angeles, California, Jan Carpenter now makes her home in Shaver Lake, California. She and her husband have been married almost twenty years and they share their home with their two sons, one dog, two cats, and three fish. She has two lovely grown daughters from a previous marriage who reside in Oregon and Michigan. She loves devoting her time to writing, reading, and sharing her life with her family and friends. She is fascinated by natural healing methods and the Native American culture, and she thoroughly enjoys a good philosophical discussion.

She began writing The Form Benders: The Sheep in Wolf's Clothing after leaving her job and finding the time to pursue her love of writing. Her wild imagination gives her a bountiful garden of ideas from which to write and create—hence, The Form Benders: The Sheep in Wolf's Clothing was born (the first in the series of The Form Benders books).

Her writings reflect her deep interest in relationships and discovering what motivates us to do the things we do.

CPSIA information can be obtained at www.ICGtesting.com
Printed in the USA
LVOW100716140212

268585LV00007B/32/P